Flokí

A Mystery Novel

Paul B Bergquist

Forfatterfabrikken Forlag AS

ISBN 978-82-94122-02-8 (ePub)
ISBN 978-82-94122-04-2 (paperback)

Book Cover by Aleksandar N.

Prologue

Geir Rosseberg loved the ocean. His entire adult life was a testament to this love. He spent it sailing abroad, crossing the world's oceans from the North Sea to the Pacific, and visiting most of its ports and harbors.

But now, he had replaced those mighty ships with a small wooden boat he navigated through the Strait of Karmsund this night.

A warm front crept in during the evening, hiding the moon's light and leaving the surrounding landscape in various shades of black, with only the lights along the streets and inside houses to testify to people living there.

He poured himself a mouthful of his home-brewed brand of moonshine and felt how his short-traveled liquor cleared his throat, warmed his body, and eased the growing tension.

The wind from the south picked up, and the waves were already creating white peaks of foam. Soon, it would rain, so he placed another lump of snuff under his lip and pulled up the zipper of his jacket.

A bulk carrier heading south passed him on the port side. There was something sad and majestic about the tall, lonely, and darkened ship. Rosseberg followed it with his eyes for a while before taking another mouthful of liquor.

He glanced at his watch as he passed the Karmsund Bridge, and the lights of the small town of Haugesund unfolded before him. Punctual, as always–whatever the circumstances.

He approached his destination, the quay at the north end of Bakarøy island, and let his boat glide into the darkened quay area. He liked that it was dark; darkness had often been his best friend.

Rosseberg inhaled the sea breeze, tar, rotting seaweed, and the distinct smell of herring, checked the fenders, observed a lone blue Audi A6 parked at the back of a warehouse with its lights off, and took another mouthful of liquor while he moored his boat.

A figure emerged from the shadows of the nearest warehouse and approached the boat with quick, determined steps. The stranger entered the boat swiftly and with boat-savvy motion. "Thank you for meeting me at such short notice. I'm so excited!"

The man smiled and gave Rosseberg a firm handshake, and he returned the smile as he spat to the side over the rail. A drop of snuff got no farther than his white beard, but Rosseberg didn't notice.

The stranger glanced around the boat. "I understood you had some documents for me?"

Rosseberg straightened his back and said: "Yes, I took pictures and kept records of everything. Suppliers, contacts, backers; banks, companies, and account numbers; everything worth knowing and then some." He paused, then continued studying a stain on the deck. "It was supposed to be my life insurance."

Rosseberg saw a sparkle in the stranger's eyes. "Fantastic! You have no idea how long we've been working on this case. But we've never had any firm evidence against him until now. And you've had to carry this guilt all these years? Not being able to confide in anyone? Not even your wife?"

Rosseberg stroked his shiny face and said: "No, not to her. This has been a secret I couldn't share with anyone. It sure ain't something I'm proud I've been part of."

The stranger nodded. "Well, I'm glad you've decided to come forward and get rid of your guilty conscience. I can't promise you a reduced sentence for your participation in this, although I'm pretty sure the judge will consider your contribution to solving the case."

Rosseberg sighed and pursed his lips. *Cop's got his back well covered, but I don't have so many years left,* he thought. He took a deep breath and nodded. Out loud, he said, "It's only now, after my wife passed, I can go public with all of this. She would have died of shame. Don't worry about me, though."

The man looked at him with extreme severity and said: "None of this must get out before we're ready to strike. Do you copy?"

Rosseberg squinted at him. "This will be a nice feather in your cap, won't it?" The policeman didn't answer but smiled weakly back while nodding almost imperceptibly.

Rosseberg spat snuff again. Luckier this time. "I thought so. Follow me." He balanced along the boat's edge until he reached the foredeck, bent over the railing, and pulled on a thin, light blue nylon thread hanging down from the boat's bow into the sea. A small container covered with kelp and slime emerged from the dark sea.

As he reached for it, something wrapped around his legs. He went headlong overboard, hit the water head-first, and lost his breath for a moment. The icy sea clawed at his face.

He waved his arms frantically and raised his face above the water for a moment—enough for him to catch his breath. The policeman grabbed his legs and pulled him back toward the boat. He hoisted him out of the water with solid hands—but stopped halfway. Rosseberg hung with his legs up and his upper body underwater.

Rosseberg tried to turn around. *Get me the hell out of here.* But his legs were stuck. He couldn't bend backward or forward to get out of the water and breathe. He needed air soon, or he would die.

Then everything became crystal clear. This was not an accident. He would die in this godforsaken place tonight.

Like he had never experienced, adrenaline rushed through every vein. Every nerve in his body was on high alert. *No! I will not go down like this!* He fought to get free and get his head above water.

He held his breath, his muscles aching from the lack of oxygen. The pain exploded and attacked every inch of his body. He opened his eyes. His white beard drifted in the dark sea before him. He closed his eyes again. He couldn't bear to look and tried to focus on something else. Had to avoid breathing at any cost. His heart pumped wildly as every cell screamed for air.

The old body jerked in convulsions. Rosseberg had to hold back, refrain from breathing, and get his head above water. *Come on!* Then he gave up and took a deep breath. Ice-cold seawater poured into his lungs.

I don't want to die! Not now. He wasn't ready. An intense pain shot from his heart, and flashes of lights danced before him. One of them stood out, approaching him. *That you, ma?* She smiled at him as she had in his childhood. Warmth and love flowed toward him, filling him with happiness. The light surrounded him.

The stranger sat in the boat and watched Rosseberg with great interest. Like a cat watching its prey, he followed the last convulsions of the old body as life ebbed away, amazed at how long Rosseberg had lasted for such an older man.

Now, as Rosseberg's splashing had stopped, he scrutinized his surroundings. Everything was still quiet. Not a person in sight and no alarms or excited voices, just the relaxed sound of waves lapping against the bottom of the wooden boat.

He loosened the rubber strap around Rosseberg's legs and let the dead body slide into the dark sea. The body reappeared a few meters away and floated on with the current. He turned around, picked up the small, overgrown aluminum container, twisted open the cap, and emptied a tiny key onto the deck.

It was a key that would fit in a standard padlock. He frowned. Was that all? He cursed.Should have waited and secured the full explanation, but Rosseberg had been in a good position, and he couldn't count on such an opportunity to present itself later.

He shook his head and laughed. He couldn't be stopped. Not by this old fool. Not by any other idiot, for that matter. He weighed the key in his hand. All he had to do was find the right padlock. And if he didn't find it, that wouldn't be a problem either. Everything would still be under control if no one else saw those papers.

He grinned to himself, untied the moorings, threw the hawser on board, and pushed the boat off the quay.

Part One

Forfatterfabrikken Forlag AS

Chapter One

In the hours before I get up, I often alternate between dream and reality, oscillating between the past and the present, between what is and what was, and all the things that didn't turn out as intended. That morning was no exception.

Apart from the rain drumming against the window, my bedroom was quiet and dark, but my cell phone interrupted the silence by vibrating and illuminating the worn edges of my bedside table. Like an eager child, it demanded my immediate attention, but I didn't feel like talking to anyone, so I let it buzz.

Outside, it was still pitch black, broken only by the faint light of a street lamp. From his bed in the corner, I could smell our German Shepherd's wet fur and hear all the noises he made in his sleep.

I squinted at the phone's screen. It was Sunday morning, quarter past five, and the caller was unknown. I wanted to throw the phone against the wall and go back to sleep, but I feared it might be about my dad and felt a pang of guilt. Maybe something had happened—a fall, a heart attack, or worse?

I grabbed the phone, stared at the unknown number, and realized my life would change the second I picked up this call. It might be some jerk drunkenly dialing the wrong number, but it had to be bad news if it was for me.

I could postpone the problem by ignoring it and letting it go to voicemail, but if it was about my dad, I had to answer. I took a deep breath, steeled myself, and pressed green.

"Yeah... hello?" My voice sounded strange, as if I was speaking with helium in my lungs. Sleepiness still covered my brain like a heavy blanket. I tried to clear my throat, but it felt like it had been treated with a rugged sandpaper, and my tongue couldn't move.

I fumbled for my bedside Coke, but it was empty, and I realized I should have brought an extra.

A woman cleared her throat. "Are you Flokí? Flokí Wilhelmsen?"

It was an unfamiliar voice. "Speaking."

The woman cleared her throat again. "My name is Cathrine. Cathrine Runevik."

The name meant nothing to me, and the world tilted to the right.

Cathrine paused and collected herself. Her voice trembled. "I'm a friend of Olav's. We need to talk."

I wanted to say something funny about how this dialogue should be delivered at the end of a relationship, but I couldn't stand my dry wit and let it go. I couldn't count the number of times I'd had to comfort women whom Olav, my younger brother, had disappointed.

With a grunt, I fell flat on my pillow and closed my eyes. It took care of the dizziness. There was one drop of Coke left in my can. It was warm and tasted awful, but at least it moistened my tongue.

Irritated, I squeezed the phone harder. The metal edge dented my palm. "No, we don't need to talk. You got any idea what day and time this is?"

She started crying. "He's missing."

Something in her voice told me she was serious about this. The adrenaline took over, and my heart rate increased. It focused my mind as I sat half upright in bed with my elbows for support. The bed creaked beneath me, an old piece of furniture long since seeing its best days. "Say again?"

She blew her nose. "Olav. He's disappeared."

Her voice was anxious and despairing. I rubbed the back of my neck to liven up my brain. "Tell me what happened." I tried to keep my voice calm and professional, though it sounded light.

She took a deep breath. "Olav was supposed to meet me at the airport in Malaga yesterday afternoon, but he never turned up. I couldn't reach him on his cell phone, so I took the train to Fuengirola and then the bus to his apartment in Elviria. He wasn't there. He..."

She paused before continuing, "... still hasn't turned up, and he's still not answering his cellphone. No one has any idea where he is."

I calmed down. I pushed the cushions around me and got more comfortable. It was as I expected. Olav not making it home after a night out was nothing to get all worked up about. I lowered my voice a few octaves. "Where are you now?"

She spoke slowly and precisely, as if she were talking to a toddler: "In Spain, Marbella."

I closed my eyes. I couldn't take this anymore. "I meant, where in Marbella? But ... whatever. Forget it."

She laughed, a nervous laugh. "I'm in Olav's apartment at Elviria del Sol."

She was full of surprises. "And how did you get into his apartment, Ms. Runevik?"

I sounded condescending and old-fashioned but was too tired to care.

"Cathrine. Or Cath, if you like. That's what most people would call me," she said.

Lord have mercy.

"So, how did you get into his apartment?" I repeated.

She hesitated again. "Olav gave me a key to his apartment just before he flew to Spain. 'Just in case you might need it,' he said."

This differed from the Olav I knew. Under normal circumstances, Olav would be very concerned about protecting his private life and possessions. "So he figured there was a chance he wouldn't be able to pick you up? Did he say why?"

She was silent for a moment. "No, he... He didn't say anything about that. I mean, I didn't ask him either. Didn't think about it. He was always a bit secretive about his plans, but it's not like him to disappear like this."

I disagreed. "Has he disappeared, or was he prevented from picking you up? Have you spoken to anyone about this?"

She sounded unsure. "What difference does it make? He's not here. I've tried to contact some of his friends, but nobody has seen him for a while."

It was time to end this call. "So why are you calling me in the middle of the night on a Sunday morning?"

Her voice vibrated again. "He gave me your number. He said I could call you if need be."

My irritation got the better of me. "He told you to call me? In Norway? At this hour?"

She fell silent for a few seconds. "You're in Norway? I had no idea."

Logical, I guess. A question surfaced in my mind. "His apartment seems normal?" I asked.

She shrugged. "What do you mean? It's a bit of a mess."

I closed my eyes. "No signs of a break-in? No signs of a struggle?"

She sounded puzzled. "No. Why?"

I trailed off. "Listen, Olav will probably show up soon, Cathrine. It's way too early."

She hesitated once more. "Can you call him? Can you get in touch with him? Maybe he'll answer you?"

I groaned. I desperately needed sleep and go back to my dream world where Jo-Ann was waiting for me. I couldn't stomach another jealousy drama and dropped onto my bed again.

My trusty Glock 19 slipped out from its hiding under my pillow. The cold barrel tickled the back of my neck. The contour of the rifled stock pressed against my cheek. I tucked it back in.

"We have to give him some time. It's far too early on a Sunday morning. Nicky Beach has yet to close. Olav sometimes needs to remember the time and place. I'm sure he'll be there soon."

She hesitated no more. "You have to call him now," she insisted. No wonder my phone never gave up calling me. It wasn't an allowed option. "I need to know Olav is okay. What if something happened to him? I don't care where he's been or why he didn't pick me up. I need to know that he's okay. Please!"

I took a deep breath. "Okay, okay, I'll call him. I promise I'll call." I instantly regretted it.

"Thank you!"

"No problem," I lied like a politician in the run-up to an election. The phone went silent for a moment, and then she hung up.

I lay on my side, closed my eyes, and wrapped my arms around the worn duvet lying on the empty part of the bed before I hugged it close. Jo-Ann still felt as if she were there, as if the warmth of her body were close to mine, and for a moment, she was in my arms again.

I buried my face in the covers. Her wise eyes found mine. The faint scent of her favorite perfume calmed me, and for a moment, I forgot all about the loss and grief that threatened to choke me every day.

I stayed like that for a while, but the conversation with Cathrine kept coming back and kept me awake. The peace and slumber would not return, and in the end, I gave up. With an effort, I rolled out of bed.

The night let go, and the day claimed my presence.

Chapter Two

The small village of Mølstrevåg was quiet this morning, its silence broken only by the distant cries of seagulls and crashing waves hitting the pier.

I opened the window and inhaled the smell of fertilizer from the fields on the other side of the road. A fly buzzed and thumped against the window in an annoying rhythm. I couldn't watch such pointless self-harm, so I pulled aside the curtain, opened the window, gave the poor thing a swat to get out, and watched it hum away without as much as a whisper of thanks.

Life in Mølstrevåg was miles away from my prior life in San Francisco, and that was the whole point, I guess. In this isolated area, I had complete control over any strangers visiting.

Last night's self-medication still weighed heavily on my body. I picked up the Balvenie bottle from the floor and put it in the cardboard box at the back of the cupboard so it wouldn't feel as lonely.

My conversation with Cathrine still churned in my head. Could she have other details I should consider? Was there anything I'd missed?

I didn't want to worry about his issues—not my circus, not my monkeys—he was a grown man.

But he'd given Cathrine my cellphone number, which was unusual. If something prevented him, I could not pick her up at the Malaga airport because I was in Norway. So why would she need my number? It seemed so pointless.

I stood up, turned off the alarm, and checked the outdoor cameras on my phone, but nothing unusual happened.

I wore my new black sweatpants and a white T-shirt with the San Francisco Police Department's logo in blue and gold, but removed the sweatshirt, pulled on a neutral white T-shirt instead, and attached the Glock to the holster on my back.

It's illegal to carry a gun in this country, except for a select few. Even the police didn't carry. But as a police officer in the United States, I've carried a gun my entire adult life. Without a weapon, I might as well be walking around naked. To me, the gun was a constant reminder to be vigilant and fair and to protect what was most important to me: my daughter. Protect and serve had become this very personal slogan to me—even though I'd nicked it from my colleagues down in LA.

I pulled on a loose-fitting track jacket to hide the weapon and entered the hallway. I retrieved a fresh tea light from a bag in the dresser, lit it, and placed it in front of the black-and-white portrait of Jo-Ann, straightened up the red rose in the vase next to it, and studied the face smiling at me from the broad, black frame. Studied her eyes—still just as warm. Her face—still as beautiful. Her smile—precisely the way I wanted to remember it.

The futility of her no longer being with me washed over me. I hurried down the stairs.

Catch followed with eager panting, his wagging tail hitting the wooden floor. His contagious joy made sorrow go away for a while. I petted his muscular chest, told him what a good boy he was, put out some dry food, and filled his bowl with water. He deserved that much. Therapy sessions would be much more expensive.

I opened the kitchen window. The scents of damp grass and garden filled the room. I sat at the massive wooden table and admired the flowering rhododendrons and the sparkling fjord view.

Olav had given Cathrine his apartment keys a month and a half before he left for Spain. Even then, he must have realized he might not pick her up at the airport. Why hadn't he mentioned this to me or my father? And why did he give her my phone number without checking with me first?

I had neither the time nor the desire to clean up his eternal chaos. But there was something about this situation that was different.

What the hell are you up to, Olav?

Something had changed with Olav while I was living in the States. The tiny, kind schoolboy I left behind had become a young man. Okay, fine. Expected. But he had become so... I searched for the word... irresponsible? He didn't show up for the jobs he had accepted, was in constant money trouble, and was a real pain in the ass who still stayed in his old bedroom when home.

For a while, our dad had his hands full, keeping him on his toes, out of the clutches of debt collectors, and doing grief work among rejected female acquaintances.

However, Olav was a thoughtful, kind, and helpful brother who was also concerned about our little family. He always understood when I needed support or someone to talk to, and he would help with everything from practical work to listening to long, self-pitying monologues when I needed it. That had been often in recent years.

When our mother died, he used much of his inheritance from her to buy his apartment in Spain. He spent about half the year in Spain but called our dad weekly and stayed in his childhood room whenever he was home.

I shook off these thoughts about Olav. The weather cleared, and the sun peeked out. On the fjord, seagulls helped themselves to the cargo of a fishing boat. I picked up my tiny military binoculars from the windowsill and watched the ship, the seagulls, and the ship's surroundings. Then, as I always did, I scanned the terrain.

In the mid-9th century, the Viking King Flokí Vilgerdsson lived in this area. He had fallen out with the mighty king Harald Fairhair farther south in the Strait of Karmsund, or Norvegr—The Way North—as the strait was called then. He took his people and cattle and settled on an island west of the Orkney Islands, which he later named Iceland.

The Vikings have always fascinated my father, Godtfred. He found my mother in Mølstrevåg while searching for Flokí's old royal court. They got married and had me, Flokí, the firstborn. Ten years later, Olav was born. He, too, got a royal name from Viking times.

I laced up my old running shoes and ran the four kilometers to the Ryvarden Cultural Lighthouse. Catch ran alongside me, happy as could be.

As I rounded a rocky outcrop, the old lighthouse area appeared as a white-painted oasis at the end of the rocky sea gap. The bright morning sun reflected off the white wooden buildings. A breeze brought the fresh, salty August air from the sea outside.

There were no tenants in the old lighthouse keeper's house this weekend, but soon, coffee-thirsty hikers, couples in love, photo enthusiasts, and tormented souls who needed to vent would invade the area. People like me. But for now, I had this paradise all to myself.

I let Catch loose, breathed the sea breeze, and jogged down to the concrete slab before the lighthouse while I stepped around and shadowboxed against an imaginary opponent. I like imaginary opponents. They don't fight back.

Sletta, this weather-exposed piece of sea where the North Sea pulls right up against the land, surrounded me in all directions.

The magnificent view, the sunshine, and the fresh salty air gave me a euphoric feeling of freedom.

A container ship from the Helman-Larssen shipping company passed me into the shipping lane. I met with the company's owner, John Helman-Larssen, a few years back. He was an excellent and amicable guy and a typical man with tons of New Money. You've met the type: expensive cars, watches, and houses with enough square meters to make a mall manager envy him.

He paid a handsome amount to take over part of the property Olav and I inherited from my mother, so I'm not complaining. But I kept her childhood home, and Olav kept a small plot of land next door, where he planned to build a cabin.

I flopped down onto a blue-painted concrete block and fished out my cell phone. Was it okay to call Olav now? A glance at my watch, and I let it be. Should I call at all? And if so, how should I phrase my concern? I could complain about being woken up in the middle of the night. That should be kosher. After all, he was the one who gave her my number.

I sat staring at the rusty railing, turned my head to the wind, and scouted out the sea to the north.

Bloksen, the reef where Sleipner sank in 1999, was a couple of Olympic-sized stone throws out. It was peaceful on a beautiful late summer's day like this, but seventy-six souls fought against the icy, raging sea that night in November. For a moment, the small farming community of Mølstrevåg filled with helicopters, ambulances, blue flashing lights, and TV crews.

Olav was just a boy. He and his mother often spent their weekends in Mølstrevåg. He called me all excited and told me what he'd seen and heard that day. He did not know I was sitting in a hospital ward in San Francisco, having my arm patched up after a shooting. I still haven't told him.

I took out my cell phone again, sent him a brief message, and asked for a swift reply. There was no response.

When I returned to the house, Charlene, my fifteen-year-old daughter, was busy doing her homework in the kitchen. This morning, the sun had given her half-length blond hair that extra shine.

She put on her worried looks, rested her index finger on her lower lip, and looked at me over the rim of her reading glasses. "Good morning, old man! Did you remember to park the walker so it doesn't block my driveway?"

She lisped and put on a poker-faced expression. Then, her face broke into a big, hearty smile. "Morning, Daddy!"

Seeing her like this warmed my heart.

"Morning, sunshine! Very funny." I tried to look smug. "Has this cheeky young lady had breakfast while I was out?"

"Figured you'd be back soon, so I did my homework while I waited. But now I'm hungry." She packed away her glasses, books, and the Mac.

I looked at her. "What makes you get up early and do your homework on a Sunday morning, huh? Teenagers don't get up early on their own." She met my gaze with an innocent expression.

I inhaled the air and squeezed my eyes shut. "Wait a minute, girl! You're up to something, aren't you? You've either done something stupid and want my forgiveness, or you're planning something stupid and want my blessing. So, what is it?"

She ignored the question. "Who called you in the middle of the night?" She'd already learned that attacking was the better defense.

"Someone who was looking for Uncle Olav."

I hoped she would leave it at that.

She squinted at me. "A lady?"

"Yup."

"Did you talk to Uncle Olav, then?"

I stared out the window, unsure why I hadn't called him. "Thought it was too early to call him. But I sent him a text message."

"Has he replied?"

"Not yet. Do you want eggs and bacon? Sunny side up?"

She didn't get distracted. "Maybe you should call him? Just in case?"

She peered out the window, watching me in her peripheral vision.

I picked up the phone and dialed the number with a determination that surprised even me. The phone rang for quite a while, but no one answered it. Then, Olav's recorded voice told me I had reached his voicemail, and I asked him to call me back and ended the call.

She scrutinized me with a grave expression. "Voicemail?"

I nodded.

"Let's hope he calls you back, then," she said, looking at me with the dark, warm eyes she had inherited from her mother.

I nodded.

As we set the table and prepared breakfast, it was as if we had a normal life. These moments of everyday normalcy with Charlene got me through my days.

"Daddy," she began, seemingly at random. I prepared myself. "Could Vivian and I spend the night at Grandpa's next Friday? We're going to the movies."

She looked at me encouragingly. Despite the tragedy she had experienced, her face still radiated childlike innocence.

I would have loved to let her have that pleasure, but the risk was too high. "There's no need to stay overnight. I can drive you both to the movie theater, visit your grandpa while I wait, and pick you girls up afterward. It's best if we spend the night here. You know damn well why!"

"Please don't give me that. I'm fifteen, and my grandpa takes care of us."

"And I'm over forty and sleep well here. We've discussed this before, hon. Nothing has changed. Did you want eggs?"

She didn't reply. Her face closed. The joy disappeared. We ate in silence.

"Do you think something might have happened to him?" she asked when we had eaten.

"No," I said. A bit too quickly; I needed to sound more convincing. "Olav has forgotten to pick her up. He can be quite absent-minded."

The young woman's face had a hint of a smile. "Maybe he's met his true love," she suggested.

I smiled, too. "Sure, he does that all the time," I said.

We both laughed, but my thoughts drifted back to the conversation with Cathrine.

Charlene studied my face and became serious again. "Are you going to Spain, Daddy?" Her eyes didn't waver. "I'll be fine if you want to," she said.

I grabbed her hands. "Nope," I said. "You'll be fine without me, I believe you, but how would I survive without you?"

Chapter Three

The fall sun cast its razor-sharp colors over the property. The white wooden house with the old red frames glowed and stood as a silent witness to my parents' life together, and in front of the house was the green lawn where Olav and I ran around as kids.

The leaves on the trees and bushes swayed in the wind, and the garden beds were full of flowers. Everything was kept just how my mother had once decided; it was beautiful. It was two o'clock, and time for the Sunday dinner at my childhood home in Hauge.

My dad had always loved to cook and sailed at sea as a steward when I was a child. He always cooked dinner on those few occasions when he was back home, and as he retired and became a widower, his Sunday gathering with children and grandchild was a sacred ritual. I had long since given up trying to get him to Mølstrevåg to let me do the cooking.

The smell of braised beef, potatoes, carrots, and onion gravy lured us from the car and into the house, and I felt starving.

Out of habit, I scanned the surroundings and memorized the details: the two crates the neighbor had yet to bring in, the black, freshly polished Golf parked farther down the street, and the forgotten red scarf on the picket fence on the other side of the road.

"Come on in, folks! This will be a treat!" he chirped through the open front door. Then my old man stood in the kitchen doorway in a red plaid apron, smiling, with his head on a swivel and his arms ready for a real sailor's hug, and although he wasn't as vigorous as his youth, his eyes still glowed with the same energy.

Charlene embraced him before disappearing with her knitting yarns and a thick novel under her arm. The sharp scent of furniture polish mingled with the smell of dinner as she opened the door to the living room. Godtfred watched her with pride: "Look at her; she's growing older every day. Our little girl's already a big girl now." He said it with a mix of pride and sadness. "But she will always be my little girl and never outgrow that."

I put my arm around his shoulders, and we went into the kitchen to lift the iron pots off the stove. Dad closed his eyes and tasted the food, smiled and nodded, and signaled us to pour the food into the serving dishes.

He cleared his throat and looked troubled as he said: "I've been trying to call Olav over the past few days, but he's not answering; you heard anything?"

I hesitated.

"Daddy!" came accusingly from the living room. "No," I conceded, giving him a summary of my phone conversation with Cathrine. "I feel sorry for her. Olav probably found himself a woman and forgot all about her."

"Let's hope so," he whispered as an afterthought.

"Do we have any reason to believe otherwise?" I said, more brusquely than I intended.

Dad didn't answer and remained thoughtful as we finished setting the table.

After a hearty dinner, topped off with my dad's "Queen Maud" pudding, I stretched out on the sofa in the living room and let the Sunday peace settle in. My thoughts turned to the day we all traveled to my wedding in San Francisco; the taxi had arrived, and the luggage was loaded, but Olav was nowhere to be found.

I ran around the house looking for him. I found him in my empty room on the second floor, at the bottom of the wardrobe, where he threw himself around my neck the moment I opened the door. "You take care of yourself, bro," he cried. "I'll take care of Mom and Dad," and we hugged like that until Dad came and chased us off to catch the plane.

When we did the dishes together later, Dad couldn't hold back his worry anymore and whispered so that Charlene wouldn't hear him: "There's something I've never told you."

I met his gaze; something hurt and unfamiliar was in his eyes, and my anxiety rose again. "What?"

"I have no idea how to tell you this," he said, scraping his foot along the floor like a shy teenager.

I gave him a disarming smile while concentrating on scouring the bottom of a pot with steel wool and said: "Try to start at the beginning; that's the best place to begin."

"Well, it ain't easy," he said before he continued. "We had problems with Olav while you were living in the States. He hooked up with people he should've had the sense to stay away from."

I held my breath for a moment. "What kind of people, Dad?"

"He, uh... He got caught dealing cannabis one Saturday night," he said and eyed me before he looked out the kitchen window. "Got into trouble with some guys who weren't peaceful, if you understand; we had them at our front door one night, and I paid them what he owed them. A debt of honor, they told me. Fortunately, we never saw them again."

My rage grew, and my blood was throbbing in my temples. "Why the hell...," I said and paused momentarily, catching my breath, "... haven't you told me this before, Dad?"

He fell silent, and his body shrank. I gave in to my anger and frustration and roared at him. "Why the heck...?"

I glimpsed Charlene's startled face in the doorway. She looked from me to Dad and back. "What is it, Daddy?"

I took a deep breath. "Forget it, Charlie. This is between Grandpa and me, okay? It's not as bad as it sounds." She looked at us both wide-eyed. She stood demonstratively still, saying nothing, then turned and left.

We carried on with the dishes. He continued in a low voice: "I'm truly worried about him. It isn't like him not to call me back. Olav always prioritizes his family. Something is wrong. I can feel it in my bones."

He bent his head over the sink without looking me in the eye. We worked in silence for a while. "One more thing. I know you don't believe in such things, but I imagined Olav standing in my living room on Thursday. In the evening. As I was resting on the sofa before the evening news. He was frightened and asked for help. I haven't had peace of mind since. That's why I've been trying to call him."

I couldn't take it anymore, so I calmed him down with a dampening hand gesture. "Calm down. Olav is okay. He's just been partying a bit last night. He'll be calling soon, and you've been worrying for no reason."

"No, I think he needs help. The people he got into trouble with at home will be like the Boy Scouts compared to those who operate in Marbella. The big money attracts the worst kind of shit. If we don't hear from him tonight, you must get on the first flight tomorrow."

"Let's give the boy a chance to get home and charge his cell phone before we go off the rails. I can't fly to Spain for every minor incident in his restless existence. I have a daughter who needs me here. Besides, I'm not a cop anymore, and you know why. If Olav is in trouble, the police in Marbella should help him. There's nothing I can or should do that the local police can't do just as well or much better. They know the environment; they know the people. I'm the last person Olav needs if he's in trouble. I only make things worse."

But he didn't budge. "What nonsense! Do you think the police in Spain's most corrupt city will help your brother? They locked up the entire city council! For corruption." He was about to raise his voice again. "You were the best damn investigator in San Francisco. The highest clearance rate for five years in a row. You need to stop blaming yourself for what happened. If Olav needs help, you need to be there! He is your brother, damn it."

I gripped the kitchen worktop and stared at the table surface. "Dad!" I hissed through clenched teeth. "I don't blame myself for everything. But Jo-Ann is dead because of me and my recklessness. It's my fault. If I hadn't taken that case, she would still be here with us, with Charlene, you, and me. We both know this is true."

He looked distraught. "The only person responsible for Jo-Ann's death is the man who killed her. And while you blame yourself, your life is slipping away from you. I can't stop it, but it's about your family this time! Your brother, for God's sake. Something may have happened to him. One of us has to be there for him. If you don't go, I'll go myself." His old body trembled in excitement.

"You have to go, Daddy!" Those words came from the living room door.

I turned around. Charlene was back. "He's right. You have to go. Me and Catch will stay with Grandpa. We'll have a good time here, and I'll be fine without you. We can't bring Mom back, Daddy, but you can help Uncle Olav if he's in trouble. You have to."

Her words were simple, and it wasn't a request but an order. She looked straight at me with her mother's warm, determined eyes. Her gaze never wavered an inch.

Chapter Four

That Monday afternoon, the departure hall smelled heavy of bacon, sausages, and coffee. Rain from the North Sea whipped against the windows. The stream of drops transformed the world outside into a blurred, darker landscape, in stark contrast to the bright lights of the hall.

The Norwegian Air Shuttle flight was lined up on domestic and ready to depart. A small private jet slid in place in front of a hangar farther away on the tarmac. And that was about it. The Ryanair flight would land in an hour at the earliest but would be airborne again in less than twenty minutes.

I bought a baguette, a Coke, and the local newspaper—more by habit than a conscious decision. It's a fixed routine of mine when traveling. I found a small table with an excellent overview of the room and a chair with my back to the wall—another habit I have.

All around me, people were traveling. Many traveled together, while some, like me, the loners, sat alone at their tables. Regardless of the company we kept, most preferred scrolling their cell phones. It was a strange world.

An SAS flight from Oslo dropped out of the low-hanging clouds. The engine roared in protest as it slowed down on the short, slippery landing strip.

I opened today's newspaper. A notice about a drowning accident caught my attention. Someone found the body of an older man floating in the harbor.

Part of the article read: "'There is nothing to indicate a criminal offense caused the death. It appears to be an accidental incident,' says Police Inspector Vik at HSPD. In a press release, he also stated they would not draw any conclusion until after the autopsy, which the Gades Institute will carry out this coming Tuesday. The police say they have completed their initial investigative steps and will further review the case when the autopsy report is available."

I hate drownings with a passion. As an officer in San Francisco, I often fished dead people out of the ocean. Sometimes, it was some poor bastard who had jumped off the Golden Gate; other times, it was boaters with too much alcohol or people who had fallen out with the triads or other gangs.

Whatever the reason, it was just as unpleasant. A body floating in the ocean is not a pretty sight and often a terrible strain for everyone involved.

Satisfied, I put the remains of my baguette in the trash and headed for International.

Like many airports, a wall of duty-free goods protected Haugesund Airport's international gates. Duty-free alcohol, tobacco, candy, and perfume bombarded travelers, marking their first encounter with the decadent outside world free of any political correctness.

I studied a bottle of Dom Pérignon Brut. Champagne, particularly Dom Pérignon, had been Jo-Ann's and my guilty pleasure. I left it on the shelf. It wouldn't be the same on my own.

A woman stood staring at me from Arrival. She was dressed in a white Dior suit, tailored and elegant, as if she had walked straight out of a fashion magazine and landed herself in my drab gray life. The short jacket stressed her curves with perfection. Her half-length raven-black hair was hidden behind a white shawl, and dark sunglasses covered her eyes and parts of her tanned face.

I'd met her before but couldn't place her in my memory. Maybe I was out of practice, or perhaps the resemblance to Jackie Kennedy confused the synapses in my brain.

A radiant smile spread across her deep red lips as she approached me. Her steps were calm but determined. "Flokí, isn't it?" Her voice was soft. She held out a white-gloved hand, and I remembered who she was.

She held her hand in a position and at a height, inviting me to kiss it, but my Norwegian spinal reflexes stopped me. "Anita?" I said instead and shook her hand. She removed her sunglasses and fixed her hypnotic green eyes straight on me.

She was Anita Helman-Larssen, the shipowner's daughter and the general manager of several of his companies. Among other things, she headed the company buying the property we inherited from my mother. It was a pleasant surprise that she recalled me from a meeting many years ago.

I threw out my arms. "I'm sorry I didn't recognize you right away."

She laughed—a low, melodic sound—and removed her shawl with a practiced movement, shaking her hair so it fell around her shoulders. A seductive, elegant perfume wrapped itself around us—guaranteed to be a brand I wouldn't find at the local duty-free shop.

"It has been far too long. Do you still live in your charming little house in Mølstrevåg?"

I let my gaze drift toward the exit and freedom. "Yeah. Same place. Like it there."

She followed my gaze and nodded toward the departure area. "Are you going far?"

"To Spain. Marbella." I prayed she wouldn't ask any more questions.

She nodded. "Fantastic area. I've had a week in Copenhagen. It's a lot of fun in Copenhagen, but not the same as Costa del Sol. Especially not the weather." She laughed softly, then touched my arm while her eyes searched mine. "What do you say we have coffee together soon? That would be nice." She was close to me, and her voice was low and intimate as if she were sharing a secret only the two of us would know.

I blushed. I couldn't help it. The physical evidence of the battle between desire and reason ravaged me right then and there. "Yeah, sure."

"A man of your talents could be... interesting... to us," she said after a pause, locking her green eyes in mine again. She pulled out a business card from her small handbag. Even that Dior, of course. "Call me when you get back."

She didn't expect me to say no. "Okay. Sure. Yeah. Right," I said intelligently, studying the selection of chocolates on the shelf behind her. I hated that I didn't decline her right away. It would have saved me the embarrassment of calling and canceling later.

She smiled back at me with a perfect row of pearly whites. "Then I'm looking forward to it," the red lips said.

The warm blush once again spread from my neck to my hairline. She gave me one last look full of promise, turned, and swung elegantly away on her high-heeled Blahnik shoes.

Watching her mesmerized me. The second before she disappeared, she turned around, looked straight at me, smiled to show she knew I had been watching her, and swung on behind the mirrored customs wall.

I stood like that for a while, caught in my conflicting emotions. Why had Anita's presence aroused such emotion and uncertainty? Had my starving hormones taken control of me? Was I that easy?

Part Two

Forfatterfabrikken Forlag AS

Chapter Five

I spotted her as I came out of the baggage claim at Malaga Airport. Not because I knew what she looked like but because she was holding a poster with my name on it.

She was in her late twenties. She had long, dark blond hair that fell in light waves over her shoulders and a long, narrow torso. Freckles scattered her summer-brown face, and she wore a simple but elegant jacket over a sporty figure.

She was the kind of woman who would survive in the wilderness with nothing more than a backpack and a Hershey bar yet maintain effortless elegance. Her blue eyes were vibrant and smiling. I liked her.

I walked toward her, boldly offered her my hand, and introduced myself. "Flokí," I said.

"Cathrine," she said, studying my face as your dentist does before attacking. "You're a lot like your brother, only older."

I wasn't sure if that counted as a statement or a compliment, but I believed the latter since she was a friend of Olav's. "Nice to meet you, too, Cathrine." I clasped my hands together. "All right! Would you like us to get going?"

"Sure," she said, turning 180 degrees on her gray and white Converse shoes. Then she started walking toward the exit.

As we exited the terminal, the Spanish night wrapped its soft, warm arms around me and thawed my air-conditioned body. It felt good after the cold and rainy departure from my hometown. I ran after Cathrine with my suitcase in tow. It threw itself at the cobblestones like a reluctant partner in a dance out of control.

When we reached the parking garage, Cathrine pressed the remote control, and the lights of a silver Ford Focus flashed at us a few rows away. "I rented this for less than a hundred euros a week. Automatic and all," she said, turning around and dropping the keys into my hand.

I found her concern for my finances surprising and nodded. "Thank you. Looks fine, but you drive. I'm unfamiliar with these roads, but you know your way around."

Cathrine maneuvered us from the airport area onto the A7 motorway toward Cadiz with quick, familiar movements.

As the car turned onto the highway, I wondered what to do next. Although Cathrine was friendly, I'm not a social person by nature. I got claustrophobic just thinking about sharing an apartment with a stranger, even more with a woman so much younger than me.

I thought about my meeting with Anita. It was hard, but I had to admit it: Anita had seduced me. The way those soft red lips moved, the smile playing along her mouth, her breasts rising and falling as she spoke, and the invitation in her eyes. I got caught up in the closeness and intimacy. The game ignited a desire I hadn't felt since Jo-Ann. I wanted her with a burning passion.

I lay back in the seat and rested my eyes. What would Jo-Ann think of me if she saw me from her place in eternity? I had to pull myself together. I had to focus on my mission and keep my sanity and equilibrium to deal with what lay ahead.

I stared out the windshield. Roadside signs flared up as the headlights hit them, fluttered past us, and disappeared into the wing mirror. The lights of myriad holiday homes and apartments twinkled like stars on the dark hills on both sides of the road. But the asphalt before us was like a black hole that swallowed all light and movement.

"Would you like me to move out of the apartment tomorrow?"

The question came out of nowhere. "No, that's fine," I heard myself say. "Olav invited you to stay in the apartment. Of course, you'll be staying as you've agreed."

"Thanks! I don't have much of a budget for this trip."

What I said was logical and correct, but I wanted something else. I wanted to be left alone, without having to relate to anyone but myself, to have complete control over my time and surroundings. I had to find a hotel, and I had to deal with it tomorrow. I was too tired to start now.

I closed my eyes. One thing was sure: it was out of the question for me to push around strangers while I was trying to find Olav. That was where I drew the line. Finding Olav - that's family business.

Cathrine turned off the AP7 highway and drove through Calahonda. An older man sat alone at a table in an outdoor restaurant with a glass of beer. He stared at us. I sank farther back in the car seat and let my mind wander again. The Sunshine Coast, with its vibrant nightlife and beautiful beaches, had always seemed like a place where people came to escape their cold Norwegian lives and enjoy their vacation or retirement. But it was also a place of loneliness, quiet longings, and lost dreams.

"I've been thinking about something," Cathrine began, interrupting my melancholy thoughts. "Olav seemed somewhat distant when he was home in Haugesund this summer, as if he had a lot on his mind. I didn't think much about it then, but I've been thinking about it for the last few hours. I remember him having long conversations on his cell phone out on the lawn. It seemed like it was something important. It was like he was only physically present at the party. Something bothered him, but he didn't want to discuss it. He laughed it off when the other wondered if he was having girl trouble again."

This could have been important, but we still needed the most essential pieces of this puzzle. Who was he talking to, and what were they talking about? Out loud, I said, "There could be a connection, of course, but it's not certain. By the way, there's one thing I wonder about. When did he give you the key to the apartment?"

"It was at the same party at Runar's, a mutual friend in Haugesund. At an after-party. Olav took it off the key ring and gave it to me."

"And my phone number?"

"He sent it to me on Messenger about a week ago."

"Didn't you think that's strange? That he gave you the number of someone in Norway?"

"No," she said, frowning, "it was a cellular number. I thought you were here, in Marbella. When I spoke to you, I realized you were in Norway. That's when it got weird."

The answer made sense, but it raised more questions. "Do you still have that message?"

She pulled off the main road at Elviria, stopped on the sidewalk, and pulled up the message on her phone.

"Hi, Cath! If I can't pick you up on Saturday, please call Floki. See contact info above. He'll understand. Olav."

I stared at that last sentence.

He will understand.

Chapter Six

I pushed the glass door aside and stepped out onto the terrace where Cathrine sat reading a Spanish interior design magazine with her legs crossed, a glass of Chablis balanced in her left hand, and a baguette in her lap.

The heat was palpable, although it wasn't yet ten o'clock in the morning, and splashes and laughter from the pool mingled with the chirping of birds.

Cathrine squinted in the bright sunlight and smiled with a cheerful "Hi!" as I stifled a yawn and nodded. "Morning!"

White plastered houses spread inside a fenced area with a vast, well-kept lawn and colorful flower beds with bougainvilleas. It was stunning, and I had no trouble understanding why Olav was here so much.

"Did you sleep well?" Cathrine asked as she studied an ad for bathroom equipment.

I wanted to say no, but I didn't. "Yeah, thanks," I said instead.

She had a breadcrumb in the corner of her mouth, and I had to fight the urge to wipe it away. My time as a single father had left its mark on me.

"I've bought baguettes, ham, cheese and wine. You'll find it all in the kitchen, along with jam," Cathrine said without taking her eyes off the magazine.

"Thanks," I muttered.

With a challenge in her voice, she looked at me and said, "So, what's your plan today?"

It was an innocent question, but it annoyed me, and I held back my answer to avoid sounding sour.

"Well, first, I want to talk to the police," I replied.

"I'm going to shower, and then I'll be ready," she said as she scrutinized my face.

I broke eye contact and let my gaze sweep over the azure sea shimmering in the distance. "I'm leaving now," I said. She focused on the magazine again. "Do you always prefer to be on your own, Floki?"

How was I supposed to respond to that? I did not need to defend myself from anyone, but before I could reply, she stood up, picked up her wine glass, and marched to the bathroom.

The service office for Elviria del Sol was on the ground floor of the building, facing a small side road, and a tanned, middle-aged woman with long blond hair opened the door when I stepped onto the walkway.

"You're early," she said with a smile. "We just opened." She studied me and said: "Are you Olav's brother?" more like a statement than a question.

I confirmed. "I'd like to talk to the local police. Do you know where they are located?"

A shadow of concern slid across her face. "Is it something serious?"

"No, it's just an insurance matter," I lied.

"A burglary? We've had a few."

"Nope."

"I'm sure Hernandes can help you out."

"Where would ..."

"If you see a Policia Local Segway outside the LIP building across the street, you'll find him there. They have a regular bridge tournament about this time."

Life as a policeman in Elviria sounded way more relaxing than being a cop in San Francisco.

The blue and cream building that housed the security company LIP Seguridad stood at the end of the area's only significant public parking lot. LIP's offices were on the second floor, at the end of a Bollywood-inspired brick staircase from street level to the front door. On the roof stood a sign proclaiming that the company cared for your home, and above the sign, a series of antennas strutted as a physical confirmation of the company's seriousness. Heavy curtains in front of all the windows kept out the scorching sun and any prying eyes.

A Segway with the Policia Local logo stood at the foot of the stairs, so I rang the bell. No one answered, so I rang the bell again, and the intercom cracked.

"Si?" said a toneless, metallic voice.

"I'm looking for Hernandes. The policeman."

"Un momento." A click broke the connection.

After an eternity, the door opened, and a man in a police uniform with dark sunglasses stood in the doorway. He had his cap in his hand, was of medium height, had dark hair, and had adorned his upper lip with a heavy mustache. "How may I help you?"

"Is there somewhere we can talk privately?"

He turned, shouted something to the back of the room, and then waved me in.

We entered a small anteroom with gloomy furnishings. By the window, a dusty fan whirred on a small table. He asked me to sit in one of the oversized, worn English leather armchairs, and with a stiff back, he sat opposite on the chair's far edge. "Well?" he asked, letting his sunglasses fall in a string around his neck.

I cleared my throat. "It's about my brother, Olav Wilhelmsen, a missing Norwegian citizen."

He stared at me. "Missing," he repeated. "I know who your brother is. When was the last time you saw him?"

"I came from Norway yesterday. A friend of Olav's called me on Sunday. She arrived from Norway on Saturday, and he had arranged to meet her at the airport but didn't attend. We haven't heard from him since."

"A friend," he said, studying the police cap in his hand. "Olav has a lot of girlfriends, isn't that so?"

I ignored the insinuation.

"He's a bit of a ladies' man?"

I locked eyes with him. "I'd like to report him missing."

He studied the cap again. "It's too early and a lot of paper-work. I saw him on Thursday afternoon with a blonde. It's only been a few days, and he may have dumped this girlfriend you're talking about and found himself another one." The cap spun around in his hand, and he raised his eyes and looked at me. "Unless you have reason to believe he has been exposed to something criminal?"

I shook my head.

"I hope you didn't come from Norway because of this?"

I said nothing.

"So you're Olav's famous brother, the American policeman? He's talked a lot about you." He nodded and appraised me with his eyes. "Are you a Dirty Harry kind of cop, Flokí?" He pretended to pull a revolver out of his holster. "You've gotta ask yourself one question: Do I feel lucky? Well, do ya, punk?" He rendered Clint Eastwood's immortal line with a Spanish accent and blew the smoke away from his imaginary revolver.

Maybe he had a future in spaghetti westerns. Who cares? "I would like to report Olav missing."

He grimaced and waved his hands. "This is Spain, señor, not Texas. I must remind you that we are in charge here. If he doesn't show up within a few days, we can report him missing." He put on his cap. "Most of the time, they'll show up long before." He stood up and stroked his mustache. His bridge-game was waiting.

"San Francisco," I said.

"Que?"

"San Francisco, as in California, not Texas."

He looked at me uncomprehendingly.

"Me and Dirty Harry," I said.

I skipped the elevator and walked up the stone steps to the apartment. The visit to the police ended as expected, but I needed to figure out where to go next. I reached the second floor as Cathrine ran down the stairs and past me.

"Hi," she said in passing, stopped a few steps below, and turned. She had freshly washed hair, makeup with a slight shadow around her blue eyes, and a pink mouth. There was something alien about her when she wore makeup like the sporty girl with mountain-wide eyes was gone. The woman standing in front of me was a lot more female.

"Things weren't going well with the police, huh?" she said.

I shrugged. "It was too early."

She thought for a moment. "I'm on my way to the city center," she said. "To meet a friend." Then she tilted her head. "Gustavo, a mutual acquaintance of Olav and me."

There was a slight smile lurking and a challenge in her eyes. "Would you like to join us?" she asked.

I hesitated, but I had no better plan, and talking to Olav's friends was a natural place to start. Curiosity got the better of me. "Okay," I said.

"I guess I should warn you, Flokí. Gustavo and I had a thing going a few years back. Just so you're prepared." She turned around. "Hurry," she shouted and ran down the stairs.

I felt like an uninvited guest at a party for two, so I stood still for a few seconds and considered the pros and cons.

Chapter Seven

We ordered Americanos at the counter and found a place to sit at one of the low, round mahogany tables at Café Intenso, on a narrow and busy side street in the old town in the center of Marbella. It was one of those modern coffee places where the menu was written with chalk on a blackboard, though it never changed.

The air was rich with the aroma of freshly brewed coffee, a comforting contrast to the pastries, which seemed to lack any distinct scent. Well-upholstered leather armchairs, reminiscent of my childhood, encircled plain tables, each chair unique yet standardized.

As I sat, I couldn't resist running my fingers over the shiny leather of the neighboring chair. My gaze wandered, taking in the books lining one wall and the vintage typewriter pictures adorning the others.

"Gustavo is a classmate from high school," said Cathrine. "He was my boyfriend back then; his father was Spanish, lost his job, and got divorced, so he and Gustavo moved back here."

Then she added: "I'm not good at long-distance relationships. Neither is he."

I nodded, thinking this didn't have to be as awkward as I feared. "Are you divorced?" she asked, looking at people hurrying past the window.

"A widower."

"For how long?"

"Five years. Ten months... and a few days."

She fell silent.

"You never found your Mr. Right?" I could have banged my head against one of those unique tables. To turn the conversation away from me, I'd made Cathrine sound like an aging virgin. "Don't get me wrong, you've still got time," I said to salvage the situation, but it only worsened. I wonder why I'd asked, as it wasn't my business, and I didn't care about her private life.

"I tend to choose the wrong kind of men. I guess that's just the way it is."

There was an awkward moment before anyone spoke. We both picked up our cell phones and escaped. Interrupted by a coffee grinder, the low-key conversation acted as a protective filter between us.

A young man in a bright Armani suit, black shirt with silver-gray tie, dark Ray-Bans, and pointed, hand-stitched Italian shoes came strolling along the sidewalk and stopped outside. Cathrine enthusiastically waved at him through the window. He waved back and came inside.

"Gustavo!"

He smiled at her and kissed her on both cheeks. Behind her back, he made a slight movement toward the man behind the counter. The barista brewed his coffee. Gustavo let go of Cathrine and turned toward me. "We haven't met, I believe," he said in Spanish, displaying his impressive teeth.

"Soy Flokí," I said, showing off some of my sparse knowledge of Spanish.

Gustavo nodded. "Yes, of course! Olav's brother. Should have seen the resemblance right away." He studied me like I was a fly in his ointment.

I showed him my not-so-perfect teeth and gestured toward the nearest leather chair. "Have a seat," I said.

"How long have the two of you been together?" Gustavo asked.

It took me a few seconds to realize what he was asking before I blurted, "Oh, my God, no! We're not together," and blushed.

Cathrine looked at me teasingly. "What a rapid save!"
She laughed.

"Cathrine and I have known each other for a very long time," Gustavo said as he studied my face. His smile still stuck around his teeth but didn't reach his eyes.

The barista put a latte on the table in front of him.

"And Olav? Is he also an acquaintance from way back?" I asked.

"Yes, but not in the same way."
Again, this strange smile, as if he was challenging me.

"Sure." I didn't want him to go into details.

"Do you know his whereabouts? We've been trying to get hold of him the past few days, but he's not answering his cell phone, and no one knows where he is."

"So maybe he doesn't want to talk to you?"

Cathrine sighed. "Get a grip, Gustavo! Have you seen him this week, or haven't you?"

Gustavo looked at me for a long time before returning to Cathrine. "I spoke to him on Tuesday last week. One week ago today. He's had some worries. Owed someone a ton of money. But on Tuesday, he seemed relieved. Said everything would work out fine."

"Right! Do you have any idea who he owed money to and how much?" I asked.

"You have to ask him about that. I may have said too much already."

He studied the white, handleless coffee cup in his hand, and I sat silent until I got his attention again.

"Olav is my brother," I said, emphasizing the word brother.

Gustavo nodded as he scrutinized the cup in front of him again. "You're his brother. The policeman." He emphasized the last word—the policeman.

This guy annoyed me to no end. "Listen, son! I'm not a cop anymore. If this is about drug money, then tell me straight up, now."

"No … It wasn't drugs," he said and put his head in his hands. "Olav didn't touch drugs anymore."

"But he owed a lot of money?"

Gustavo didn't answer.

"To whom? How much? For what?"

Gustavo still didn't answer.

Cathrine cleared her throat and waited until she made eye contact. Then she tilted her head understandingly and said, "You're trying to protect him, Gustavo, but this could be serious. Olav has been missing for many days. He was supposed to meet me at the airport but never arrived. Flokí needs to talk to him; I need to know he's okay, and we need your help."

Gustavo wriggled and sighed, avoiding her eyes. "He owed some money. Quite a lot of money. But no, I don't have the details. I swear I don't. But I can confirm it sure wasn't the Salvation Army."

He drank his coffee but didn't put his cup down. Something exciting on the inside of the cup demanded his attention. "But I can think of a guy who might know more. Someone closer to him than me. I can ask him if he wants to meet you."

He took out his cell phone, dialed it, put it to his ear, stood up, and walked outside.

"Can we trust this guy?" I asked Cathrine as the door closed behind him.

"Gustavo may have a strained relationship with the police, but he's a loyal friend. Not the faithful boyfriend type, I know all about that, but always loyal to his friends."

Outside the window, Gustavo gestured with his arms while talking on his cell phone. "Okay. Let's go with it," I said, draining the last drops of coffee. It had become cold.

Gustavo returned. "I've promised Cool J you'll buy him dinner at Antonio's. He'll meet you there at eight o'clock."

"That late?" Cathrine couldn't hide her disappointment.

"Believe me, that's an early bird for him. He's a creature of the night."

"Does he have a real name?" I asked.

"I have no idea what name is on his passport. Here, he's just called Cool J."

"So we're going to meet this Cool J at Antonio's at eight o'clock," I said. "And where can I find Antonio's?"

He seemed surprised. It was as if I'd just said something inappropriate. "It's on Banús."

"I know where it is," Cathrine interjected.

"Okay, Antonio's on Banús, eight o'clock," I said and got up to leave.

Gustavo turned to Cathrine. "I'd like to have a word with you." He nodded in my direction. "In private."

Cathrine pointed her head toward the door.

I went outside and stood for a while, enjoying the sun and the warmth. The window on the other side of the street reflected me in full figure. Age had given me more pronounced facial features. It was no longer round and childish, like when I patrolled the streets of San Francisco, and my nickname was Baby Face.

Probably because I came from the same exotic country as Ole Gunnar Solskjær, but that wasn't the only reason.

I liked what I saw. The dark glasses. The hair, with a hint of a silver streak, which I had combed to match the short beard that needed a trim. I looked a lot more manly than I felt and a little… rough. Perhaps it wasn't surprising that Hernandes mistook me for a reckless Dirty Harry type?

The smell of freshly baked pizza at a sidewalk restaurant reminded me that it had been a long time since breakfast.

I was about to turn back and ask Cathrine if she was ready for lunch when I noticed something in my peripheral vision. Cathrine and Gustavo were standing close together in the cafe. Judging by their body language, they were about to pick up where they had left off.

Chapter Eight

I strolled along the cobblestone streets in the old part of town. On an open, tiled square by a cathedral, a wedding photographer was busy taking pictures of a young bride and groom.

The newlyweds smiled at each other and the photographer, who directed them back and forth. Memories of my wedding came flooding back—the indescribable joy when she said, "I do." She wanted to be mine and promised it would only be the two of us until death did us part.

Death seemed unreal and far away. We were immortal, but death knew better. It came knocking when we least expected it.

I missed Charlene and my dad. Being in Spain while they were back home thousands of miles away felt absurd.

I was here for one reason only: to help Olav. If Hernandes was right, and Olav was living the sweet life sipping Piña Coladas and chasing women, it was not the creditors he should fear the most.

The most logical assumption would be that he'd gone hiding from his creditors, but I suspected this story was more complicated. Otherwise, I would have stayed home.

Apart from Charlene and Dad, what convinced me the most was that Olav had yet to contact us. I knew Olav would have let Dad or me know if he had gone underground. If he could prevent it, Olav would never have put Dad through this ordeal and all this uncertainty. There was no doubt in my mind. He would have taken the risk and given us some sign of life.

So what had happened to Olav? Why hadn't he reached out? I reminded myself why I flew down here—to figure this out.

My phone vibrated as I stood up. I moved away from the square and took the call while turning away.

"Hello, is this Flokí Wilhelmsen?" a cold and formal woman said.

I confirmed my identity.

"My name is Nina. I work as a nurse at the general hospital in Haugesund. This is about your father, Godtfred. "

My legs gave way, and I sat down on the edge of a fountain. I held my breath.

"Ambulance brought him in earlier today after showing signs of heart problems. He's now admitted to our care," she continued. She sounded businesslike and matter-of-fact, as if she was reading the weather forecast.

Chills and heat waves coursed through me. My thoughts whirled in all directions like dandelion seeds in the wind. Was it serious? Would I make it home in time? Was Charlene safe?

I had to get home.

"You there? You went all quiet on me."

"About those heart issues. Could you be more specific?" It was hard to breathe. Hard to talk.

"We've had him under observation for a while, but the doctors have detected no arrhythmias or other signs of pathological cardiac activity. All measurements are within the established, normal ranges."

"Which means..."

She sighed. "His heart has behaved since his admission to our care. He's no longer in the ICU but moved to the cardiology ward. Right now, he's sleeping, but you can come visit him as soon as possible." She spoke so loud that the phone was optional.

"I'm in Spain right now... trying to..."

"Sort out your thoughts. I see." She was a mind reader, too.

"Come home as soon as you can, no rush. Your father is in safe hands with us. There's no immediate danger, and we will keep you informed if there should be any change in his condition."

"Thanks! One more thing: my daughter Charlene is staying with Dad while I'm away. Is she there? Can I talk to her for a moment?"

"It was your daughter who called for the ambulance. A wonderful and bright young lady, by the way." Her voice softened. "She sat and waited for many hours while he was in the ICU, but after that, I'm afraid I haven't seen her."

"Okay, thanks..." I waited a few seconds but couldn't think of anything else to say, so I hung up.

I sat staring at my phone. My heartbeats were pounding so hard I could hear them. Charlene was a child, only fifteen years old. She had to be both terrified and lonely now. I should go straight home. Olav would have to sort out his problems.

I closed my eyes and hyperventilated a few times to calm down. It didn't help; my head felt like cotton. I dialed Charlene's number. The call went straight to voicemail, and her cheerful voice asked me to leave a message.

"Hey, sweetie, it's Dad. Call me back as soon as you can! I'm coming home on the first flight with an available seat. Thank you for getting Grandpa to the hospital. Proud of you, sweetie. Everything will be okay."

Going home was the only solution. I could only be in one place at a time, and Charlene was priority number one.

"Damn it, Olav! Why don't you give us some sign of life? Tell me you're okay so I can go home with a clear conscience?"

I checked my phone and found a direct flight home the following day, landing in Haugesund at two p.m.

I called Torstein. He had been my best man and best friend since first grade in elementary school. The only one I could trust besides family in a crisis like this.

"Am I interrupting?"

"No sweat, buddy. What's up?"

Everything tumbled out in a more or less coherent stream: "It's Dad... He's in the hospital with heart issues, but he's out of the ICU now. I'm in Spain because Olav is missing, and he hasn't been in touch for several days; Charlene is staying with Dad while I'm here, and now she's on her own, poor thing. I'm flying home, but it doesn't leave until tomorrow morning. Now I don't know what to do... and..."

"Relax, buddy. Take a deep breath. Listen, I can take care of Charlene. No sweat. She can stay with us until you're back. You should sit down somewhere, have a glass of wine, and think it all through; things will work out. The more wine, the better solutions, that's my experience. Well, there are exceptions. Ha-ha. I remember one night in..."

He interrupted himself. "I'll keep you in the loop about what's happening."

"Thanks a million. You have no idea..."

"Cut it out! We'll get things under control at home. I'll get right on it. But what's this about Olav gone missing?"

"Long story. He's been missing for some days. Dad got worried, so I came here to figure it out."

"You think it's some kind of woman trouble again?"

"I have no clue. The whole thing is one big mess."

"Yeah, Flokí, ha-ha, you live up to your name sometimes, buddy. But if the Olav thing was important enough for you to go down to Sangria-land, you might as well try to chat with him before rushing home. Talk to you later; I gotta get moving." He hung up without waiting for my reaction.

The photographer and the newlyweds had disappeared. I walked back toward Café Intenso with lighter steps, rounded a corner, and halted.

Gustavo wrapped his arms around Cathrine and kissed her on the mouth—not a friendly kiss on the cheek this time. His hand wandered down her back. Cathrine smiled and pushed him away, saying something that made him laugh.

They hadn't noticed me. I slipped into a side street and got out of sight but stopped as quickly. Why was I doing this? Cathrine and Gustavo had a special connection. Who Cathrine kissed wasn't my business.

I was here to find Olav, not to get tangled up in complicated feelings and relationships. There was enough drama in my life already. I straightened my back and walked back toward Café Intenso.

Cathrine was sitting alone at the table when I arrived. She looked up and smiled at me.

"There you are! Where did you go?" she asked.

I forced a smile. "I needed some air." Then I told her about Dad being admitted to the hospital. "I have to go back home tomorrow," I said.

She looked disappointed. "And this thing about Olav?"

I shrugged. "It's difficult, but I can't leave Charlene alone."

The phone in my pocket vibrated. It was a message from Torstein.

"On my way to the hospital. Take the time you need in Spain. Find Olav, will you? I'll hold down the fort. Breathe. Drink wine."

Torstein delivered the goods. Knowing Dad and Charlene were in safe hands until I got home lifted a burden off my shoulders. The ice cube in my stomach melted, and I could reason again.

Cathrine put a hand on my arm. "Shall we go?"

I nodded. "Yup."

The phone rang as we approached the car. It was Torstein again.

"I have some excellent news and some that may not be good. The good news is your dad has recovered. He believes he will get discharged in a few days. We'll see. He didn't look as sharp right now, though."

"The bad news?"

Torstein hesitated. "Well, um, I haven't been able to reach Charlene yet. She wasn't at your dad's place, not at the hospital, and the hospital doesn't know where she's gone either. Her phone goes straight to voicemail. Typical teenagers to turn off their phones and blame it on a dead battery or something."

The ice cube in my stomach froze up again. "She has a friend, Vivian Holmen, in Mølstrevåg. I can check with her."

"I've already talked to her, of course," said Torstein. "I've called all her friends, but she's not with any of them. The only exception is Vidar. He's not answering when I call, so I wonder if she might be with him. He lives right around the corner. I'm on my way there now."

I stood up and started pacing in front of the window. "Vidar, who?"

"Her boyfriend."

"Boyfriend?"

"Come on, Flokí, I thought you were keeping up. Vidar is a nice neighbor kid who's been in and out of our house since he was knee-high and realized my wife could bake. Ha-ha. And he'd always bounced along when Charlie and Vivian came over, even when my wife hadn't baked. I figured out early on something was happening there, you know."

He chuckled.

Chapter Nine

Even at full blast, the air conditioning couldn't penetrate the heat inside my head. I rolled down my window and let the wind cool me.

Charlene, a boyfriend? Since when? I shook my head. This would explain why she'd been so eager to stay overnight at her grandpa's in Haugesund. But why had she kept this a secret from me? Had Dad known about him for a long time? Probably.

Since I was a little boy, Mom and Dad preached the importance of family. They engraved the importance of family and loyalty in Olav's and my cerebral cortex. So why had my dad kept Olav's problems and Charlene's boyfriend hidden from me?

Cathrine slammed on the brakes for a red light.

"Why aren't you answering? Hello, are you still here?"

I turned to her. She threw her hands up in a frustrated gesture.

"What? Can you repeat? I'm not following," I mumbled.

She rolled her eyes. "So, what's our plan? Are we having dinner with Cool J tonight, or do you have other plans? I need answers. Talk to me!"

Dad called while I sorted my thoughts and tried to respond intelligently. I raised a hand to Cathrine to signal it was a priority call. She stared at the road while shaking her head in exasperation.

I answered the call: "How are you doing?"

"I'm much better now. It must have been... uh, the food. Perhaps the trout had been lying around too long. These cute nurses are taking good care of me, and the doctor says I'll be out tomorrow or the day after. Torstein and Vidar are caring for Charlene and Catch, so you don't need to worry about us. Have you met him, by the way? Vidar, I mean?"

There it was again. Vidar. It irritated me immensely that Charlene had a boyfriend everyone else knew about except me.

"Yes, he's a fine young man," Dad continued without waiting for my answer. "And he has wonderful parents who've raised him well. Charlene visited them last night. Torstein knows his family."

How often had I, during my time as a homicide detective, heard neighbors and friends describe men exposed as cold-blooded, cynical murderers as "fine young men"? How could he be so naïve?

"Why hasn't anyone told me Charlene has a boyfriend?"

There was a pause.

"Maybe because you insist on living in your past, son. A past where Charlene is still just a child." He paused. "And because you'd stalk the poor guy until he couldn't take it anymore."

I swallowed hard. There was quite a lot I'd like to say on the matter, but I couldn't risk him getting all worked up and having another episode.

"We'll cross that bridge when I get home."

"The very reason I called. Don't come home now; there's no point. Everything's under control, and there's nothing you can contribute that still needs to be handled. You're the one best positioned to help Olav. You're the one who knows him and understands how he thinks. Stay in Spain. That's where you can make a difference. Not at home."

I wasn't sure about either, but I let him continue. Should I tell him about Olav's money problems? Would he be able to handle it? Should I wait until he was out of the hospital? Olav was his son. He had a right to know. Loyalty, right? I decided and cleared my throat.

"I've received information that might explain why Olav is off the grid."

He went quiet and braced himself. "Tell me."

"He owes money. A lot. We need to find out to whom. But they're more to fear than the..."

"Listen to me. Olav may owe money and can go off the grid all he likes, but he'd always stay in touch with his family. Something is wrong. Find him. Don't quit until he's back home and safe."

His words were as I would have expected.

"I'll go to the police with this new information and see if it makes them understand the urgency and take action. Then I'll come home."

"Forget the police. You are way ahead of them. Keep going until you find him. You have no time to waste. That's where you can make a difference, not at home."

His trust in me touched me, but I couldn't meet his expectations.

"But okay, talk with the police, too. I know this police officer in Haugesund who can put you in contact with the right officer in Marbella. He's been to the Costa del Sol quite a bit in connection with his drug cases," he said,

"All right, but don't tell him more than you have to. I don't have a full picture of what this is all about. If nothing else, he could push some buttons to get them to take it seriously. Is it someone you trust?"

"He is Jonas Vik. I know him, and more importantly, he knows Olav. He was the one who caught Olav with the drugs. Gave him a second chance and took care of him. He's a good man," Dad said.

Cathrine parked the car outside Elviria del Sol.

"Okay. We've reached our destination. I'll call you later."

"Be careful. Trust your instincts. Olav needs you." He hung up.

"What's going on?" Cathrine studied the nails on her left hand.

"Dad's better, and Charlene is staying with a childhood buddy of mine." I couldn't bring myself to mention Vidar.

"And she has a friend no one's told you about?" She compared her nails on both hands. As far as I could tell, they were long and equally many.

I opened my door to get out.

"Flokí!" She was serious and determined.

I turned and looked at her.

She looked at me. Her eyes were dark.

"She's a big girl now. Deal with it!"

Chapter Ten

Puerto Banús, the harbor west of Marbella, glittered in the late afternoon sun. We had arrived at the Spanish version of St. Tropez, a playground for the super-rich and famous where everything you could wish for is readily available, absolutely everything, as long as you can pay.

Tourists in shorts, Scandinavians in tracksuits with backpacks, party girls in tight miniskirts, and older women in evening gowns strolled around the harbor area. Some stopped to take pictures next to a neon green Lamborghini; others admired the luxurious vessels moored side by side in the harbor, while some sipped overpriced drinks at the many bars and restaurants nestled between luxury boutiques along the quay.

Antonio's, an uncompromisingly authentic Spanish restaurant, sat in the middle of the harbor. The place oozed charm from an era where waiters wore white shirts and burgundy vests, each with a white towel draped over their arm. Inside, flames from candles flickered on small tables covered with white tablecloths, and the scent of saffron and grilled seafood filled the air, accompanied by the sound of a classical Spanish guitarist.

We got a table by the sidewalk and ordered a bottle of white wine and three glasses while waiting for Cool J. A blue and black Bugatti Veyron glided by on the narrow road along the quay, a dream of a car worth well over fifteen million kroner - before Norwegian taxes.

Behind the dark windows, I glimpsed the man behind the wheels wearing a traditional white robe and a broad black agal on his head. Next to and behind him sat two bodyguards in black suits, without visible necks, just muscles.

"Exclusive watches for your beautiful daughter, sir?" An African with arms full of "exclusive" watches and bags stared at us.

Cathrine giggled, but I ignored his comment about her being my daughter and shook my head. Selling fake bags and watches was a well-organized trade. I was certain there was a connection between the masterminds of this trade and the smugglers who transported people in those half-sinking boats across the Mediterranean Sea.

It wouldn't surprise me if the same criminal masterminds owned some boats moored in this very harbor. Some became filthy rich from other people's misery, and the engine of this cynical human trafficking was our willingness to adorn ourselves with those false feathers.

A flaming red Ferrari swung into an empty parking space by the quayside as we tasted the white wine. The door popped open, and a man with wild, black hair, dark sunglasses, white pants, and a thin white silk shirt unbuttoned to his navel stepped out. He was a strange mix of a rock star and a reincarnation of Saturday Night Fever, but he had something about him that made it seem natural and not weird.

He waved to someone he knew with a broad smile before heading toward our table. "Hope you haven't been waiting long."

We stood up. "Cool J," he introduced himself and kissed Cathrine on both cheeks before turning. "And you must be Flokí," he said, grabbing my hand. "Funny name. I understand it means some kind of trouble or entanglement in your language. Do you try to live up to it?"

He laughed. I smiled and nodded back. I had heard this comment many times, but his entrance and cheerful energy gave me a positive impression of him.

We sat down, and the waiter gave us our menu.

Cool J put a hand on my arm. "Fantastic to meet Olav's famous brother. A real sheriff!" He rolled his eyes. "Almost hard to believe," he said.

That made two of us. I didn't believe it either. Granted, I have worked in the San Francisco Police Department as a homicide detective, not a sheriff, but in another life entirely.

I was about to ask him about Olav when our waiter interrupted us to take our orders.

Later, as we enjoyed the well-chilled wine, I got another opportunity and leaned forward across the table. "I need to talk to you about Olav," I began.

He stared at his glass, twirling the stem back and forth, but said nothing.

"We cannot get in touch with him. He has yet to respond to any attempt to contact him, and no one knows where he is. It's... unusual for him."

He drank some wine. "There's not much to say," he said. "I don't know where he is, and it's better that way. Olav sometimes needs to... uh... be left alone."

"He can have his peace," I said. "But we'd like to know if he's okay."

"I don't know how to get in contact with him."

I scrutinized him as he studied his wine glass and avoided eye contact.

"Listen, look at me."

He met my gaze.

"We know Olav had money problems. Is that why he's gone underground?"

He didn't answer, but his eyes darted around.

"If Olav needs help, I want to know!" It came out more intensely than I'd meant.

He still didn't answer. The waiter bringing our appetizers glanced at us uncertainly.

"Why did you come here tonight if you didn't want to help us?" I asked more softly.

He didn't look as worldly and confident now and lowered his voice. "It's better this way. The less you know, the better. Olav is lying low for now. That's all we need to know."

Frustrated and needing venting, I excused myself and went to the bathroom.

When I returned, Cool J and Cathrine had their heads close together and were talking confidentially. She saw me over his shoulder and signaled for me to disappear. With a quick U-turn, I returned to the bathroom.

I called Charlene again, and this time, she answered. "Hi, Dad! I was almost out of battery when I called for the ambulance for Grandpa. Then it died completely while I was at the hospital."

"Was Vidar's phone also out of battery?"

She didn't answer. It was very awkward, and I let her off the hook. "We'll talk about this when I get home. What's important now is that you're staying with Torstein tonight, and I'm coming home tomorrow."

"But, Dad…"

"My plane lands at two o'clock."

"Dad! You don't need to come home for my sake. We… I'm at Torstein's and having a great time. The hospital will soon discharge Grandpa. We visited him, and he seemed fine again."

"You and Vidar?"

"Dad, stop it! Torstein and I, and yes… Vidar was with us. But you need to find Uncle Olav, which is much more important. Grandpa won't get better if you come home now and leave Olav in the lurch, and you know how much it means to him. And Dad, if Grandpa and I are fine, why do you want to come home then?"

She said it without reproach, but her words hit home. There was only one reason I wanted to go home now. Vidar. And she knew it. But Vidar could wait as long as Torstein vouched for him. Olav was more important right now.

I sighed. "Okay, I'll stay a few more days and see if I can get in touch with him, but when I come home, we need to talk. I must be able to trust you; we're not done with this matter."

When I returned to our table, where Cathrine and Cool J sat, my food was served. "Sorry, my daughter was on the phone," I said and sat down. "Drama at home. Where were we?"

After we had eaten for a while, Cathrine cleared her throat. "Flokí, Cool J has something he wants to tell you."

Cool J finished chewing and wiped his mouth with the napkin. "I should have told you right away," Cool J said. "Cathrine vouches that you can handle hearing it, even though you are, or were, a cop."

He took a deep breath, let it out, and straightened up. "Olav has a huge gambling debt. I don't know the exact amount, but with interest, compound interest, and all that, it's come up to more than a hundred thousand euros. Olav had already mortgaged his apartment to the hilt. That was enough to get rid of that first debt he gambled himself into. He thought he could win his money back. Now he's in a pickle."

He studied me. Then he lowered his gaze to the table as he continued. "I work as a DJ at the Shoot Out nightclub around the corner. Last Friday, Olav argued with a VIP guest, a filthy rich Arab named Al Sayed. He is the type of Arab prince who wades into money, drugs, and women abroad while his family runs a hardcore Sharia regime back home. Maybe they were arguing about money. That Olav owes money to Al Sayed."

He paused for a moment. "If so, I understand why he's gone underground 'cause Al Sayed has contacts everywhere and enough resources to make his life a living hell."

I sat there gaping. More than a hundred thousand euros? Over a million Norwegian kroner? In gambling debt? To an Arab prince?

"The good news was that he'd met someone who wanted to help him. Don't know who, but think it was a female, maybe this new girl he'd met. I don't know."

He tilted his head and winked at me. "I'm not too keen on women, but I could probably sacrifice myself for such a generous lady."

"How can I get in touch with Al Sayed?"

"He lives in a well-guarded villa by the sea on The Golden Mile. A fantastic place. I've been there both for parties and gigs; getting in requires an invitation, not to mention if you want an audience to talk to him privately. But Olav hung out there a lot, and if he's the one who lent him money and Olav has gone underground, he might want to talk to you guys."

"Can you arrange a conversation?"

He shrugged and grimaced. "I'd like to help Olav, but I'd rather not get on the wrong side of those people."

I opened Google Maps on my phone. "Okay, at least show me where he lives."

Chapter Eleven

"Look, there it is!" Cathrine exclaimed as we approached Al Sayed's villa. A castle would be a more accurate description of the house. Only the upper floors and two domes were visible above the wall encircling the property, but the gate, secured only by an electric barrier, gave an impressive view. The building comprised a two-story primary structure with two side wings in neoclassical style and a long driveway leading from the gate to the house.

They kept the brick building's facade in shades of beige with white contrast lines, adorning it with enough ornaments and columns to make King Solomon jealous.

This is madness, a voice screamed inside me, but out loud, I said, "Seems about right."

Before I knew it, we stood before the gate, where a security guard came out of a guardhouse and scrutinized us. We prepared an envelope filled with blank A4 papers, and Cathrine placed it in her lap. I pointed to it. "Documents for signing," I mumbled while my heart pounded.

"Which company?" he asked.

"Trusted Alliance Couriers. They asked us to keep a low profile."

Judging by his facial expression, we had succeeded in that.

"Identification?"

I handed him my driver's license, already regretting my bluff. He went into the guardroom and consulted with someone via a screen. I got my driver's license back, the barrier opened, and we could drive in.

Cathrine glanced back. "Is this smart?" Her voice was tense and uncertain.

"No," I said, and I meant it. But it was too late to turn back.

We rolled up the alley where well-groomed cypresses stood at attention. I stopped the car by a small fountain in front of the entrance.

On the opposite side stood a long, single-story garage building in the same style. One garage door was open, and inside, the shine of a blue and black Bugatti Veyron's paint caught my eye.

The Veyron is a rare car, and even in Marbella, there were hardly two blue and black 2022 models. It was the exact car I had seen in Puerto Banús the night before.

A servant in his fifties wearing a white suit and gloves opened the door for Cathrine while a young African man in a chauffeur's uniform opened my door and held out his hand. "Your keys, sir!"

I gave him my keys. He accepted them and drove our rental car to a more suitable parking spot, which wouldn't be visible to other guests.

The white-clad servant waited for Cathrine and me. "To the right, follow me," he said with a glimmer of sympathy–or was it pity?

We walked in through the open, massive door. Each step echoed as we stepped onto the shining marble tiles. Sunlight from outside reflected and cast back against cream-white walls framed with wide, profiled gold moldings, and from the ceiling hung an impressive chandelier with sparkling crystal. A fresco painting, a portrait of an Arab with the traditional white head-dress and black agal, either of Al Sayed himself or his father, dominated an entire wall.

It was open at the other end of the room, and a slight breeze from the sea played with the white, transparent curtains hanging from ceiling to floor. Behind the curtains, between us and the azure Mediterranean, stood six white columns and an artistic green, blue, and gold fountain. Offshore from the beach and pier, the sun glinted off a white luxury yacht anchored.

"In here, sir."

The servant took us through a side door and into a smaller room with a security check, not unlike what you'd find at an airport. A bodyguard, likely one of those who had been in the Bugatti the night before, put forward a tray. "Place mobile phones and metal objects here."

We complied, and the security personnel waved us through the detector. "These will stay with us for now," he said, lifting away the tray with our phones. "You may wait there," he continued, pointing toward a door at the end of the room.

We entered the office, where a massive oak desk dominated the room, surrounded by bookshelves stretching from floor to ceiling. Behind the desk hung a painting of an Arabian desert and an oasis, framed in a heavy gilded frame. We sank into the deep armchairs upholstered in dark blue velvet.

All was quiet except for my breathing and a discreet ticking from a wall clock. I realized this room was well sound-proofed but refused to ponder why.

Cathrine drummed on her chair's armrest. "How long do you think we'll have to wait?" she asked, shifting her weight from one side to the other.

A woman came in and placed a glass of water with lemon in front of each of us. "The Commander will be here shortly," she said.

A few more minutes passed, and an Arab man in a black military uniform entered the room. He nodded; the curt gesture signaled both authority and self-assurance.

"Flokí Wilhelmsen," he said and met my gaze. "Olav Wilhelmsen's brother, I presume. My name is Commander Aws Amhari. I am His Royal Highness's security attaché. I'm glad you left the stack of blank papers in your car so we can dispense with this charade."

He neither smiled nor seemed irritated. He was formal and correct, with an alert and intelligent gaze. As he spoke, he dabbed a medal on his uniform. I tried to determine if it was a sign of pride or uncertainty.

"His Royal Highness is not available for an audience. How may I assist you, Mr. Wilhelmsen?"

So much for my bluff. I was sweating now, and it wasn't because of a lack of air conditioning. I had to place my cards on his table.

"It's about Olav. I gather from what you're saying that you know who he is. We cannot contact him, and I'd like to ask if he has been in contact with His Royal Highness recently."

He studied us both, more cautious now. "His Royal Highness is in contact with many people daily."

For a moment, an imperceptible smile crossed his lips. "How long has it been since you were in contact with him? Please forgive my lack of empathy, but how does this concern us?"

I ignored the diversion and went all in. "One of the last sightings of Olav was in connection with an altercation between him and Al Sayed at a nightclub in Puerto Banús. Are you aware of this?"

His gaze became flat, moving from me to Cathrine as his head swayed from side to side—like a cobra. The tip of a pointed tongue moistened his lips. Thankfully, it was a regular tongue without a split.

"No. Neither His Royal Highness nor I are aware of any such incident."

He was lying.

"Perhaps you could ask His Royal Highness? Just to be sure?" I said.

"His Royal Highness is a very busy man. He has nothing to add to this matter."

"But maybe he remembers some important details. We're grasping at straws here."

"Is there anything else we can do for you?" he said, springing to his feet. His voice was colder, his words sharper, a clear warning that we had reached the limit of his patience. It was not an invitation to ask more questions, but he had probably gotten the answers he needed—what we knew and didn't know.

I backed up in alarm into two burly men standing right behind me. I hadn't even noticed them entering the room, but from how they held my arm, it was clear this audience was over.

"Please excuse me," he said, straightening up even more, and left the room.

"This way," one of the muscle-bound men growled.

The pool area was one floor lower than the entrance level. On our way out, I glimpsed the splendor as we passed through an archway.

Amhari and another person sat in a cabana by the pool, smoking a hookah and talking. The Commander pointed with his mouthpiece in our direction. You didn't need to be a genius to understand who the topic of conversation was.

Outside, our car was ready, with the front facing the gate, the key in the ignition, and our phones neatly placed on the seats. We got in, started the Ford, rolled down the hill, and out the gate, which closed behind us.

Cathrine shook her head.

"So we're back where we started."

Chapter Twelve

We drove home without saying a single word, lost in our thoughts. I was thinking about Charlene. I called her in the morning. The hospital had still not discharged my dad. No one knew why.

"I'm fine staying with Torstein and his wife for a while," she'd said.

But who would care for her if I disappeared and Dad became dependent on care? Was it a mistake to stay here and continue this search? I rested my head in my hands and tried to think.

Cathrine steered the car with one hand and drummed on the wheel. Her gaze kept flicking to her rearview mirror. We reached Elviria, and she parked our car in front of LIP Seguridad.

We sat like two hypnotized lemurs staring ahead before she broke her silence.

"Did you want to talk to the police?"

"The Segway," I said.

"Huh? The Segway?"

"It's not here."

She turned. "Should I be worried about you now?"

"Hernandes, the cop," I said, unable to form complete sentences.

"Should I be worried about Hernandes?" She still seemed more concerned about me.

"He rides a Segway. It's not here, so Hernandes isn't here either."

Now, she grasped the connection.

"Where is he then?"

"Out patrolling on his Segway," I said. "Chasing hooligans or lonely housewives."

"You're not very respectful of your Spanish colleague."

She was right, of course, but I hated this situation. Hated feeling powerless, of not getting through, of having to fight against people with power and resources. Against all the Al Sayeds and fucking Hernandeses of the world, against people who hid behind authority and wealth to undermine justice and who treated the world as their private playground or harassed others with their power.

A real estate baron in New York swindled my father-in-law. He worked for months and paid for materials and subcontractors, but the idiot refused to pay. The scoundrel hid behind a wall of lawyers, making it futile to hold him accountable. It shouldn't have been like that, and I wanted to be one of those who ensured it wasn't. That experience was why I applied to join the police.

"When you were a policeman, would you put heaven and earth in motion to search for a young man, a man in a certain way with women, who had only been gone for a few days? Would you?"

She was right, of course. Men sometimes disappeared for days and weeks and turned up on their own. Looking for all of them would be a stupid use of police resources.

"We would have reported him missing after a few days, but only used a few resources so early. I understand his decision, but it was how he said it, as if he had something personal against Olav and me. As if he... relished the situation."

She studied me. "I did not intend to criticize."

I had answered her through clenched teeth. I let out my breath and lowered my shoulders. "Sorry," I said. "I didn't mean to get so worked up. This trip to Al Sayed..."

I threw up my hands and shrugged.

Cathrine focused on something behind me. "I believe we have our local 'Mall Cop' inbound."

I turned and saw Hernandes coming rolling on his Segway.

Cathrine was already out of the car. "Leave this eye candy to me," she said, striding straight toward him.

I remained standing by the open car door.

"Are you Hernandes?" she called out in Spanish.

He stopped his Segway. "Si..." He straightened his back, smiled, and looked her over. His gaze moved on. He wasn't as happy to see me.

"Can I help you with something?" Hernandes asked with a professional smile. He still studied me, but I doubted he intended his question for me.

Neither did Cathrine. "I have some information. Do you have a few minutes?"

He parked his Segway. "If it's about your boyfriend who disappeared, I can't do much now."

Cathrine smiled at him. "Olav isn't my boyfriend! He's just a good friend from high school."

She tossed her hair back and laughed, then turned serious. "But yes, it's about Olav," she said. "Some information you might want to know about has come up."

He nodded toward LIP Seguridad. "Vale ... Come with me inside."

They started walking toward the stairs. I followed, half-prepared for Hernandes to ask me to wait outside, but it didn't happen.

Everything was like a replay: same room, Hernandes and me in the same chairs, the same dust circling in the air, his sunglasses on the cord, and his cap spinning in his hand. The only difference was Cathrine.

"We've talked to some of Olav's friends," she began. "There are indications Olav had money trouble. He'd borrowed tons of money and couldn't pay it back."

Hernandes nodded. His cap spun. "So you think he's gone into hiding, eh?"

"That's one possibility. Another might be that something has happened to him. We don't know right now, which makes our situation difficult."

He studied her, then me. "It's still too early to put out an APB on him."

"But isn't there anything you can do?" I asked.

"Si... I could look into it. Unofficially. Ask some people I know. Informants. But that's all for now."

"Thanks," I said.

His skeptical, almost hostile expression softened.

"I'll do my best, but remember this: If Olav has gone underground of his own free will, he might not want to be found. Not by anyone. Do we understand each other, señor?"

Chapter Thirteen

The nightclub Shoot Out was like a forgotten set from the '70s, where modern EDM had replaced the disco, but the decor and patrons still suited the Bee Gees better. Middle-aged women dressed in skin-tight dresses and diamonds, and older gentlemen were accompanied by what I hoped were their daughters.

It was where the upper crust came to see and be seen, but the man we were waiting for was still absent.

Cathrine handed me a double Balvenie and let her gaze wander over the pulsating venue. She checked her wristwatch—it was almost a quarter past one, but still no sign of Al Sayed.

"Do you think he'll show up tonight?"

"Cool J told Gustavo that Al Sayed gets by here on Wednesday nights. It's a long shot, but it's our only chance to have a word with him," Cathrine said.

I was about to respond when a door to a private booth opened, and five people took their seats around a table. Ahmhari wasn't with them, but two heavy guys in dark suits took positions on either side of the guests. Their stone faces, earpiece wires, and the outline of concealed weapons under their suits signaled they were providing security, whatever that entailed.

Al Sayed arrived last and slid into his seat at his table with an almost imperceptible movement. His intense eyes and calm confidence signaled power and control.

Next to him sat a platinum-blond woman in her early thirties. Her elegant attire and confident demeanor revealed a person accustomed to luxury and influence. She lifted a cigarillo with a small mouthpiece; Al Sayed gallantly lit a lighter and held it up before her. She chuckled at something he said, concentrated, and lit her smoke.

Cathrine gazed at the group. "So, what do we do now?"

I continued studying them without answering.

"Do you wanna dance?" she asked.

She stood and moved dancingly toward the dance floor without waiting for my answer, and I followed.

We danced closer to the booth, where Al Sayed was engrossed in a conversation with one of his guests. He leaned forward, nodded, and gesticulated eagerly. The blonde stood, stubbed out her cigarette, and danced onto the floor with her eyes closed.

This was the opportunity I'd been waiting for. A glance toward Al Sayed showed he was still focused on his conversation, and his two bodyguards weren't bothered.

I led us closer to the woman. She opened her eyes and locked them with mine with a small smile, closed her eyes, turned around, and bumped her hips against mine. Cathrine let her into the dance. The blonde was still smiling and dancing with her eyes closed.

I leaned in toward her and tried to overpower the music. "I need your help. Need to talk to Al Sayed; it's important—life-or-death important."

She turned to me and continued dancing while studying my face before abruptly returning to her booth. One guard monitored us.

We shuffled back to the bar and sat down. "Oh shit," Cathrine muttered and nodded behind me. I turned around. One of the muscle men crossed the dance floor with no sign of rhythmic hip movement.

He stopped in front of me with a slight nod and handed me a card.

"Miss Silvestre would like to invite you for a drink in booth number three. Please show these cards at the entrance."

As quickly as he'd come, he was returning, still showing no signs of being swept up by the dance.

Miss Silvestre glanced our way. I lifted the card and signaled that we were on our way.

After finishing our drinks, we showed our invitation cards to a booth guard, who led us to Silvestre's table. The guards lost interest in us and scanned the venue, possibly for a man with an out-of-tune machine gun in a worn violin case.

"Miss Silvestre," I said.

"Call me Victoria," she said and studied me again. "You look like someone I know."

"Olav?"

She nodded. "You must be Olav's brother…" she searched for my name.

"Flokí," I helped.

"I've heard a lot about you." She glanced toward Al Sayed, who was still engaged in conversation. She leaned closer, her eyes narrow with concern. "What do you need help with?"

"Olav is missing; no one has seen him since Thursday afternoon. He was then reportedly with a woman. A woman who could resemble you, according to the description."

She paled and stared at something behind me.

"Won't you introduce me to your friends?" Al Sayed had ended his conversation and positioned himself behind me. "You must be Flokí, Olav's brother, I presume," he said, extending a hand with three diamond rings toward me.

I stood up and shook his hand.

"And who is your charming companion?" he said before I introduced her.

"I'm Cathrine, Cathrine Runevik, Your Excellency." She curtsied for the occasion, and Al Sayed bowed in return.

"Flokí says Olav is missing," Victoria said. She met Al Sayed's gaze with an expression of concern and anxiety.

Al Sayed dropped his gaze and addressed me. "And now you think I have something to do with it? My commander told me you knew about our little quarrel."

"Since you mention it, Your Excellency."

"Call me Mickey," he smiled, showing off a perfect row of pearls. "As in the mouse man." He laughed heartily before turning serious. "Let's put it this way: Victoria has been my faithful... partner for many years, and I don't tolerate anyone trying to make a move on her."

"Stop it, Mickey!" Victoria exclaimed irritably.

"We cleared up our little misunderstanding. Victoria is one of my most important advisors, and Olav brought her into this when he asked her for help to get a loan from me. He was in trouble with some heavy-handed creditors."

"Did you lend him money?"

He gazed into nothing. Thought for a moment. "Your brother didn't have much to offer as collateral for such a loan."

"So you refused to lend him the money?"

"I couldn't help him. I try to keep friendship and financial transactions separate. You understand the necessity, even in your brother's unfortunate but self-inflicted situation."

He looked at me with sorrow.

"Have you sent people after him?" I locked eyes with his.

He looked, if possible, even more sad and threw up his hands. "Never. That's not my style. That's why I don't lend money to friends."

"So, who did he borrow money from?"

"I'm afraid I don't know. Now, I must end this evening." His eyes flickered, and his jaw tightened. He was lying; I was sure of it.

He nodded to one of his bodyguards. "Escort my friends out," he said and signaled departure.

Chapter Fourteen

*S*he approached me on the path along the harbor. The cool morning air mixed with the scent of salt water and oil from the ships docked at the pier. In the background, the Golden Gate Bridge bathed in early sunbeams. A few strands of hair fell before her eyes, and she brushed them away.

Behind her, a Norwegian tanker rushed toward San Francisco. A deck boy gazed toward the big city, just as I once did from the deck of the tanker John Knudsen. Gazing toward America and the grand adventure, back when America was still the promised land, that summer when I first met her.

She approached me, and I held her tightly around her waist. I pressed my body against hers and reacted immediately. She smiled at me through her unruly bangs.

"We have a bond that can never be broken. Never. I'm a part of everything you are and everything you do."

A shadow passed over her face. Then she smiled again.

"But you need to move on with your life, baby. You need to become the man I met and fell in love with back then. Charlie *needs your strength. A father who lives. Someone alive in her world, not living in mine."*

My heart tightened, and my sorrow pulled me back into darkness. "No, Jo-Ann!"

She vanished as suddenly as she had appeared.

Something was wrong. My room was lit. I opened my eyes. Cathrine stood in the doorway wearing a simple nightgown. "Is it okay if I sleep here? I'm not able to sleep. Keep hearing strange noises, and it freaks me out. I'll keep my distance and won't bother you."

"You can take my bed; I'll sleep on the floor."

"Don't be silly. We're both adults and can share a bed without it being more. I don't wanna be alone, is all."

"I can't." I lay down and closed my eyes. This was very uncomfortable.

"Is something wrong?" she asked and sat on the edge of my bed.

I moved to the opposite edge and lay with my back to her. She got into my bed and packed the comforter around herself. Suddenly, I was left with no cover.

"Can't we share this comforter so you don't have to freeze?"

"I can't," I said.

Her hand gripped my shoulder and turned me. She looked at me questioningly, but my boxer revealed it all. She smiled warmly. "Are you sure?"

"Yes, I'm sorry," I said.

Her eyes dimmed. She sat silent for a while, then hurried out of the room with my comforter wrapped tightly around her.

I lay awake all night, freezing, but couldn't bring myself to turn off the air conditioning. My thoughts churned incessantly.

Only as God lit his enormous light did I fall asleep.

Chapter Fifteen

Loud knocks on my door awakened me. It was quarter to nine, and I was cold and exhausted after a poor night's sleep.

"What's going on?" I mumbled, rubbing sleep from my eyes.

Cathrine cleared her throat in the hallway but didn't open my door. "Gustavo called. He wants to meet us at La Cañada. Now. He said it was important."

Fifteen minutes later, we were in the car. An awkward silence marked the drive. Neither of us wanted to talk about last night's incident. Rarely have twenty minutes in a vehicle lasted that long.

I was less comfortable with our collaboration and preferred to go alone, but Gustavo was her contact and source. We'd have to sort out other stuff later.

Gustavo waited at one of the cafe tables. As soon as we came in, he stood up, looking nervous and restless.

"There's something you need to see. Right now."

He walked toward a door beneath the escalators, and we followed suit. The door led to a control room with screens showing video from various parts of the mall. "I found this footage this morning," he said, pressing a remote control.

The screen displayed a video of an oversized parking garage. The clock on the screen sped up. People and cars whizzed by, while some vehicles remained stationary as if not part of reality anymore. The time and date on the screen set the recording for last Thursday after lunch. "The garage below," Gustavo explained, pointing at the floor.

He pressed his remote again, and a man appeared at the bottom of the frame, walking toward a row of parked cars. His face turned away from the camera, but it was Olav. He walked toward a Peugeot parked next to a dark van and fished out a remote. His Peugeot responded with two rapid flashes.

Just as he got into his car, the van's side door slid open, and two masked men jumped out. They moved quickly, pressed a cloth against his face, and dragged him into the van. The van drove out of the frame without rushing.

The incident was over in seconds.

Chapter Sixteen

Once again, it was all my fault.

I'd been here before, caught in a personal tsunami of desperation as darkness pulled me into its abyss. Once again, life had struck in the most brutal way.

In hindsight, I should have taken Cathrine's desperation seriously, listened to my dad, and left as soon as I got Cathrine's message. I'd lost precious time—time that could mean the difference between life and death.

I pictured Olav as a nine-year-old. I'd gifted him a Hardy Boys novel for Christmas, but he refused to read it unless I sat with him. It was too scary for him to read on his own. Life was innocent back then compared to the dangers he was facing now. He was in serious trouble. How did we ever end up like this?

Everything must have fallen apart for him when I moved to San Francisco. To me, it was just another grand adventure. I was the lucky guy who'd won the princess and half the kingdom, but Olav must have felt abandoned. He was used to having a big brother who was always there, someone he could confide in. A big brother he could talk to about everything he couldn't share with the adults. A big brother who fixed things, protected him, understood him, and made sure he didn't fall in with the wrong crowd.

It was unbearable that I'd been away when Olav started using drugs. After all, I was his brother. I was a cop. I should have been around to pick up on the signs. Not acting as some superhero on another continent. I'd failed him and had no valid excuse. I had failed him.

But how could I help him now? I was in a foreign country, without the police authority I'd always relied on, and I was unarmed. Despair came rushing back.

"We need to track them down! Every second counts," Cathrine said with conviction. "We can't give up. We have to find him before something serious happens. These people mean business."

I looked toward Cathrine, unable to focus, but her straight-forward gaze lifted away from the fog surrounding me.

"What if something serious has already happened?"

"I choose not to consider that option. I'm not ready to write his obituary yet," she said.

Simple words—the signs of a sharp mind.

Cathrine read me and held my hand. "We'll find him. But we have no time to lose. Come on!"

The determination in her voice cut through my despair and pulled me out of my apathy. I studied her face for signs of doubt or uncertainty but found none.

My strategy stood clear to me. I would shake down his rotten network, every branch of that damned tree of life he had planted in Spain. Provoke a reaction, see what happened, see if anything fell out. And then shake it again and again.

But my memories from the last time I'd used these tactics made me sick.

Chapter Seventeen

"Gustavo sent me his recording. We should talk to Cool J. I bet he knows these guys," Cathrine said.

We stood and took the escalator down to the parking level. I avoided looking around so as not to recognize where Olav got kidnapped. Instead, I fixed my gaze on Cathrine's sneakers until we reached the car. We exited the parking garage in a hurry.

Soon, we were on the highway, heading toward Puerto Banús again. While I battled the traffic, Cathrine talked to Gustavo on her cell. He figured we'd find Cool J at a bar near the restaurant where we met him last.

His Ferrari parked outside Sinatra Bar made it easy to find him. He was flirting with the male bartender over in the far corner of the bar. Cathrine walked us through a group of well-dressed, middle-aged couples chatting eagerly over full champagne glasses. Their crystal glasses clinked, and the sun glinted off their jewelry and bling.

Sinatra was singing over the speakers, urging us to come fly with him. I had plenty of fun just keeping up with Cathrine through the crowd.

Cool J stared at us, a bit surprised. "Hey," he said. But this time, his smile didn't reach his eyes. Where had the confident, worldly man of yesterday gone? Had someone or something spooked him?

"We need to talk to you," Cathrine replied. "It's important, it's urgent, and it's about Olav."

She pointed to an empty table on the other side of the bar. "Coming?"

Cathrine walked toward the table. Cool J considered his options, but I kindly blocked his path and smiled at him. "Nice to meet again, buddy. It's about Olav," I repeated, nodding toward Cathrine.

Resigned, he shuffled over to Cathrine's table. I blocked all escape routes, but he didn't seem inclined to run off.

None of the surrounding people cared. The sound of their conversation and laughter was drowning out Sinatra's song.

Cathrine took out her phone and showed him the video of Olav's abduction. "Do you recognize any of these men?" she asked, gazing at him.

He glanced at the video before fixing his gaze on the table surface, visibly uncomfortable.

"Gustavo already sent me that video, but I've never seen these guys before," he mumbled.

Was this jerk lying to us? We didn't have time for such nonsense. I slapped my hand on the table in frustration. "Cut the bull... Now isn't the time to cower. You know more than you're telling us."

The voices in the room quieted. But Sinatra still wanted us to fly with him, and the buzz picked up again.

"I'm not a coward," Cool J said. "But those people…"

He studied his fingers and fiddled with a napkin. "Don't mess with them if you want to stay alive."

I kept my voice steady. "But you know who these guys are," I pressed. "If you're withholding information, you're complicit in anything happening to Olav!"

Cathrine placed a hand over his. "I understand this is difficult, but you're our best chance of finding Olav alive. Please."

He took a pen from his inner pocket, jotted some words on the napkin, looked around, and pushed it toward Cathrine.

She put her purse on the napkin, pulled it toward her, and unfolded it in one fluid motion. She then waited a few seconds and checked the room before reading.

She held my gaze. "You've got something on your cheek, honey. Here, use this," she said, handing me the napkin.

I wiped my cheek, unfolded the napkin, and read what he had written. "Ricardo Sanchez's goons—don't say that name out loud. Ears everywhere. RS owns Shoot Out." I crumpled up the napkin and put it down on the table.

"Olav used to owe money all over this town. He mortgaged his apartment and settled up. Then he tried to win it all back and lost even more. That's all I know. On my honor."

I took out my phone and wrote, "Do you have the address?" before placing it on the table between us.

He wiped the corner of his mouth with his napkin. "You should take this case to the police. Only they have the resources you need to find him."

He picked up my phone while talking. "I have to get to work," he said, standing up. He kissed Cathrine on both cheeks, shook my hand, and hurried to his Ferrari.

After a few seconds, he opened the door again and came running back.

"I'm so sorry, but I think I picked up the wrong phone," he said. "This must be yours."

Cool J put the phone back on the table, picked up his own from the chair, and rushed back to the car. Then, he quickly reversed out of his parking spot.

I put my phone in my pocket, and Cathrine waved to the waiter.

After walking some distance from the bar, I opened my phone.

Cool J had pinned a point on my map.

Chapter Eighteen

Cathrine floored it, throwing the car onto the highway, ignoring the puny speed limits. She maneuvered safely through the dense traffic despite quick and less-than-thoughtful lane changes in front of us. A sun-scorched landscape with scattered bushes and billboards whizzed by on both sides of the road.

Ricardo's address was a ranch high in the mountains above Marbella. I needed to find out if Olav was being kept there and how to get him out.

I scrolled through satellite images on Google Maps and zoomed in on Ricardo's property; the details were blurry. I needed more accurate and up-to-date information. A plan took shape.

"Where are we going?" Cathrine interrupted my thoughts.

"Back to La Cañada."

"What are we doing there?"

"We're going shopping."

She gave me a sidelong glance but said nothing.

My phone rang. Siri announced it was my dad.

"The two of you okay? Anything new?" I asked.

"I'm doing fine, son. Sister Gunnlaug and I have become best buddies. She's as beautiful as an angel and as kind as the day is long."

He was chewing on something. "Charlene stopped by during a free period and smuggled some tea cakes for me. Gotta eat them before Gunnlaug sees and confiscates them," he said. "Good to hear your voice, by the way, but you sound a bit tense. Any news about Olav?"

"Uh, no. We have some names and tips about people who might know more about Olav's debt."

"Jonas, the police officer I mentioned, asked a colleague in the Marbella police to contact you. I gave him your number."

"Well, let's hope we can trust his colleague," I said.

"You can trust Jonas. He's capable and has known his Spanish colleague since way back."

"We'll see. We're almost at our destination. Anything else?"

He hesitated. "There's something you're not telling me. I know you."

He said it calmly, but his voice vibrated toward the end. What should I tell him? I didn't want to risk another heart attack when I was thousands of miles away. But as Olav's father, he had the right to know anything I knew.

"Still there? Your silence is telling, you know. If you're worried about my heart, it's not getting any better by your withholding information. I'm not stupid, even if I am old."

I drew a sharp breath as Cathrine swung onto an exit so fast she just had time to brake. I closed my eyes to concentrate on my conversation.

"A gangster by the name of Ricardo Sanchez kidnapped Olav last Thursday. Olav owes him money. We're following that lead."

I held my breath as I'd given him the news. He remained silent for so long that I had to check if the call had dropped. His voice became weaker when he replied, "Be careful, son."

His voice broke. I took a slow breath. "I will. We'll both come home safe and sound."

I lied. The odds were terrible. But what else could I tell the old man?

He said nothing. He understood what I was thinking, but he couldn't say it aloud, either.

I gave him a few more seconds. "Gotta go. Give Charlie an enormous hug from me when she's home."

Cathrine parked outside this time, not in the basement. We ran toward the entrance of La Cañada. Just inside the doors was a FNAC store, my first stop.

"What are we doing here? Buying books?" Cathrine asked.

I turned to her. It was time for the difficult conversation.

"You should go home," I said. "This will be too dangerous. I need to get Olav out of Ricardo's ranch on my own. Can't be responsible for you, too."

She turned and pressed her hand hard against my chest. "I'm not going anywhere. We're in this together, and you need me, whether you admit it or not."

Her eyes sparkled, and her words came between clenched teeth. She spoke so quietly that only the security guard watching us understood what was happening.

"This isn't a game or an action movie. It's real, and it is dangerous. We're dealing with sociopaths who don't follow normal rules. We and others could get hurt or killed if we make just one wrong move."

"I'm not going home. I'll have Gustavo look after me while I figure this out on my own."

I didn't like the thought of Gustavo and Cathrine together; she knew it.

"That's not my point," I insisted bravely. "It's not safe for you here, and if you're looking for Olav, it will not be safe for Gustavo either."

She planted her hands on her hips and met my gaze with a hint of a challenge. "I'm not going anywhere. Right now, we should focus on how we can rescue Olav from Ricardo."

"We'll have this discussion later," I said, knowing full well I'd already lost.

"So, what do we need?" she asked, turning and entering the store.

Chapter Nineteen

The road wound in long loops up along the mountains north of Marbella. We were heading toward the village of Ojén. I rolled down my window and forgot about the manual I'd been studying since we left La Cañada. The air was fresher, and my view was fantastic. In the distance, I could make out Gibraltar, also known as "The Rock."

I checked my tablet to ensure we were still on course to his property. "We're getting close now. According to Google Maps, there's a gravel patch around the next bend where we can park. His ranch is within our drone's range, so we don't need to get any closer before inspecting his place."

"Okay," she said, took a deep breath, and gripped the steering wheel with both hands. Moments later, she maneuvered us into our lookout spot. The gravel crunched under our tires as we braked. Below us lay green hills and clusters of whitewashed houses. Behind the mountain was the sea. A perfect place for a couple in love to stop and enjoy the view in case we were being watched.

We sat for a while, staring out over the landscape. "It's so beautiful here! Those vivid colors of the sky and sea, the green landscape, and the white houses." She had concentrated on traffic rather than studying the view while driving.

"Yeah, the landscape is beautiful," I said, "but beauty can be deceiving. Not all predators walk on four legs. Many fates in their wake. Our job is to ensure Olav doesn't become one of them."

Through the mirror, I studied the traffic on the road, but nobody paid any attention to us. "Right now, I'm glad you didn't choose an Aston Martin," I said. "We don't need to attract more attention than necessary."

"Well, we're not James Bond," she replied with an ironic smile. "And like you said, this is no movie," she added through gritted teeth.

"Let's get started," I said.

The drone we had bought was small enough to be hidden under a jacket. I held it close to my body as we walked down the mountainside. When we were out of sight from the road, I prepared it for takeoff.

We set down the drone and went back to our car. On my tablet, I sketched out the route our drone would follow. It would first take a loop toward Ojén, then fly in toward Ricardo's ranch from a different angle than where we were sitting. Our drone would circle his property at a height where it would neither be heard nor seen.

I added pause points on the round over his property to direct our drone manually toward areas of particular interest. Before returning, the flight would take about twelve minutes, with at least ten minutes for reconnaissance. The return followed the same path, in an arc around and below us, before returning to its starting point.

A glance confirmed we were still alone. I pressed the start button and pulled the goggles over my eyes. Video images from the drone camera were displayed in my goggles.

Sand and grassroots filled my field of view before the drone jerked away and flew toward Ojén. As it flew its predetermined route, I turned my head to steer the camera toward areas of interest. Cathrine followed the video transmission on her iPad.

Over Ojén, our drone changed course and climbed toward Ricardo's ranch. A long gravel road led from the main road up to a cluster of buildings. The landscape was barren and naked, without many opportunities to hide in the terrain. Halfway up the road, a fence surrounded his property. A sturdy gate blocked the road. A person sat outside a guard house. Two people patrolled the area inside the fence. One had a Doberman on a leash and a short weapon in a strap over his shoulder, while the other carried a rifle. I took some pictures to study them later.

The drone continued and stopped at its first reconnaissance point. I took manual control and shot some pictures before zooming in on an extended garage with four doors. A Hummer parked halfway inside one of them. Outside the other stood a dark van, identical to the one used in the abduction of Olav.

Jackpot!

Everything went wrong just as I put the drone back on automatic flight. The sky, horizon, a bird's wing, and scorched ground flashed past the camera. Then my VR goggles went dark.

"Damn it!"

"What happened?" Cathrine stared at her tablet. "Connection Lost" glowed red on her screen. The map marked the point where the drone had lost communication. She slammed her fist on the dashboard.

I pressed the "return home" button and tried to enter an alternative route and start over. But nothing helped. The drone didn't respond.

"A falcon took it, I assume. Probably trained to take out drones. Nothing left to chance at this place. Let's hope they think it's a tourist who flew it."

"This was a mistake! Now, they'll tighten security and vigilance. We must carefully plan what we do next and consider they're on alert."

"Getting in there and getting Olav out will be challenging. Fortunately, we have secured pictures and video on your tablet."

She grabbed her tablet and studied a picture of the ranch, which she enlarged. "I have an idea."

I grabbed her tablet as Cathrine started the car and swung toward Marbella.

"Hope I still can get Gustavo on board," she said.

Chapter Twenty

"The CCTV at the ranch is offline. This was the simple part, I guess. The rest is up to you guys."

Behind Gustavo stood a thin, shy girl with a long ponytail, tattoos, and dark jeans over a dark top.

"This is Edmina. Violin virtuoso in the Orquesta Ciudad de Granada by day, hacker legend by night. She just cracked Ricardo's security system for us."

He nodded toward the timid girl and seemed pleased with their achievement. Edmina didn't look up, just rocked back and forth.

"Great job, both of you."

I let my gaze drift from Edmina to Cathrine and back. "Just make sure I won't be visible in the back of the car. If they see me, it's game over."

Gustavo shook my hand and nodded. "Cathrine will take care of it," he said. "I informed the security guys at the ranch that we're sending Manuel to fix the glitch. They know him, and he's clueless about our plans. He also does the annual maintenance on their equipment, so we believe they will check his car sparingly."

He scratched his head. "Edmina and I can keep him engaged for about half an hour, but then I'll have to turn their cameras back on. I hope that'll be sufficient time to check for Olav and get him out."

He checked his pocket and found a car key. "Here are my spare keys to the service vehicle in case you and Olav need to bolt without Manuel."

Cathrine and I rushed down a back staircase to an outdoor area, where we found the service vehicle parked. It was a small van with the security company's logo. Dented and rusty, but drivable, I hoped.

She stopped me. "Do you think you can find Olav and spin out of there in under thirty minutes?" She studied me. "Is that realistic? Is it possible?"

"Well, it might be possible with some luck," I said.

"Okay, listen to me. I'll take the Ford and follow you at a distance," she said. "I can track you on this tablet."

She pointed at my smartwatch. "That's your tracking device. I'll pick you up if necessary. Got it?"

"Thanks," I said, settling in among various boxes and cases behind the driver's seat. Cathrine wrapped a tarp around me and placed chains and heavy objects on it. I hoped that would keep everything in place.

The click of the lock and her receding footsteps marked the start of our rescue operation. The rest was up to me.

The tarp was thick and blocked out both light and air. The sun was blazing outside, and I sweat. Lying wrapped up like that without air conditioning was claustrophobic. Each breath was warmer than the previous, so I tried to breathe more slowly.

Manuel got into the car without noticing me, started the engine, and put it in gear. We were on our way to the ranch.

I couldn't enjoy the view this time, but in return, I got acquainted with every turn and bump of the road. A metal edge cut into my back. When I tried to change my position, it only got marginally better. I had to grit my teeth and hope it would soon be over.

I thought about Olav again. On my way, bro. I'm on my way. I was ready for action.

After an eternity, we turned off the main road and onto the gravel road up to the property. The road bumps threw me hard against the metal edge. Finally, the car slowed down and halted. My battered body got some rest, but the sudden silence was frightening. It was crucial that I'd stay still and hope for the best.

They tightened security. Three people were talking beside Manuel. Someone opened the back door and checked, but only superficially. There was the sound of a thump in the car, and then someone said, "Continue!"

I was in.

We drove some more and stopped. Manuel opened the side door and lifted something out. He tugged at my tarp and mumbled in Spanish but left it at that.

His footsteps receded, but the side door sounded open. This posed a risk if someone outside looked into the car where I was lying. I had just half an hour and had to take a chance, so I lifted the tarp off me, crawled to the door side, and peeked out. No one saw me.

We had stopped outside a large villa in classic Spanish style. On the second floor, a terracotta-colored veranda wrapped around the house. After studying the drone images, Cathrine and I agreed this was most likely where Olav was being held captive, mainly because of those solid iron bars in front of the windows.

I looked right and left, sprinted to an open door, peeked in, and saw a utility kitchen. It was empty. I slipped in. I planned to check all rooms on the second floor, where we assumed the bedrooms were located. Also, I would take a round in the basement if necessary—both natural places to keep prisoners.

But he might be in one of the other buildings on the premises. I had to take a chance and improvise if necessary.

I crept up the carpeted stairs to the second floor. My feet made no sound. I listened to each door before opening it. I found four empty bedrooms. Only one was in use. Olav wasn't in any of them.

I stood still. The only sound I heard was the steady ticking of a grandfather clock. I hurried back down the stairs to the first floor.

The staircase continued to the basement, but a sudden sound of voices forced me to try a side door. I kept the door ajar.

Two women were rolling a cart with cleaning supplies. They stopped and chatted right outside the door while time ticked away. Fifteen minutes left.

Finally, they went their separate ways. I slipped out and continued down. Cool air hit me as I stepped into the basement. In front of me lay a long basement corridor with thick, gray-painted metal doors on both sides. It smelled of mold and rust.

A camera hung from the ceiling. I crossed my fingers, hoping the red LED light beneath it didn't mean the camera was active again. I had to trust that Gustavo and Edmina controlled the technology.

I could hear Manuel having an agitated conversation in a room at the end of my corridor, arguing with someone with a darker voice. That's probably where they had the equipment monitoring the property.

I slipped into the first room on my left. The room was pitch dark. I didn't turn on the light; it might be visible from the hallway. I used my phone to look around. A metal bed and a nightstand. An empty gun holster hung over the end of the bed. There was a lump under the blanket at the foot of the bed. I lifted the blanket and checked. It was a semi-automatic P08 loaded with 9mm Parabellum. I secured it, tucked it into the back of my waistband, and covered it with my t-shirt.

I opened the door and checked back and forth in the hallway before trying the next door. It was locked. A movement at the end of the corridor made me sprint to the opposite side and open the door. I tumbled in. The light came on.

Chapter Twenty-One

"Can I offer you a whiskey?"

The plastic sheeting along the walls rustled as his musclemen moved about. Ricardo sat relaxed behind a massive oak desk. They had brutally zipped-tied my hands behind my back and taken the gun I'd borrowed from the adjoining room. Two burly guys lifted me and unceremoniously dropped me in front of Ricardo's desk.

"I guess not. Well, I'll have one myself. Hope that's okay," he said, smiling as he filled his glass.

This didn't bode well. The man before me bore little resemblance to the American godfathers I'd encountered. He was much younger than expected, in his late thirties, tanned, fit, and dressed as if for a family lunch or garden party in a short-sleeved polo and shorts in light colors.

He could have been a family man working at a reputable accounting or law firm.

But I knew better.

Ricardo smiled, but his eyes were cold. "You're either a brave man or don't understand who you're messing with."

He let his gaze glide over the plastic-covered walls before meeting mine again. "But I think you understand the value of keeping an agreement, something your brother only grasped... to a certain extent."

He grimaced, then brightened. "The camera system in this basement is independent of what you managed to disable. We knew you were coming, and we appreciate that you dropped by. We have important matters to discuss. But you shouldn't underestimate the consequences of this little game of yours."

He emptied his whiskey glass, winced, and looked at me again. "Your brother owes me money. A lot of money."

"Where's Olav?"

"That is the hundred-thousand-euro question. And you're the one who's going to find out for me."

"Cut the crap. I know you kidnapped him, and you're holding him somewhere on these premises."

"You don't know a damn thing. Your brother came here one afternoon after my... well, let's call it an urgent request."

He smiled crookedly, then turned serious.

"But I let him go because he promised to pay within seventy-two hours, and I was stupid to trust him. Now he's disappeared without a trace."

"I don't believe you."

He studied me. His voice made the room temperature drop several degrees. "It doesn't matter. But I consider this debt as a family obligation. If Olav won't pay, you pay. It's that simple.

Alternatively, you must find your brother and make him understand he has to settle."

He signaled to a man behind me. This audience was nearing its end. I had to keep him talking.

"How was Olav supposed to get money to pay you off? What made you think he could pay you?"

He studied me again and shrugged.

"He told me he'd met someone who would help him," he said. "Someone with access to lots of money. He was sure he'd get help."

"And why should I believe you?"

"Because you have no choice. To ensure you remember the gravity of this situation and to mind your own business, we have a small parting gift for you."

The first blow hit me in the stomach. My vision went black. The next one turned out the lights.

Chapter Twenty-Two

A rhythmic sound cut through the silence from some-where to my right. I waved my left hand toward the noise without being able to open my eyes, but my hand refused to obey, and I gave it up.

"You awake?"

Her voice was familiar, the voice of an anxious woman, but I couldn't place it. A searing pain stabbed the left side of my waist, and I whimpered. Running footsteps. Someone said something in Spanish, and it all went dark and lovely again.

The next time I regained consciousness, I was alone. I was lying in bed in a small, sterile room, surrounded by wires and with IVs in both arms. The room had green doors and walls painted white. Next to my bed was a nightstand and a chair. Behind me was an impressive collection of equipment. It was dark outside.

Cathrine came in with a Starbucks coffee in hand. I smiled but was unsuccessful since my mouth was numb. It ended in some charming drooling.

"They operated on your jaw, and you're pretty bruised all over, but you'll be your good self again soon."

She put her coffee on my nightstand and wiped the corner of my mouth. Then she sat on a chair and looked deep into my eyes. She became serious.

"You're stumbling around like a blind man on the edge of a cliff. Putting both your own and others' lives at risk."

She grabbed her coffee and took a sip.

"Next time, there might be no one to catch you when you fall. You're lucky to be alive this time, and we both escaped with no bruises from Al Sayed's."

She looked at me again.

"We need to think through risks we're taking, plan, and, most importantly, work together on what needs to be done."

She took advantage of my fragile state and inability to respond to give me a verbal dressing-down. I didn't protest. I just closed my eyes and let myself fall back on my pillow.

She was annoyingly correct, of course. My approach had been too impulsive and primitive. What would have happened if they had been hiding Olav up there? Maybe fed to the sharks of Gibraltar tonight?

Much to my surprise, I believed Ricardo. He wasn't holding Olav captive and didn't know where he was. It was a dead end, and we were back to square one.

I fell asleep again and dreamed about Olav. He was on a train, waving to me from a window. His train disappeared into the fog, and the sound of his train continued until I woke up for the third time.

I still couldn't open my eyes. I did not know what time it was or how long I'd been sleeping. My mouth was bone dry, and it took time to pry my eyelids apart. When I could see her again, Cathrine was still there. She was knitting something colorful and smiled at me, but she said nothing. Just continued knitting.

Then she spoke again.

"I just had to finish counting," she said. "How are we feeling now?"

She asked with an affected doctor's voice.

"Better," I said, surprised I could speak again.

She leaned toward me.

"What happened? Was Olav there?"

I shook my head. Shouldn't have done that.

"No," I said, swallowing as much as I could to suppress my nausea. I then gave her the bullet points from my visit to Ricardo's ranch.

Afterward, it was her turn.

"I parked where we sent up the drone and watched on the tablet where you were. I was relieved when you came down the road again. Based on the speed, you were in a car, and I hoped you had Olav with you."

She paused for a moment.

"But just when I thought everything was fine, the big dark van from La Cañada passed by instead of the service car, and you were not in the driver's seat."

She swallowed and stared ahead.

"I was scared, but I knew you were alive. Your smartwatch was still registering a pulse."

She collected herself and continued.

"I followed at a suitable distance. The van stopped on a quiet side street near the old town of Marbella. The side door opened, and they pushed you out before the van drove off."

Her face flushed, and tears gathered in her eyes.

"I called an ambulance. An ambulance arrived and took you to Hospital Costa del Sol."

She wiped away her tears while looking the other way.

"You goddamn selfish idiot!"

She wanted to hit me in the chest but restrained herself. A lightning bolt that even Thor would have been proud of replaced her tears.

I knew she was right. We had to change our tactic, or this could end just as tragically as last time. I had put us all in mortal danger, contributing nothing to help Olav.

"Sorry," I said. I understood her anger. It was only because of her care and common sense that the outcome wasn't much worse.

"We need to approach this more systematically," she said.

I nodded. It wasn't a brilliant move, but the aftereffects were milder.

"Together?" she asked. "Together" implied a lot: a way forward and a confirmation that we were a team now.

"Together," I said.

She nodded and handed me a business card.

"This was in a pocket in your suit jacket. I found it when I was home getting you new clothes. Anything you'd like to share?"

I stared at the card in confusion. It was the business card of an unknown woman with dark skin, pictured in an erotic pose. According to her card, she called herself Snow White, with the subtitle "everything a gentleman could wish for."

Cathrine studied me but saw I was just as confused.

"There's a V handwritten on the back."

I turned the card over.

"Victoria?"

"Maybe," she nodded. "It was in the pocket of your jacket used at Shoot Out."

"Could you call her and ask if she knows Victoria?"

"I'll take care of that," she said. "I'll go to the waiting room and call from there. Do you need anything? There's a kiosk at the reception."

I didn't dare shake my head.

"No, thanks."

She took the business card and disappeared.

I stared at the damn second hand ticking. Every tick and tock was a reminder: seconds became minutes, and minutes became hours. It was pointless to lie here, unable to do anything.

As Cathrine returned, the sky outside started taking on the characteristic soft blue-purple color—the area's signature color. Before long, the sun would rise, and the day would return.

Cathrine was excited.

"How did it go?" I asked eagerly.

"She knew Victoria and had been waiting for us to call."

She laughed. "But she didn't expect me to call in the middle of the night. I got her address. We will go there together when you are able."

"Together," I said. "I get it now."

She glanced at me with a tenderness I hadn't seen before.

"I think she has something to tell us," she said. "The nurse thinks they can discharge you tomorrow if you don't get worse."

"Tomorrow? I'll be okay in a little while."

I knew I was lying, but we had no time to waste. With a jerk, I sat up, planted my feet on the floor, and stood up.

Just as the sun cast its bright daylight over the landscape outside, I plunged back into darkness.

Chapter Twenty-Three

I came to a lot quicker this time. The nurse brought me some breakfast, but I wasn't ready for food.

"Nauseous?" she asked.

I nodded. This time, my nodding went fine. She helped me into a sitting position.

"I'll keep your food on the nightstand in case you get hungry later." I thanked her with my eyes.

Cathrine entered, her presence a welcome sight. This time, she had two cups of coffee. The aroma of coffee displaced the smell of disinfectants, and my mood lifted. Having a friend to keep me company inside these sterile premises felt comforting.

She looked worried as I brought the cup to my mouth, but my numbness had gone, and I drank without drooling. The coffee brought me back to life.

She smiled. "Look at him; he can drink all by himself!"

The coffee and the smile did me good—so good that I regained my appetite. My breakfast consisted of a croissant with cheese and ham, and although my jaw was still tender, chewing went fine.

Cathrine took out half a baguette wrapped in plastic. She bit carefully into her baguette, chewed thoroughly, wiped away a crumb from the corner of her mouth, and again broke her silence.

"You're Olav's brother..." she began. "And a widower with a teenage daughter."

Here goes.

"You're also a cop, but..."

"Used to be a cop. In San Francisco. That's a part of my life I left behind back then."

"Okay, used to be a cop. You live in Norway, but I don't know much about you. So, tell me, who is this mysterious Floki Wilhelmsen?"

"You've pretty much got the important stuff, no mystery."

"And that's all there is to know about Floki?"

I studied her for a while. I noticed the uncertainty in her eyes and my resistance to our path. "How about you? Besides Gustavo and Olav, anything else I should know?"

"Grew up in Haugesund with Mom. My parents got divorced. My dad lives in Bergen with his new wife, who is only ten years older than me."

She rolled her eyes. "Mom is bitter and can't move on with her life. Since high school, Olav has been my wailing wall for existential and non-existential issues."

She bit her lip. "So he invited me down here when he realized I needed a breather and to experience something else."

And then you just disappeared, Olav? I thought. Out loud, I said, "And so you ended up in this mess?"

She nodded. "Out of the frying pan into the fire, but why did you move back to Haugesund? And your daughter... what's her name?"

"Charlie. Or Charlene after her mother."

"Her mother? Was your wife's name also Charlene?"

"No, my wife's name was Jo-Ann. Her mother's name was Charlene."

"Jo-Ann? You mumbled a name... when we didn't... I thought it was Johann."

She smiled.

I realized what she was uncertain about. "Still on the hetero team, if you're wondering. I understand Olav has been very private about his family, but he must have told you something, though?"

"Not much about the important things in life. Mostly about parties and women he'd met. That kind of stuff. He seemed like he had his life under control. And I believed him."

"He ever mentioned Victoria to you?"

"Not by name. But he talked about a woman he'd met who sounded more than a casual acquaintance. He mentioned she had some influence out of the ordinary. He was cautious when he talked about her, as if he had to hide something. I thought maybe she was married."

"Could there have been something between Olav and Victoria? Something more than helping him get a loan? Relationships rarely start with soliciting a loan from someone. Must be a backstory."

"Then, the real question is, did Al Sayed believe in Victoria's explanation? He did seem like the controlling and jealous type."

"Hard to tell. We should ask Victoria about this."

"Listen, there's one thing I'm still wondering about. If you don't want to talk about it, I'll accept it, but... it's kind of important to me. There's one thing Olav never talked about. Please forgive me if I'm overstepping it now, but how did Jo-Ann die?"

There it was. The question I knew would come.

"Killed. Someone killed her," I heard myself explain.

I continued. "I was a homicide detective. The murders of several women in the Bay Area had many similarities. I believed there was a serial killer on the loose. My clearance rate was high, and I was certain I would catch him, but it was a race against time. I knew he would strike again."

I closed my eyes. I kept my emotions in check but couldn't stop talking. "Serial killers, in particular those who mark their prey with some kind of signature, are often narcissistic sociopaths. They want to tell us how smart they are and how powerless we are. It's as if it's programmed into their DNA."

She observed me with furrowed eyebrows.

"I called him out in the media. Called him a coward and a not-so-smart asshole. Called him an amateur who'd made big mistakes, left traces, and said we would catch him soon."

I needed a sip of water. My hand shook, but I drank and put my glass down without spilling. I had to get this out.

"It was a fatal mistake because he decided to go after me in the way he knew would ruin my life. He killed Jo-Ann, the very foundation of my life, and I knew it was only a matter of time before he would attack Charlie."

I couldn't hold back my tears. It was a relief to tell my story. Many knew my story; the media in the US had feasted on it for weeks, but I had never talked about it outside my family.

Cathrine was the first person outside my inner circle to whom I talked. It was as if I had been carrying this hand grenade in my soul for so many years. I had pulled the pin. The explosion was inevitable and felt so strangely liberating.

"That's why you moved back to Haugesund?"

I wiped my eyes with a corner of my duvet. Cathrine fetched a strip from a paper towel roll in the bathroom.

"To protect Charlie," I explained. "It was impossible in a city like San Francisco. Too many people. Too many possibilities. We had some protection for a while, but eventually, someone would cancel it. So, instead, we live in this small rural community on the outskirts of Haugesund. No strangers poking around without everyone knowing. Without me knowing."

Cathrine got up from her chair and sat on my bed. She put her hand on my chest, and my breathing became more manageable.

"I'll never fathom the horrible things you've been through. Never really understand. But I see who you are. And what I see is a wonderful man."

I closed my eyes. Drew in her scent.

"Can I ask you one last thing?"

She said it so casually that I knew it was something that'd bothered her for a long time. "Mmmm."

"Was it because of... her, your wife..., you didn't..., we didn 't..., you know, last night?"

She was embarrassed. She avoided eye contact.

"Yeah... I haven't..."

We sat for a long time in silence. I knew what was coming, but it felt neither awkward nor scary.

She watched my face. "You think you might find room for someone new in your life ever again?"

She was nervous after saying these words. I understood how brave she was to be so direct. She deserved that I'd be equally courageous.

"If you'd asked me a few days ago, my answer would have been no. But now..."

"You've lost a lot. Jo-Ann and Charlie mean everything to you. They should mean everything to you. But my dad, of all people, said something important on the day I saw my half-sister for the first time."

She made a face and rolled her eyes. "He said love increases whenever you let someone into your heart. That's why you don't need to love someone less to love another person. You can love everyone you care about just as much."

"It's been Charlie, Dad, and me for a long time. That's all I've needed and all I could handle. But with you... I'm just so happy to have you here... I'm alive and feeling again, no longer only existing."

I wasn't sure if I should have told her all this, but I meant every single word, and it felt right. A few days prior, that conversation would have been unthinkable. The cat was out of the bag, and she seemed relaxed.

"So maybe we can figure out if there's something here. If you are the person I believe you are," I said with a crooked smile. "We'll take some small steps at a time, okay? This is an unfamiliar territory for me. And I have some people to consider who are important to me."

She smiled. "And what kind of person do you think I am?"

I checked her out. "Hmmm. I think you're Cathrine. Olav's friend from high school and Gustavo's ex."

"Dork."

She laughed, threw a pillow at me, and leaned over.

A nurse came in, and Cathrine straightened up.

"Time for medication," he said, placing a tray with a glass of water and a couple of pills on my nightstand. He found my pillow on the floor and returned it to my bed. "Need help with those?" he asked, nodding toward the tablets.

"Nah," I said, washing my pills down with water.

The nurse took his tray and left.

"Where were we?" Cathrine said as he disappeared out the door.

"I was a dork, if I remember correctly."

She smiled slyly. "I rest my case. We'll wait with the rest until you're out of here."

"The rest?"

"Keep on fantasizing for now. We don't want to risk getting thrown out of here before you are back on your feet."

I wasn't as sure. Maybe it would be just as well to get thrown out of here. Olav was still missing, and every hour was crucial.

Chapter Twenty-Four

Cathrine slept with her head leaning against her shoulder and her mouth open. Her knitting had slipped to the floor. Before she woke, she made a light snoring sound and moistened her lips with her tongue. Her head straightened up but soon fell back. She slept on.

Even while sleeping, she was beautiful. She radiated warmth in contrast to the cool, impersonal room. I felt a need to protect her from everything threatening us.

The hospital's rhythm was a mix of haste and routine, quick footsteps and muted conversations, interrupted by doors opening or slamming shut.

The clock on the wall read eleven. It was Friday. A lot had happened since I landed and met her for the first time: Gustavo, Cool J, the abduction, Ricardo, Al Sayed, and Victoria. Who could I trust?

Was Cathrine the person she claimed to be? I studied her. I couldn't believe her being fake after all we had experienced and shared. It was unthinkable. I felt sure about her. She would never betray me. Without her, I wouldn't even be looking for Olav right now.

As Mom often said, trust is the cornerstone of any relationship. I had unlimited trust in her.

But Ricardo had been well prepared when I came to his ranch. It seemed he knew about my contact with Gustavo and our manipulation of his security cameras. Had Gustavo tipped him off? It wasn't impossible, but he also seemed upset when it became clear Olav had been abducted.

I shook my head in frustration. *Shape up, Floki! Don't let your jealousy impede logical analysis.*

Instead, I thought about Charlene and Dad. Charlene was at school; the last time I talked to Dad, he was still at the hospital. I couldn't call and tell him what had happened. It had to wait.

Lost in thoughts, I felt a hand on my shoulder. A nurse was trying to get my attention.

"You have a visitor. It's from the police," he said. "If you need rest, I can ask him to leave. Just let me know."

"It's okay. Let him in."

He disappeared back into the hallway. Cathrine was waking up.

"We're getting a visitor," I explained. "From the police."

She looked confused for a moment.

"Maybe I should ask him to come back later?" I suggested.

"I'll just pop into the bathroom and be right back," she said, disappearing.

I sat watching her. I wanted to hide in the bathroom with her.

The door opened, and a clean-shaven man in a white T-shirt and khaki shorts came in, his arms tattooed. His gaze swept across the room, taking in all the details.

"I'm Horacio Almenada, narcotics investigator with the Guardia Civil," he said.

His voice oozed determination and authority. He extended a hand toward me. Not to shake hands, but to give me his business card. "I'm an old friend of Jonas Vik. At least that's what he thinks," he said, winked, and guffawed.

I took his card and met his intense gaze. He didn't let go of my eyes while talking about himself. I was more concerned with how he knew he could find me at this hospital.

Horacio eyed my empty chair. "Is it okay if I sit here?"

I was about to protest, but he'd already sat down, so I let him stay.

"How are you doing, by the way? Jonas asked me to give his regards and wish you a speedy recovery. You sure need it, but I've also promised him to find your brother..."

He checked a notepad. "Olab."

I had to correct him.

"Olav. Yes, I've tried to report him missing. But your colleague wasn't very interested."

"I see. Olab. And that's when you started investigating on your own? I understand, but as you've noticed, the Costa del Sol is dangerous for the curious. I know you have police experience, but not from Costa del Sol. You also do not have the jurisdiction or protection you have as a police officer. From now on, I will handle this, but to do so, I need some information from you."

He pulled a ballpoint pen from his inner pocket and flipped to a blank page in his notebook. Cathrine exited the bathroom and sat at the foot of my bed.

Horacio studied her before nodding and continuing. "How well did you know about your brother's activities in Spain?"

"Not well."

"I understand he worked as a DJ at parties and yachts in the area. Do you know if he was involved with the drug trade?"

I hadn't been able to think that through. But it had been nagging at my subconscious for a while. "Not as I've been able to find out. Not according to those I've talked to so far."

I was uncomfortable with the direction this conversation had taken. It seemed like Horacio had decided on a direction and only wanted me to confirm it. With his background, it might be natural, but I needed more time to decide whether to define this as a drug case.

"He owed someone money," I said.

"For drugs?"

"No, gambling."

"Do you know who he owed all this money to?"

"No."

He sighed and regarded me. Noticed my reluctance. "Do you know who beat you up?"

He was ready to take notes.

"No."

He looked at me, irritated. "And this had nothing to do with you being on Ricardo Sanchez's property yesterday?"

I didn't answer.

"Let me make one thing crystal clear. This is an official police matter. Officer Hernandes submitted the missing person report about your brother, and we were involved before Jonas' inquiry. You need to stay away from this investigation. We don't need anyone stomping around here like a bull in a candy shop."

In a china shop! I thought, barely contained myself.

"And we don't need a rural police officer from Norway getting hurt while visiting. Do we understand each other?"

"Sure," I said, not even trying to clarify the misunderstanding, just as I didn't care about following his advice.

"One last thing. Do you know who offered to help Olab pay off his debt?"

"No," I said. At least that bit was valid.

He asked a few more questions, but it seemed like he was treading water. After some polite phrases, he disappeared as abruptly as he'd come. We heard him talking on his cell on his way out.

"Penny for your thoughts?" Cathrine asked.

"Not worth that much. But I'm not planning to sit in Elviria staring at the wall while this clown stomps. That's for sure."

"Agreed. We need to talk to Victoria tomorrow. Nobody can deny us the right to talk to her."

Again, she displayed the determination that had fascinated me from day one. "I wonder who told him someone would help Olav with the money?" she thought aloud.

"Yeah, it's been bugging me, too. My first suspicion was Ricardo. Horacio tried to figure out if we would snitch on him. I don't trust our friend, the narco-cop."

Cathrine nodded. "We need to find 'Olab' before he does," she said.

She grabbed my hand, and we sat in silence for a while, letting everything that happened during the last twenty-four hours sink in.

She turned to me. "Are you coming back to life? You look way better."

I smiled. "I think so. Can you help me to the bathroom? Need to check if my plumbing still works."

She gave me a playful and challenging glance. "Am I going to regret this?"

"Oh, come on," I said. "You don't have to hold my hand. Just get me installed, and I'll update you later."

She rolled her eyes but smiled. "Jeez, Flokí, sometimes you're just such an old geezer."

As I returned, I pressed the button above my bed, and a nurse came. "Can I help you?" he asked.

"I want to be discharged."

He stood lingering, looking at me, considering how to react. "One moment," he said and hurried to fetch the doctor on duty.

It turned out to be a middle-aged man who in no way resembled any doctors found in romance novels.

"I can't force you to stay, but you should know you're not ready to be discharged and are leaving this hospital at your own risk. You've had a severe concussion and should be grateful your kidneys are still functioning. You're putting your health at risk by leaving this hospital."

He stared me down.

I shrugged. "I risk more by staying."

He glanced from me to Cathrine, seeking her support. But he got none. He took a deep breath and let it out.

"Fine. I'll give you some pills. Try to rest as much as possible and avoid strenuous activities. If you feel unwell, you come right back here."

He shook his head.

"And one last thing," he said, "you are not to get behind the wheel for the next forty-eight hours. That's an order, not advice."

Chapter Twenty-Five

We drove into the parking garage beneath Avenida del Mar, the avenue stretching from the tranquil Parque de la Alameda down to the tourist harbor. We parked and wandered through the narrow cobblestone streets to the address we'd been given.

I was not in good shape, so I tried to calm my breathing. Cathrine radiated determination as if nothing could shake her.

Snow White's apartment was in a modern complex. The building had shops on the ground floor, offices on the second floor, and flats on six floors. Conversation flowed at a small Italian cafe on the sidewalk.

The smell of freshly ground coffee was tempting, but we hurried past, found the correct apartment, and rang the bell. Snow White, in a neon pink tracksuit, opened the door. She checked the stairs behind us before removing her security chain and letting us in.

Her apartment was devoid of sound—like when you use noise-canceling headphones. Her walls displayed dark brown, almost black tones, starkly contrasting the sunlight and bustling life outside. Three large portraits of Snow White wearing a carnival mask and different facial expressions hung on the walls.

The hallway led to a dark living room. However, she guided us through a side door to a small adjoining room. The room had sparse furnishings in a Scandinavian style, and she had had it painted with lighter colors.

"Victoria's just around the corner," Snow White said.

She studied me. "So you're the cop? Olav's big brother?" She smiled.

I bowed. "Guilty as charged."

I wanted to correct her misunderstandings about my profession, but let it slide.

"Had this apartment long?" Cathrine asked to break the ice.

"I don't own this apartment. Let's call it my creative service office."

She laughed a little. "You understand. You've seen my business card, so you know what my... 'day job' is."

She turned serious. "There's so much lying in this city. I prefer to be honest. Let everyone answer for themselves when this life is over. But this room is my oasis of normal life. For me, it's perfect to live close to everything. All I need is within walking distance. So this is where I choose to live."

She turned to me. "How about it, officer? Are you comfortable with who I am?"

"I've met many questionable individuals throughout my career. You're not one of them. Not based on what you've told us so far. I appreciate honesty and openness. Speaking of which, I assume you weren't christened Snow White?"

"I guess you wouldn't believe me if they'd christened me Pitch Black, either?"

We laughed.

"Black is correct, by the way. Miranda Black. You owe me at least one drink next time we meet. Everything has its price."

Her doorbell rang. I hoped it was Victoria arriving and not some client or Al Sayed.

Miranda rose and went to the door. We heard Victoria's voice. Then, they both came into the room.

"Sorry you had to wait," Victoria said. "Mickey asked me to entertain some important business associates at Santiago. But here I am."

Victoria shifted her focus to me. She looked concerned and surprised. "What in heaven's name happened to you?" she asked, studying my face.

"If you think this looks bad, you should see the other guy," I said, acting much more upbeat than I felt.

I was still pretty beaten up, and the effect of the painkillers was wearing off.

"Was it Ricardo's men?" she asked, studying my face.

"Why?"

"Because I know it was Ricardo who lent Olav the money. That's what I wanted to tell you today. I'm sorry I couldn't tell you at the nightclub. Especially if what happened to you is his doing."

She seemed distressed. Cathrine and I exchanged glances. We were unsure if she was being open because she knew about our meeting with Ricardo or if she wanted to help. It was hard to tell.

"Who told you Ricardo was Olav's creditor?" I asked.

"Olav, of course."

Her face suggested she was pondering something more, so I waited. "And Mickey. He was the first to tell me Olav was in trouble. In a fit of jealousy, he said I shouldn't go after someone who owed Ricardo money unless I wanted to end up floating in the harbor with him."

Burning stomach acid threatened to take the quickest way up. I swallowed and swallowed to avoid throwing up. The pain felt acute again. I was sweating, even though the air conditioning kept the room chilled.

"Are you okay?" Cathrine asked.

I stammered: "I think I need to take that pill now. For my pain."

Cathrine stood up. "Come on. I'll help you." She turned to Miranda. "Where's the bathroom? And can you get us a glass of water?"

Miranda showed us to the bathroom. I swallowed one pill I'd gotten from the hospital. Cathrine moistened a towel. She wiped my forehead, lifted my t-shirt, and wiped my chest. I came back.

Looking toward the door, Cathrine whispered: "Do you trust her?"

"Maybe. And you?"

"I think so. Let's hear what else she has to say. I haven't made up my mind."

We got up. Before returning to Victoria, I whispered: "We need her help. She's all we've got."

Both seemed relieved when we returned.

"You look better," Victoria said.

"I feel better, too."

"It's amazing what a loving hand can do," she said, smiling at Cathrine.

We sat down.

"There's something else you should know," Victoria said, looking at us both before focusing on me. "The day before Olav disappeared, he asked me for a favor."

"Okay. Go on."

"He claimed he had a chance to get rid of his debt to Ricardo. Said he knew someone who might be willing to help him."

"We know that. Someone with money and influence. We figured it might be you."

I studied her reaction.

She ignored me. "Then he asked me to drive him to Hacienda Las Chapas."

I took a breath. We were one step further.

"Hacienda Las Chapas? Where's that?"

"A hillside east of Elviria. Large villas and estates. Well-established. You know, high walls with climbing roses, camouflaging barbed wire, and cameras. I haven't been there since the restaurant La Hacienda closed—the most romantic restaurant in Marbella ever!"

"Do you have the address?"

"No address. I drove, and he directed me."

"Can you take us where you dropped him off?"

"I believe there's a tracker in my Bentley. It's not my car, you know."

She winked.

"If he's holed up there, I don't want Mickey to know. But if you drive, I can show you."

I understood her thinking. And I understood something else: Victoria was the last person to see Olav before he disappeared.

Chapter Twenty-Six

"Right here, at this intersection, this is where I dropped him off that evening," Victoria exclaimed.

Cathrine pulled over to the side and stopped. We were in the upper part of Urbanización Hacienda Las Chapas. Secluded villas lined the road we had driven on. Behind high fences, we glimpsed flowering gardens, roofs, and gables with a layer of the patina of time.

"He walked up this road to the left. That was the last I saw of him."

Cathrine turned onto the road she pointed to.

"Stop!" Victoria seemed nervous. "I think I should leave now. Don't want to be seen. I'll walk down a bit and order an Uber. You'll have to manage the rest on your own."

Victoria got out and walked back toward the main road.

Cathrine looked at me uncertainly. Then, she retook the lead. "Shall we park the car and walk so we don't miss anything important?"

I nodded, and we began walking up the side road. There were discreet villas on both sides, with even higher fences and hedges than the previous.

Where the road ended, an impressive, white functionalist villa made of brick and glass stood. A white wall and a perfectly trimmed hedge surrounded the property. Unlike the neighboring houses, the sizeable wrought-iron gate with no back panel made it easy to peek inside.

The property offered a peaceful escape from the noise of the main road. But in this discreet residential area, it screamed of nouveau riche narcissism.

Seeing the bronze plaque on one of the gate pillars made me gape.

Cathrine's voice snapped me back to reality. "Something wrong?"

"The sign," I said, nodding toward the bronze plaque.

She read the name on the plaque: Villa Helman-Larssen.

She raised an eyebrow. "Helman-Larssen? As in the shipping dynasty?"

I nodded, confused. "The very same."

"Do you know them?"

"Kind of."

I ran a hand through my hair. "Olav and I inherited some land from our mom. I kept the old house; he kept some land. The Helman-Larssens bought the rest. Olav bought the apartment in Elviria with the money from the sale."

"This is no coincidence," Cathrine stated.

Did Olav ask Helman-Larssen to help him with the money? Why didn't he ask me? Dad and I would have sacrificed everything to help him.

"No," I repeated as if in a trance. "It's no coincidence."

She stood right in front of me and looked me in the eye. "This is where Olav went that evening. If you want to know where he is, you'd better get to that gate and chime the bell."

I did as told and pushed the intercom.

"Si?"

"Hi! Is Anita here? She has invited us over a few times, so we wondered if she was home."

"Momento."

The gate slid open, and Cathrine tightened her hand around mine. Together, we walked up the driveway.

At the top of the marble steps, we met a thin, bald man in a tailored pinstripe suit and cream-colored shirt, open at his neck. Dark Cartier sunglasses hid his eyes. He exuded controlled elegance.

"You wanted to meet Anita today? I'm afraid you've come too late. Miss Helman-Larssen left for home a while ago," he said in a polished Bergen dialect. "I believe she's in Copenhagen now."

I didn't correct him.

He studied me. "I'll let her know you called, Mister...?"

"Floki. Floki Wilhelmsen."

I drew an arc in the air. "And this is Cathrine Runevik."

"Sture Glette," he said, extending a hand. "I work with the Helman-Larssens and get to use this place as an escape from the everyday. In return, I'm responsible for upkeeping this property."

He lifted his head and took a deep breath.

"This place is more than just brick and marble to me; it has that special tranquility I seek. It's rare to find such a peaceful oasis these days. And your name is Flokí? That's a remarkable name, unusual in these times. Are you Olav's brother? The policeman?"

I studied the house and its impressive facade.

"Yes," I said, gathering my thoughts. "Have any of you seen Olav in the last couple of days? We cannot get in contact with him, and we're worried."

He nodded.

"Olav was here. I believe it was last Thursday. I spoke with him."

I stopped breathing for a moment. *Olav had been here!*

He gestured toward the open door. "I seem to have lost all my manners. It's almost a hundred degrees out here. Come, let's talk more inside. It's more livable in there."

We walked through a hall where workers were still laying the carpet on the stairs to the second floor. The hall smelled of fresh paint and tapestry glue. "Sorry about this mess," Glette smiled, "but we are working on completing it, and it will be wonderful."

Soft light streamed through the tall, sun-filtered windows, casting long shadows across the polished floors. Giant abstract artworks created by artists far beyond my budget dominated the walls.

The ceiling height was as impressive here as everywhere else. A large crystal chandelier hung down from it. The view through the glass wall toward the garden took our breath away. The garden lay on three plateaus, separated by marble stairs, with a fountain in antique style on the middle level. Behind the fountain, Marbella and the azure-blue Mediterranean opened to the horizon.

It was beautiful.

Glette came back, rolling a small bar cart. "Marvelous, isn't it? We bought this plot six years ago. It took a couple of years to complete everything, but since this terrace was finished, I've spent almost every evening under the open sky enjoying coffee with something sweet."

He stood, lost in his thoughts. "Speaking of coffee, help yourselves," he said. "Miguel takes care of all that, but he's off today. Would you like a Hansa beer? Should be something for every taste in here."

He stopped mid-sentence, distracted. Then he came to and jumped up. "Except coffee," he said, staring out the window. "Where were we... Ah, yes, coffee? Anyone want a cup?"

We nodded, and he disappeared again. "What do you think?" I asked, turning to Cathrine.

"At least we've confirmed that Olav has been here," she said.

I glanced through the window. "Let's hope he knows something more. And that he'll tell us the entire truth about his visit."

Glette returned with a tray containing three coffee cups, a pot of coffee, a milk jug, and a plate with assorted cookies. I noticed how hungry I was. I couldn't remember when we last ate, but these cookies wouldn't amount to much.

Glette poured coffee and sat down. "As mentioned, Olav dropped by last week. He was a polite young man. He talked about the property in Mølstrevåg and wondered if we would still be interested in buying the plot where he'd planned to build his cabin. I understood he needed money for some investments and wanted to check with us first."

"Did you find it interesting?"

"We had already secured the area we wanted in our previous deal. The plot he offered didn't fit our purpose. It was a small plot on the other side of your house. We couldn't use it for anything profitable."

He checked his watch.

"I advised him to sell it as a cabin plot. We sat and talked right here where we're sitting. He stayed for about an hour, then he left."

I realized this might be the last place Olav was seen before disappearing. I thought about the disappointment and fear he must have felt when his hope shattered.

"Did he indicate where he was heading next?"

"No, I'm afraid not. Nothing. He seemed pensive and didn't mention what kind of investments he was considering, but that wasn't my business. A fine young gentleman. But tell me, you mentioned it had been a while since you'd heard from him?"

"Since you last saw him," I said.

He understood the implication.

"Does that mean the police might come here? I'm anxious about causing a stir. Police may raise unnecessary attention in a neighborhood like ours. You understand that we're new here, and discretion is important. Finding your brother is more important, but I don't know anything else."

"Well, I don't control that. That's up to the police."

"Of course, of course, I understand..." He squirmed and stood up. "Well, it was nice to meet you. I have a Teams meeting in ten minutes, so I must move on."

Our visit was over, and he showed us out.

"I hope Olav gets in touch soon, so you don't have to worry anymore. And that the police can use their time on more pressing issues."

I shared his hope but couldn't care less about keeping up the Helman-Larssen facade.

Outside stood a black G-Class with a couple of suitcases next to it. Maybe he had visitors? Was that why he was so distracted and eager to get rid of us?

Construction work was still ongoing outdoors as well. By the gate, they had prepared an area to pour the floor of an oversized garage, a perfect place to display a small fleet of luxury cars.

I turned and looked back at the house. It was an exceptional property but overly ostentatious for this neighborhood.

I thought of Olav's message to Cathrine.

He will understand.

There was still something important I didn't understand.

I still hadn't figured it out.

Chapter Twenty-Seven

We sat in the car with our doors open, staring at the beautiful houses and gardens without seeing them. I was digesting everything that had happened. Olav had visited this villa to sell his property, but got turned down. That's where our leads ended, and we were back to square one.

I started the car, and humid, warm air hit my face. The air conditioning came to life, filling the cabin with a whiff of mold. We closed the doors almost mechanically and drove off.

Cathrine broke her silence.

"What's on your mind?"

Her voice was warm and concerned.

I took a breath. "It's..." I began. "Like an endless circle. I'm thinking about Olav and how he felt when they rejected him. What went through his head as he left that place?"

I realized we didn't know how he left. Had he ordered a taxi or an Uber? Could we find out?

I turned to Cathrine. "Why wasn't he open and honest about his situation? Family is supposed to be the foundation of life, like a cornerstone, right? Did he go underground to avoid Ricardo? I know how unpleasant it was to be in Ricardo's crosshairs."

"It's hard not being able to be open with your family about your problems. Even in a split family like mine, blood is thicker than water," she said.

"We try to protect them. I'm shielding my dad and Charlene in the midst of all this. I want to spare them as much as possible from anything dangerous. Maybe that's why Olav didn't tell us? Or maybe he was ashamed of his situation? I don't know."

"We'll ask him when we find him," she said.

My cell phone broke the silence as the car rolled onto the highway. It was my dad. I let it ring until it stopped.

What could I tell him? One thing was clear: I couldn't tell him about the beating and my hospital stay. I had to tell him about Olav's visit to Helman-Larssen and have him figure out more about Glette.

"Why didn't you answer?" Cathrine asked.

I sighed. Her gaze burned into my peripheral vision. "I wasn't ready."

"Was it your dad?"

"Yeah, I don't know what to tell him."

"How about the truth?"

"Yeah, but... I am trying to figure out what the truth is. And I don't want to tell him everything. He's an old man. I don't know if he can handle hearing about my hospital stay. It'll make him anxious."

"Didn't we agree it's better to be honest? Family is the foundation, the cornerstone on which everything rests."

"There are other considerations."

"Sure? Maybe we should just tell the truth? I'm tired of these half-truths."

Dad called again. This time, I answered. My voice sounded severe.

He reacted. "Anything wrong?"

"No, or yes... I don't know."

"Tell me."

I turned into the driveway to Elviria. Cathrine signaled for me to tell him. "We just heard Olav tried to sell his property in Mølstrevåg to get money to pay off his debt."

"Sell? To whom?"

"To Helman-Larssen."

"Helman-Larssen? How did they get involved? You said he tried? They weren't interested?"

"Didn't seem like it. The sale was supposed to save him from his creditors. He hoped Helman-Larssen could get the money quickly. They wanted to buy the entire area when we negotiated earlier."

"Was this before or after the abduction?"

"After. The men who abducted him had set him free."

He took a breath. "Thank God! How did you find out about Helman-Larssen?"

Cathrine gestured for me to continue. I parked in front of a twenty-four-hour store and told him about our visit to

Helman-Larssen and the conversation with Glette. Cathrine grabbed my hand.

"Do you know anything about this Glette character?" I asked my dad.

"Yeah, he's an executive at their shipping company. But I can ask Jonas for more details. He knows a few people in that company. How come you talked to him?"

"We met someone who had driven Olav to their villa last Thursday."

"I see. Then what happened? Where did he go afterward?"

"We don't know."

"How about the driver? Wouldn't he know?"

"She only drove him to the house."

"Did this Glette character tell you how he left?"

"An Uber? We don't know."

"So that's where our leads end?"

I took a breath. "That's where they end. We've mapped his movements until a few hours before he disappeared."

"Tell him about the hospital," Cathrine said softly in my ear.

"Hey, Flokí..."

Dad took a slight pause. I seized the opportunity to change the direction of our conversation. "How's Charlene? She with you?"

"No, she's at the movies. With friends from school."

"Vidar?" I asked.

Cathrine signaled for me to let it go.

"Listen, son," Dad said. "Don't you have something else you need to tell me? Something important you've forgotten?"

Cathrine's gaze met mine. Her eyes asked: What do you do now, Floki?

"What's on your mind?"

He said nothing. The silence became oppressive. I didn't like this. He knew something. He knew Jonas, and Jonas knew Horacio. That's the connection.

"Ricardo let Olav loose on the strict condition that he could get the money in less than seventy-two hours and settle his debt."

"Do you think Ricardo brought him back in? Or that he went underground?"

"Maybe. Or both. I don't know yet, but I will find out."

He was quiet for a second or two.

"When were you planning to tell me about your hospital stay?"

With a sigh, I gave up and told him about the break-in at Ricardo's property and a beautified version of the "massage" I got before being dumped in Marbella.

I could hear him trying to control his emotions. Then he took a deep breath.

"I've talked to Jonas. He's concerned about both of you and adamant that you shouldn't pursue this any further. He fully trusts Horacio and believes they have the resources and authorizations needed to bring Olav home."

But I didn't want to give it up. I doubted even Horacio, with his resources and contacts, would find him. I doubted anyone would show the same level of dedication as Cathrine and me.

"We'll be careful," I said.

Dad lowered his voice. Cathrine leaned closer to hear better.

"Jonas is concerned Ricardo, with his network's reach including Norway, might target his victim's family when he's angry. Jonas thinks you're putting Charlene in his crosshairs. Me, too, but I'm too old to care. But I am worried about Charlene."

I could not afford to make another mistake. No matter how small the risk, I couldn't expose Charlie or Dad to danger. The image of what had happened to Jo-Ann made my stomach churn. It threw me off. I felt exhausted and checkmated.

"We'll return home."

Chapter Twenty-Eight

"Will you sleep here tonight?" Her eyes narrowed, and she bit her lip while gazing at me. "I don't want to be without you for another night."

We stood by the door outside her room. She was so close I could feel her warmth and breath. I put my arm around her. The crickets provided a soundtrack for our moment through her open window. It felt good. It felt right.

She opened the door behind her but didn't break eye contact. She smiled, kissed me on the cheek, and pulled away. Her door slid open behind her. I grabbed her, pushed her against the doorframe, and kissed her. Her tongue was demanding; her passion fired me up.

She nuzzled me away, took a breath, and studied me. She wanted to say something but hesitated.

"What's on your mind?" I asked.

"Come," she said, grabbing my hand and leading me into her room.

We lay on the bed, close together, with our clothes on. The faint light from outside cast long shadows in the room. Everything was quiet except for our steady, rhythmic breathing. The hunger, desire, and anticipation made my heart beat faster.

"You know what I want," she said in the direct, straightforward manner that was her trademark. She lay in the crook of my arm, looking at me.

She sat up and undressed.

I turned and studied her. The light from the full moon outside colored her body blue and made her eyes sparkle. She was beautiful, intelligent, and had a kind and brave heart.

And me? I felt lucky. And nervous.

Afterward, we lay close together. The physical passion of the moment had consumed me, but this was more than sex. This could be the beginning of a new era in my life.

Or was it just the old Adam running out of control? No, it was more than a moment of passion - and therefore damn complicated.

"Do you think we stand a chance?" she asked, as if she'd read my thoughts.

"Right now, I'd say 'yes.' But go easy on me, girl. This is a big change in my life."

I searched for the right words. "The most important thing is we know how we feel about each other."

Was I moving too fast? Would Charlene handle a new person in our lives? And would Cathrine handle all the extras that came with me? That part of my life she didn't know yet. A teenage stepdaughter could be challenging.

"You're more than just you. I know," she finished my thoughts once again.

"Was it that obvious?" I smiled.

"Yeah. You're as easy to read as a dime store novel."

"Fair enough. This feels right to me, but I come with some heavy add-ons. Both past and present. The question is whether it's the right thing for you."

She smiled. "I haven't met the important people in your life. But I've met you. And I'm convinced the people you choose to have in your life are worth loving."

I nodded. "Yes, they are."

She rested her head on my shoulder. "But you haven't met my mom yet. What if she's a veritable dragon?" She smiled mischievously.

"Dragons I can handle, but mothers-in-law are far more lethal," I said diplomatically.

Cathrine sized me up. "Bet you've had plenty of adventures for a while, right?" She smiled, but her eyes were serious.

"I want to see if this can work out how I think it could, but I understand it's more complicated for you."

I answered without hesitation. "If I weren't ready for us, I wouldn't be in this bed with you, not like this. Tomorrow, we'll be back in Haugesund. We'll hold off on the house tours for a bit. But I think Charlene and Dad will appreciate that I have someone in my life. We need to take it step by step. Let it unfold naturally."

"So we return home tomorrow?"

I fell silent for a moment while collecting my thoughts. I needed to get Cathrine home and safe. Needed to be present to care for the three people who meant the most to me. I couldn't protect them from here.

However, this irritating, nagging feeling held me back - something was off.

After going through everything we'd experienced over the last couple of days several times over, I couldn't put my finger on it. But that feeling of something being wrong had grown stronger.

Would Horacio see it the same way and follow all leads? Persevere like a bloodhound to find Olav? Would his relationship with Jonas keep him going? Or would he settle for a superficial check before another case caught his interest?

If so, my cowardice and protective instinct for the other three would put Olav's life in danger. There was no perfect solution to this tangle. I was living up to my name.

"Anything you'd like to tell me?"

I took a deep breath. "It's complicated. Can we sleep on it? Maybe everything will fall into place in daylight?"

She sighed. "I understand it's complicated, Flokí."

She kissed me and snuggled up close. "We'll deal with it tomorrow. Right now, I'm exhausted."

The moonlight was gone, and it had become pitch dark inside and outside our room. I lay awake, listening to the silence. Cathrine's breath was like a warm, soothing heartbeat against my neck. Gradually, her rhythm became more even.

Finally, she was sound asleep.

Chapter Twenty-Nine

I plummeted through darkness, alone and at breakneck speed, waking up just before hitting the bottom.

Gasping for air, I tried to get my bearings. I tossed and turned in bed, unable to find a comfortable position. My sheets felt too hot, too constricting. I kicked them off, only to pull them back up a moment later. My thoughts were as restless as my body.

I reached for my phone on the nightstand. My fingers trembled as I unlocked the screen. It was almost three a.m., and there were no new messages.

I set it aside and rubbed my eyes, trying to rub away my worries.

Last night came back to me. I turned. Cathrine lay on her side, her back to me, her hair fanned out across her pillow. With each breath, her shoulders rose before sinking. She was groaning and mumbling something. My heartbeat steadied in sync with her breathing.

I studied the cracks in the ceiling. They reminded me of dried-up riverbeds. Dad had always said life was like a river—constantly changing but always flowing toward the sea.

My life had been like these cracks: dried up without power or direction.

Maybe my drought was over.

Dad had asked me to come home for Charlene's sake. He left Olav's fate in the hands of the Spanish police. It must have been a hard choice, a sacrifice he would make only because the alternative was terrifying.

How would Dad react? I had traveled to Spain to find Olav but returned with a girlfriend instead—a girl a bit on the young side. Would he understand? Or would he see it as a betrayal of the task he had entrusted to me? I hoped he would know that some things in life are beyond our control. They just happen.

I rechecked my phone. Still nothing. Just a notification about a memory in my photo app. I opened it. A sequence of images from my life with Jo-Ann and her funeral streamed across my screen: pictures of Charlene at her mother's grave, colleagues from SFPD in uniform, and a profound, grief-stricken young man, Olav.

What are you hiding from me? I thought as I studied his picture.

Tears welled up, and I closed my screen. The images disappeared, but it didn't help. I lay staring at my ceiling.

"I can't let Olav down. Can't lose Charlene, Cathrine, or Dad. It's not an option," I whispered.

A glance at Cathrine told me she hadn't noticed.

I'd have to choose, and none of my alternatives would be viable if the worst should happen. I groaned, disturbing Cathrine's breathing rhythm.

Cathrine had turned out to be a skilled and intelligent ally under fire. The solution might be for her to go home to care for those back home. She could take them to Mølstrevåg while I continued searching for Olav.

Would she be willing to accept this solution? Would she understand how important it was for me to protect my family without letting Olav down? Would Dad be able to handle such a situation? Or would he be stubborn and reject her?

I looked at the woman next to me, remembering how determined she was and how she got a loner like me to do whatever she wanted. It was an important reason I had opened up to her and no one else.

Love flowed through me. Lord, it had been a long time since I'd felt like this. I stroked her hair.

But how would I pursue the hunt for Olav if I stayed? It hadn't been a success story so far. At worst, his situation had gotten worse. I had barely taken care of myself and wasted valuable time lying helpless in a hospital.

What if Olav had gone into hiding, and I found him? One slight mistake on my part could reveal his hiding place to his enemy.

Was it better if I went home after all? I dismissed the thought. So, where should I look? I went through all the events from when I landed.

Had Ricardo retaken Olav? What had convinced me this wasn't the case? He'd let him go, but that was no guarantee he hadn't brought him back in.

I got up and walked across the cool tiles to the window.

Olav's strange message to Cathrine stated that I would understand. Was this some code or hidden meaning I didn't catch? Had he already known he wouldn't pick her up at the airport? If so, it could show that he had planned his disappearance.

Did Al Sayed have something to do with Olav's disappearance after all, either as a facilitator or because of his jealousy? I hadn't followed up on this lead. I made a mental note: "Talk to Victoria."

The lights and low hum of a passing car outside broke the silence momentarily.

Then there was Glette and Helman-Larssen's villa. That's where all trails stopped. Something about our visit to Helman-Larssen's villa had been wrong. I have felt this many times since. I remembered how worried Glette had been when we arrived, how distracted he had been while we were with him, and how quickly he'd gotten rid of us once we told him what we knew.

From the moment I studied the windows on the second floor, he had acted strange. What if Olav never left but was hiding in the building? What if he was being held against his will?

I felt a shiver down my spine. If Olav were there, it would only be a matter of time before someone discovered him. I had to get back to the villa first thing in the morning. We could bring him home on our flight tomorrow if I found him. We had no time to lose.

Optimism gave me energy; realism brought me back down to earth. I was grasping at straws. Glette's behavior was odd, but to relate it to me, studying the house's facade was pretty far-fetched.

Glette's stress could have natural causes. He had an important video meeting but saw our desperation and wanted to help as best he could. After all, Olav had been visiting that evening, and Glette had information that could be useful to us.

I was back to square one. Again.

I was exhausted. I noticed how pointless it was to assemble this puzzle when all the pieces were the same color as the sea. My pieces made no sense, no matter how I arranged them.

The energy that had flared up for a moment had gone. I sat on the bed with my head in my hands.

How did I believe I could find Olav like this? Did I deceive myself by thinking I was still the investigator I once had been? Had I ever been one?

I got under the covers and closed my eyes. I kept my eyes closed for a while, but the Sandman wasn't anywhere to be found.

What was the actual value of my contribution so far?

Then, everything became crystal clear to me. It was like a revelation. I knew what I'd reacted to.

I looked at Cathrine one last time, caressing the curves along her back with my gaze. Then I lifted the duvet and got up. I gathered my clothes. My belt buckle clinked. Cathrine reacted to the sound. But soon, she was back asleep, and I tiptoed out of the room.

I dressed in the kitchen, took a turtleneck and beanie from the closet, and found a small flashlight in the drawer by the entrance.

I checked my watch. It was half past three.

There was still time.

Chapter Thirty

I parked fifty yards from the driveway of the Helman-Larssen villa and killed the lights. I sat observing the villa, scanning from right to left and back to detect movement, but I saw none.

In the darkness, the house was, if possible, even more impressive. Long vertical lights illuminated the walls, architectural details like columns and reliefs were floodlit, and the lights from the pool and fountain cast ghostly shadows on the stone walls.

The property signaled power and wealth on the outside, but all the windows were dark. The house was like a monument to the person who lived in it—a dazzling exterior but dark inside, alluring and threatening simultaneously.

I was ninety-nine percent sure I had solved this puzzle. My heart hoped I was wrong. A fist around my heart said otherwise.

It was four a.m.

I had to get onto the property without being detected. That was my entire plan.

I had seen a security company sticker on a gatepost and at least four cameras covering the gate and the wall facing the road.

The cameras had motion detectors, which I had noticed during my previous visit. Guaranteed to be connected to the security company.

If I didn't find Olav, I might as well give up and go home. I had to get in. I had to know the truth.

I started the car, passed the property, and turned around a corner. The neighboring property looked abandoned and was less well-maintained than usual. I examined the gate and wall but saw no signs of a security company or surveillance cameras. If I judged correctly, one corner of this property was near the area with Helman-Larssen's best view. They lowered the wall at that end to preserve the view. This would be my best option.

I parked my car by the curb, rolled up the neck of my sweater, and put on my hat. As I was about to leave the car, I noticed the light from another vehicle coming up behind me.

I ducked down in my seat and waited for the car to pass. It was the security company's car patrolling the area. Two guards were in the vehicle.

I sat still, considering my next move. This was a break-in, and I understood the risk. If Olav wasn't here, and I got caught, I would be in trouble.

I'd made my choice. I could not leave without doing what I came for. I took a deep breath, checked that my dome light was off, and opened the door.

As expected, I got onto the neighboring property without problems. Under the cover of walls and vegetation, I found a corner to observe the Helman-Larssen property.

The garden was dimly lit, and the beautiful fountain stood prominently in the foreground. Below the well-manicured stone hedge, the terrain dropped thirty feet. A six-foot ravine, as deep as the drop, separated my vantage point from the wall. I couldn't spot any cameras along this side.

A cool breeze brushed the back of my neck. It was getting close to sunrise.

"Okay," I thought. *Make it or break it.*

I ran up, jumped over the ravine, and clung to the other side. I lay still for a moment. No signs showed an alarm was triggered, but I hadn't expected it. If an alarm had been triggered, it would be silent. Within a few minutes, the guards would be in place.

For a moment, I regretted not bringing Cathrine along. Could have used that extra pair of eyes to warn me if the guards returned.

But Cathrine was sleeping safely in the apartment. I pictured her in bed when I left.

I had a job to do, so I stood up.

I ran along the edge of the property, disappeared into the darkness, and avoided lit areas. Because of the cameras on the wall, I kept clear of the villa. I ran toward an area with gardening equipment and found myself a shovel.

Without wasting time, I ran toward the gate where the new garage was under construction. I studied the garage site and the formwork for pouring the floor. Then I started digging in the corner nearest the stone wall, far from the gate.

I dug, interrupted by small listens. No one disturbed me. The soil was soft, silent, and easy to dig, as if someone had already dug it. The fist around my heart tightened.

Fifteen minutes later, my shovel hit a plastic bag. I scraped away enough soil to open it.

A hand fell out. A hand with Olav's signet ring—the one he got from Dad for confirmation—and the wristwatch I gave him last year. I stopped digging, stunned by shock and grief. Tears welled up as I stared at Olav's lifeless hand.

No one kidnapped Olav; he wasn't hiding. Olav was dead.

My worst fear had become real. I felt nothing, heard nothing. Time stood still while that grip around my heart crushed it slowly.

The world would never be the same—not for me, not for Charlene, and least of all for Dad. Someone would pay for this. I would find the one responsible.

Then, all my emotions came rushing at once. Tears blinded me; a roar built up in my lungs and tore through the night to wake the dead.

The world spun, and darkness closed in around me.

I wasn't out for more than a few seconds. A car was approaching on the road outside. I must have triggered an alarm at some point, but I didn't care. It didn't matter anymore. *Couldn't care less.* Prison or dungeon made no difference.

The car halted outside the gate. A car door opened and slammed shut. Rapid footsteps approached.

I stood up, brushed the dirt off my pants, walked toward the gate, and got ready.

"Floki? You here?"

Cathrine's voice. My wonderful Cathrine. She was standing by the gate, peering through the wrought iron grill.

I stepped forward into the light.

"Olav is dead," I said in a voice I didn't recognize.

I noticed how cold, sterile, and unreal these words were, the ones we used to describe that a person's life is over.

"How...?" she asked.

"He's buried here. I dug a little and found..."

I gestured, unable to explain. Couldn't take anymore.

"Come," she said, stretching her arms toward me through the wrought-iron gate.

I walked over and let her hold me. She was literally the only thing keeping me up.

Would my dad blame me? I prepared for that. It was okay.

But he and I would demand someone be accountable for this crime. I would make sure of that. Olav's killer would not get away. I straightened up.

Two cars came up the hill at breakneck speed.

One had flashing lights.

Chapter Thirty-One

I stared at people hurrying back and forth between police cars and ambulances. Soon, daylight would overpower the blue lights and lamps.

But for Olav, there would be no sunrise. His days were over.

I couldn't muster the energy to be angry or upset. Had no feelings. Just sat there but didn't feel like I was present. The people around me were silent extras in an absurd play. Focused on activities that didn't concern me. Olav was dead. Nothing these people did would change that.

I held Cathrine, who leaned her head against my neck. I felt her warm tears on my skin. She cried quietly. I sat just as cold as a dead soul in an alien body.

Cathrine lifted her head and looked at me with red-rimmed, tear-filled eyes. "Are you okay?" Her voice was barely audible.

"No," I said. It was an honest reply.

She laid her head back down. There was a long silence. "Anything you need? Something I can get for you? Some water, maybe?"

"If you have a weapon, I'll take it. Any kind will do."

She was quiet for a while. Then she sat up and gazed at me. "For what purpose?"

I clenched my fists. "Glette, Ricardo, Sayed... they'll all get what they deserve."

She said nothing but stared at a dark red sliver on the horizon where the sun would soon rise. I stared the same way. We sat like that.

"We need to make sure the guilty get the punishment they deserve," she said.

Her words came slowly, as if she had to control herself. "But it doesn't help anyone, especially not your dad and Charlene, if you end up in prison."

She kissed me on the cheek. "And it doesn't help me either," she whispered. "I don't want to spend the rest of my life with an hour of conjugal visits as the highlight of my week."

She was right. "I promise you that whoever did this won't get away, no matter how long it takes and no matter the cost."

I watched the people crawling around Olav's body. A woman was taking pictures. An older man was placing markers on the findings. The big police machine was in motion.

A young, polite officer had taken our statements. I didn't know the consequences of my illegal trespassing, but I didn't care as long as it wouldn't prevent me from finding Olav's killer.

"We'll find him together." Cathrine grabbed my hand. "You and me. We make a great team, and we have an advantage. We know Olav and most of what happened before you found him. Deal?"

I considered her words. They moved me. She was right. We had been a great team, she and I. Both in our search for Olav and the friendship we had developed along the way. "Deal," I said.

She squeezed my hand. The first rays of the sun flamed over the horizon. Together, we watched the sunrise to where Olav had died.

"Did they indicate how long we had to stay around?" she asked after a while.

"They're waiting for some kind of hotshot," I said.

She sighed and laid her head on my shoulder. "They took my phone," she said.

"They kept mine, too."

I was dreading the conversation with my dad. I had gone through the conversation so often that I couldn't take it anymore. A delay was just fine.

She stroked my cheek and looked me in the eye. "No easy way to tell him something like this. So keep it brief and honest, and let him ask his questions and start grieving."

I nodded. "Thanks."

"Glette must be involved somehow," she said.

"Olav was either killed on the stairs or in the hall," I replied. "The new carpet and paint put me on the trail. This house is only four years old. The carpet on the stairs doesn't see that much traffic to be worn out by now."

"And the digging on the property," she nodded.

"Yeah. Once that thought got stuck, I had to check it out. Before they started pouring the concrete."

"But why did you start your digging in this corner?"

"That's where I would have pissed."

She looked at me with an open mouth and a skeptical gaze.

I shrugged. "Most men relieve themselves where they figure there's the least chance of being attacked or surprised. Where it feels most safe, I believe it's also the most natural place to bury a body. I was right this time, too."

A man I recognized came walking toward us. It was Horacio Almenada, the investigator who had visited me in the hospital.

"My condolences, Mr. Wilhelmsen," he said as he approached us, nodding at Cathrine. "I understand it was your brother you found here."

It wasn't a question but a statement. I nodded.

He straightened up a bit. "We won't make an issue out of you entering private property without permission. That kind of thing creates a lot of paperwork."

A smile curled his lips before he became serious. "But I need to ask you some questions and have you make an official identification now that we've dug him up," he said, looking toward the technicians.

He studied me to make sure I understood him.

I nodded.

"Enlighten me. How did you conclude Olab had been buried at this exact spot?"

I told him about our previous visit to the villa without involving Victoria. I mentioned Glette, the paint, the carpet, and the excavated plot, and explained how I had seen a pattern I needed to check out and the risk that they would start pouring the floor that morning. Then, it would have been too late.

Horacio took notes and nodded. He asked some follow-up questions.

"It was lucky you didn't have to dig up the entire plot. That you found him on your first try?"

It was a question, but I just nodded without going into detail.

He looked at me appraisingly. "We'll leave it at that."

He looked at the house. "No one home. This guy," he checked his notes. "Sture Glette."

He tried to correct his pronunciation of Sture but gave up. "This man. We're checking if he's left Spain, but the house is empty, so we assume he's not in this country. I've contacted our mutual friend Jonas Vik, who will have a chat with him if he's back home."

He shook his head. "I'm afraid I must ask you to stay in Spain for now. We will keep your passports for a short period. Until we have a better overview of recent events."

"Is that necessary? We'd like to go home to our family. We have a flight this afternoon. Nothing much for us to do here. You don't think we're involved in this, do you?"

"Stay until we have a better overview. We'll be quick about it. Manuel will help you identify Olab, escort you home, and collect your passports." He nodded to an officer who was walking toward us.

Even though we were sitting outside, I felt claustrophobic. I had to get home and talk to Glette. I needed to know what happened when Olav died.

The last thing I wanted was to sit idle with my memories. I needed to be with my dad. I needed to hold and comfort Charlene. And I needed to find the killer who had murdered my brother.

Cathrine's hand touched my arm. "We'll be okay, Floki."

I turned to her and met her gaze. I understood her look and could finally breathe normally. We were in this together. His killer wouldn't slip away. Olav was dead. Time was no longer working against us. No rush.

I lowered my shoulders and nodded. "He won't get away."

Horacio nodded to Manuel, who signaled for us to follow. Then he turned and started walking toward the parking lot. We got up and strolled after. Horacio formed the rear.

As we approached the site of discovery, the ambulance personnel were just about to close the zipper on Olav's body bag. Manuel gave a few commands. They put the bag back on the ground and opened the zipper.

Tears blurred my vision. Even though his face had changed after death, there was no doubt. It was Olav.

I saw him as a little boy in Mom's garden. Imagined my bright little brother with his big smile and light curls. I heard his joyful laughter, which greeted me as I came home from school.

All my memories came flooding, and I couldn't hold back. I cried uncontrollably.

Cathrine put her arms around me. Said nothing. She just held me and let me take the time I needed to empty my heart of grief and despair.

The body bag was closed. Through the tears, I saw the zipper glide over Olav's face until he disappeared. It was irrevocably over. Everything undone remained undone forever.

I shook off my sorrow and straightened up so fast that Cathrine jolted. "Let's go," I said, jaws clenched.

"It's time to get ready for the hunt."

Chapter Thirty-Two

I lay on my bed, fully clothed, staring at the ceiling. I should have called Dad and Charlene, but I couldn't bring myself to it. Wanted to tell them face-to-face. Hug them. Cry with them. But they were thousands of miles away.

Meanwhile, a killer was on the loose. Sture Glette was involved, and I wanted to figure out his role. Our flight was in a few hours, but we couldn't leave without passports.

When I found Olav, I promised I'd catch his killer. I had pledged to him justice. But is there any form of justice that will make good on the murder of someone you love? Arresting his killer would be essential to prevent him from killing again, but it wouldn't bring Olav back.

I've been skeptical of the death penalty my whole life. A wrongful death sentence is hard to rectify. But I also understand why many victims' families would rather have revenge. I felt the urge.

I picked up my phone and called Torstein. Gave him a brief rundown of the last twenty-four hours. With some exceptions.

"Well, I'll be damned! I'm completely floored. Why on earth would anyone want to take Olav's life?"

"Keep this to yourself, Torstein. I want to tell Dad and Charlene myself."

"Of course. You're coming home?"

"We can't leave yet. They're holding our passports. Glette is our only lead. He must have been aware of, and probably involved in, the cleanup these past few days."

"He's in the same lodge as me. Should I swing by and see if I can chat with him? He lives just ten minutes away. Tell him what you found on the property. See how he reacts?"

"If he killed Olav, that's a hazardous strategy. I was thinking more about getting some background information. Talk to people in his circle."

"Ha! Don't think that wimp's gonna be a problem as long as I don't turn my back on him."

"A gun does just as much damage from the front," I said seriously.

"This isn't the Wild West. Most people don't walk around packing heat."

Torstein insisted, so we agreed he would check if Glette was home and make some calls to learn more about him.

He called back fifteen minutes later.

"There are more cops on Glette's property than flies on a warm cow pie," he said in his usual matter-of-fact way. "Word is the guy offed himself."

The buzzing of the intercom interrupted our conversation. Cathrine answered, checked the video, and opened the gate.

"Horacio," she said, walking toward the door to greet him.

I ended the call with Torstein and followed her. She opened the door as Horacio reached the top step.

He moved without his usual energy. He came into the living room and sat heavily in an armchair. Horacio let his gaze drift from Cathrine to me and back.

"I'll be quick," he said, putting our passports on the table.

He searched for words for a moment. "Sture Glette has confessed to the murder of Olab."

He fixed his gaze on me. "Jonas found him in the garage. He had hanged himself. In an email to the shipping company, he confessed everything. Olab had discovered he was transferring money from the company to a fictitious firm in Gibraltar. Olab threatened to report him for embezzlement if he didn't pay a significant amount. An argument broke out, and in a fit of rage, Glette killed your brother."

He spread his arms. "The whole thing is so tragic."

He shook his head. Then he collected himself. "No reason to keep you here, and I understood you wanted to get home as soon as possible. So I won't keep you."

He stood up, offered his condolences to both of us and found his way out while Cathrine and I watched him leave.

We stood staring at the door closing behind him. It was as if the air had gone out of both of us. In less than twelve hours,

I had found Olav murdered, and the killer had received his punishment.

Yet it felt wrong.

Cathrine was the first to speak. "So it was Glette, after all?"

I shrugged. "I would have liked Glette to explain this face to face. Would have liked to hear him confess and accept the consequences, but that's not how it turned out."

It was too simple yet entirely logical. The crime was solved, and revenge was fulfilled. I had done my part when I found Olav; there was nothing more to do.

"We'd better get moving—three hours til our flight. We can make it," she said.

I nodded. She was right. I should call Dad. But I had to be present when I told him about Olav and Glette. Any other option felt wrong.

We packed in silence. How was I going to tell Charlene all this? Barely four years after her mother's dramatic death, she had lost her uncle in a similar tragedy. How would she handle it? How would it affect the rest of her life? How could I help her cope with two such traumatic events in her childhood? I imagined her innocent face dissolved in grief and tears.

I prayed for strength to protect her from the cruelties of this world.

"So, what happens when we get home?"

We passed El Faro. These were the first words we'd exchanged since we left.

"I have to tell Dad and Charlene about Olav. Going straight from the airport as soon as we land."

"Okay, I understand."

We drove on the highway through the outskirts of Fuengirola. It wasn't until we passed Benalmádena that Cathrine broke her silence again.

"Will I see you when we get home?"

Her voice was vulnerable, and I grabbed her hand. She rested her head against my shoulder.

"I'm sorry," I said. "I've been so focused on caring for my family back home. Of course, you can come along. We found Olav together, and they'll probably have many questions for you. But I have a favor to ask. You can come as a good friend, but I don't want to introduce you to Charlene as my girlfriend yet. We'll deal with it later. She has a lot to cope with. Is that okay?"

She nodded gratefully.

Part Three

Forfatterfabrikken Forlag AS

Chapter Thirty-Three

Dad sat on the green-painted bench in the garden when our taxi parked outside his house. I rushed toward him while Cathrine paid, and the driver set our luggage on the sidewalk.

He noticed me, looking puzzled, but then brightened up and glanced behind me.

Olav wasn't there.

Dad locked his gaze on me. His eyes grew moist. I sat down next to him and put my arms around him.

"No, no, no. I knew it, I knew it."

He rocked back and forth. His old body was tense to the breaking point. I had no words. Just clung to him.

We sat on the bench, holding each other. Cathrine was still standing on the sidewalk with the suitcases. She looked uncertain and shy. I asked her to leave our suitcases and waved her over.

Dad studied her momentarily, wiped his eyes, and pulled out a handkerchief.

"Well, where are our manners? Bring the suitcases, and I'll put on some coffee."

"This is Cathrine. She helped me find Olav. Are you sure you're up for this?"

He waved me off. "Have I ever turned down a beautiful lady?" Dad tried to be his old self, but his voice and eyes betrayed him.

I nodded, fetched Cathrine and the suitcases, and felt grateful for something practical to engage in. Dad had already set the cups on when we entered the living room.

"Coffee will be ready in a jiffy," he said after I had introduced Cathrine as a good friend of Olav's.

We sat on the couch.

"Where's Charlene?" I asked.

"At the library..."

He looked at his watch. "They'll be back any minute."

I leaned forward on the couch and met Dad's gaze.

"We found Olav. But... unfortunately, he was dead."

Dad's eyes filled with tears.

"How did you find him?"

I told him about my journey to Spain, meeting Cathrine, the following chase, about Ricardo, Victoria, and Sture Glette. Cathrine nodded in confirmation and added details I had forgotten.

"Glette? From the Helman-Larssen shipping company?"

Dad frowned. "Why is he involved?"

"He embezzled money from the company," I explained. "Olav discovered it and threatened to expose him. Olav needed money..."

Dad sank into his chair.

"So Olav pressured him for money... and it cost him his life? But why didn't he come to me?"

He threw his arms out. "I could have helped him!"

I shook my head.

"Pride, maybe? I don't know."

"And Glette? Where is he?"

I took a deep breath.

"He took his own life and left a confession."

Dad stared into space. "So much suffering... and for what?"

Tears ran unchecked down his cheeks. "I hear you. Sounds logical. But Olav... he wasn't a blackmailer, not a crook. I refuse to believe it. Must be another motive."

"I also find it hard to believe Olav was involved in blackmail, but you must understand his situation. Even the best can stumble when under pressure this intense."

"No," Dad said firmly. "It doesn't add up."

I didn't reply.

Someone knocked at the door. Dad went to answer. A deep male voice came from the entrance. We couldn't make out the words. Dad returned with a man in his late fifties, dressed in a down jacket and jeans.

The man extended his hand toward me.

"Police inspector Jonas Vik," he said. "My condolences on the loss of your brother. I was the one who found Sture Glette's body last night—a tragic outcome for both him and Olav. I knew Olav. He was a good kid despite some missteps in his youth. It's all just so tragic."

He studied Cathrine before continuing, addressing me: "Anything you'd want to discuss, contact me."

He handed me a business card. It felt more like an order than an offer. He probably wanted to talk to me one-on-one.

Jonas turned and nodded to my dad. Dad followed him out, his shoulders slumped.

I went to the terrace. The wicker chair creaked as I sank in and rested my feet on an adjacent chair. Thoughts raced through my head. My conversation with Horacio and all his questions about drug trafficking surfaced. Was this why he had emphasized knowing Olav and the references to his missteps in his youth? My stomach knotted.

I closed my eyes and felt the nausea rising.

How could I shield my dad from all of this? I clenched my fists so hard my knuckles turned white. Did the police need to dig deeper into this case? Mystery solved. The motive disclosed. Olav's name tarnished. This had to end.

They came walking along the fence. Vivian spotted me, nudged Charlene, and pointed. Charlene lit up momentarily, but her joy disappeared when she saw my face. She ran through the gate and threw her arms around my neck.

"Did you bring Olav home safe?" she asked anxiously, studying me.

I shook my head and held her close to me.

"He's dead, sweetheart," I said as gently and carefully as I could.

Chapter Thirty-Four

U dland Church stood as a beautiful paradox, modern yet timeless. Its spires and walls from behind resembled an old papal hat in copper, while the front showcased an empty cross, symbolizing Christ's resurrection.

But that day, the colors and scent of flowers—symbols of life—dominated the modern and abstract lines inside the church.

Amid this sea of flowers stood Olav's white casket.

At my first funeral as a little boy, I thought about how cramped and claustrophobic it would be to be buried in a coffin and how painful it would be to be cremated. I wanted neither. It still stuck with me.

Even on this day, while staring at Olav's casket, everything inside me tightened at the mere thought. I knew Olav was beyond feeling, but the anxiety still wouldn't let go.

Death always lurks in the background among the living—a fact of life we rarely dare to contemplate. I've chosen to believe humans have a soul, an identity, or a consciousness, something lasting that survives the body's demise. I've chosen to believe in a creative force, the soul's existence, and that Jo-Ann, Mom, Dad, Olav, and I would reunite after death.

Olav had joined those who had gone ahead.

The church was full of both mourning friends and curious onlookers. The media's attention had done its part.

Dad stared at the casket, fidgeting with his memorial booklet. He had slumped and aged several years over the last few days. Olav's tragic death and the media reports about his extortion attempt had hit us all hard, Dad most of all.

Whenever I tried to talk about the newspaper headlines, he turned pale, his voice bitter: "It's all lies. Olav wasn't this person they were portraying."

Since we sat down on the front pew, Charlene had been crying and clinging to my hand. I tried to comfort her as best I could, giving her tissues and holding her close. The three of us needed each other more than ever. It was my responsibility to get us through this crisis, especially Charlene. She's been through so much in her brief life. This had to be the end.

Vidar and his parents sat behind us, next to Torstein and his wife. Cathrine sat on the back pew. She had been patient. We had talked on the phone after Charlene had gone to bed at night. She understood we had to put our wishes and needs on hold.

I hadn't yet been able to deal with the changes in my life, hadn't found the time and place to introduce Cathrine as my new love. I couldn't bring myself to tell Charlene about my feelings for her. Couldn't tell her I was moving on.

I didn't even know if what I felt was right. Maybe it was genuine love. Perhaps it was desperation—or passion and lust.

Before Cathrine could become part of our life and family, I had to ensure Charlene's life was stable and that I was sure about my feelings.

Charlene looked at the empty seat next to her, then at me with big, hopeful eyes. "Can Cathrine sit next to me?"

She had reserved that seat for Cathrine. We turned. Cathrine looked at us with glistening eyes, twisting a tissue in her hands. Charlene nudged me to the side. "Go get her, Daddy; she shouldn't sit at the back."

Dad cleared his throat, caught my eye, and nodded.

I glanced from Dad to Charlene and back, stood, and walked along the wall to the back row. Everyone's eyes were on me. I leaned down to Cathrine and whispered, "Come with me."

She glanced up, surprised.

"Charlene wants you to sit with us."

I nodded my head to show her she should come with me.

She looked at the older woman sitting next to her, who nodded. With a gentle hand on Cathrine's back, I guided her to where we sat.

Charlene pointed to the empty seat beside her, and Cathrine sat. I met her astonished gaze and shrugged, just as bewildered.

So we sat together, the four of us.

"Who's the one you sat next to?" I asked.

"My great-aunt Margit. She wanted to come with me to this funeral."

The pastor's voice filled the room. He shared a warm and beautiful eulogy, telling stories about Olav's time as a confirmand and his care for those who struggled to find their place in the confirmation group.

The pastor's words made Olav come alive for me. That's who he was and how we would remember him.

Olav, the extortionist, wasn't our Olav.

Was he an extortionist? Only one piece of evidence pointed in that direction: the email Glette had sent and signed with his life. Thus, Olav's legacy was ruined—without a jury and without a verdict, without him getting to tell his story. I understood why Dad found this problematic.

With heavy hearts, we gathered to carry Olav's casket. Dad's face was gray and pale, his back hunched. With Dad by my side and four of Olav's childhood friends behind us, we carried his casket toward his open grave. Behind us walked Cathrine, holding Charlene. Behind them, Vidar and his parents.

As we reached the grave, it drizzled. The smell of damp earth mixed with wet, freshly cut grass. None of us had umbrellas, and no one cared.

The crowd gathered around the grave was silent. On the other side of the grave, on the crowd's edge, stood John Helman-Larssen with his daughter Anita. Their chauffeur held an umbrella over them. The police officer, Jonas, exchanged a few words with the shipowner before moving on. All three saluted me with sorrow.

A friend of Olav's sang Eidsvåg's "Kyrie" while his casket lowered. Then came the casting of the earth. I couldn't hold back my emotions. Tears ran down, making my lips salty. Dad held a firm grip on my arm. Charlene's warm hand grasped my free hand. She didn't let go of Cathrine with her other.

The funeral director approached with red roses heavy with raindrops. He handed them out to us, one for each. I held my rose for a moment, feeling the silky surface of its petals against my fingers, before letting it slide down into the grave as a last farewell.

Then, it was time to receive condolences from those present.

When it was Helman-Larssen's turn, they took our hands and offered condolences. Anita became uncertain when she shook Cathrine's hand. Her questioning gaze flickered between me and Cathrine a few times.

The shipowner cleared his throat. "We are, of course, stunned that it turned out to be one of our employees who killed your brother," he said. "We can never make it right, but we want to talk to you about a memorial fund in your brother's name. When you feel ready."

He glanced uncertainly from me to Dad. "With both of you, of course."

"Thank you for your concern. We'll talk some other day," I replied.

"Yes, of course. Whenever you're ready."

Anita cast a last glance at Cathrine before they left the cemetery.

One of the last to come forward was the older lady Cathrine had been sitting next to in the church. After giving Cathrine a wonderful hug, she turned to me.

Cathrine tucked away a lock of hair covering her eyes. "This is my great-aunt Margit," she said.

Margit took my hand and offered her condolences. Her eyes glowed. "There's something I need to discuss with you," she said. "Call me or drop by when you're able."

She glanced around her, afraid someone might hear. Cathrine took my arm. "You should hear her story. She's tired. I'll drive her home now. Shall we talk on the phone later?"

I nodded. Then she cradled her great-aunt's arm, and together, they walked toward the parking lot.

I heard Jonas's voice behind me. "My condolences. It was a beautiful ceremony, and many followed him to his last resting place. He was a good boy."

We stood looking at the open grave for a while. Then he thanked us and left.

I felt Dad's hand on my shoulder and Charlene's seeking mine. I felt exhausted and dreaded driving home to my dad's.

But it was time to leave Olav to rest in peace.

Chapter Thirty-Five

The drizzle had turned into large drops slamming against the living room window. The rain beating down on the grass and the terrace was the only sound in the darkened living room. We sat in separate chairs, still wearing outdoor clothes with the lights off. No one spoke.

Nobody had spoken on our way home—nothing left to be said. Emptiness hung over the three of us. Dad had invited no one this time, even though he had prepared food and decorated for her memorial when my mom passed.

I was grateful.

Dad stood, breaking the silence: "I couldn't even find the energy to invite his friends over."

His voice grated like old porcelain. He cleared his throat, and a tear ran down his cheek. "Not until his name is cleared."

I got up and put my arms around him. His knees buckled, but I held him up. "I understand, Dad. It's just too much for all of us."

"He wasn't a blackmailer. That's a damn lie."

I didn't respond. We'd been through this many times before. It led nowhere. Only made things worse. Dad needed time to process it all. The truth would dawn on him one day. I'd pledged I'd be there for him when it did.

Still, I couldn't believe Olav had been so desperate that he tried to extort money from Glette. He could have gotten the money from Dad and me if he'd explained his situation and asked. It would have cost him some pride, but he'd be alive and out of Ricardo's clutches.

I went to get rid of my coat when someone knocked at our front door.

Cathrine stood outside. She held an umbrella, but rainwater ran down her cheek. "You okay?" she asked, giving me a wet and cold hug.

"We're all exhausted."

We went into the living room. Dad perked up. "I guess I haven't removed my wet clothes," he excused himself. I helped him out of his coat while Charlene hurried to the hallway and hung up her wet jacket.

Cathrine hugged Dad before Charlene held her hand and pulled her to the couch. Dad went to the kitchen to make coffee.

"Charlene, I need some help," he shouted.

"Great-aunt wants to talk to you," Cathrine said after checking that the other two were busy in the kitchen.

"Yeah, she mentioned that," I said with minimal enthusiasm.

She leaned in closer and whispered: "Hear her out. She believes there's a connection between great-uncle Geir's drowning accident, Olav's murder, and Glette's suicide. Believes powerful people in this town are hiding something."

"And you believe there's this grand conspiracy going on in Haugesund?" I asked skeptically.

"Just talk to her, is all. If there's nothing to it, at least you've made the effort."

"We already have an established connection between Olav's murder and Glette's suicide, so that case isn't mysterious at all. That your great-uncle's drowning accident would be connected to this case, however, seems a bit far-fetched. Why would Glette kill an old sailor just because Olav blackmailed him?"

"I don't know, but Margit is convinced. You should at least listen to her story."

"I sailed with Geir," Dad said from the doorway. "He was floating around outside Aibel the same week Olav got killed. 'Drowning accident,' the police said. You must investigate if there's a connection and if someone has been hiding something. For God's sake, talk to her. For my sake and Olav's."

Charlene stood behind him. "And for me."

All three looked at me. There was a massive conspiracy, and it was right here in this room. Its power was so overwhelming that I surrendered.

"Fine," I said. "I'll talk to Margit. Tomorrow."

"Great! Then Charlene and I will finish up the treats."

He turned to Cathrine: "And you're going nowhere. You don't want to miss out."

We were still sitting on the couch an hour later when Charlene and Dad came in with freshly baked raisin buns and coffee. We exchanged stories about Olav late into the night.

Occasionally, when Cathrine would touch me while talking, I could notice Charlene's reaction.

Chapter Thirty-Six

Margit Rosseberg lived in a blue wooden house by the sea. Her home was surrounded by a well-kept garden with lawn, flower beds, and fruit trees. The scent of lavender and apples greeted me as I walked down the asphalt strip from the main road.

"Thank you for coming," she said, closing the door behind me. "Coffee's almost ready, and I've made waffles."

She brought her coffee pot and waffles. She had set the table with cups and saucers, reminding me of my grandmother's.

"Try the jam," she said. "I made it the old-fashioned way, with strawberries from my garden."

I took a spoonful of jam and tasted it. "Fantastic. You wanted to tell me something?" I asked, eager to begin.

She chewed and swallowed. "We were three siblings, but I'm the only one left. Geir died, as you know, and Cathrine's grandmother Inga died before Cathrine was even born."

She smoothed her skirt. "Geir was a sailor like your father. When he was home, he visited me often. He kept his boat in my boathouse."

She pointed to a wooden shed by the sea.

"Geir sailed with your father for a long time with Knutsen shipping company. But he drank himself out of his job. Later, he changed companies so often I couldn't keep track."

She took a sip of coffee. "When his wife, Jorunn, died, he moved into my attic. As payment for his lodging, he maintained everything. He was so skilled with his hands."

I wondered if she just needed someone to talk to. Margit fiddled with her cup. I glanced at my watch, and she noticed.

"I'll get to the point. Geir claimed he knew about a crime committed by some powerful people. He had evidence and documentation he wanted to give to the police. He confided in me because he feared arrest when it became known."

She hesitated. "He'd been involved in it."

She put down her cup. "The evening he drowned, he took his boat out late. When I asked if he was going fishing in the dark with such bad weather coming up, he just smiled and said it was the day it would all happen. Then he left. I think he was going to confront someone. Maybe Glette?"

She lifted her cup, but her hand shook, so she set it back down.

"Geir didn't drown that evening. Even drunk, he could balance on a boat better than anyone. Someone killed him."

Margit sat for a while before shaking her head. "Geir was the best sailor I knew," she said. "He didn't drown by accident. I'm sure of it."

Margit wiped a tear from her cheek and looked at me straight.

"I've never believed the official explanation," she said firmly.

I believed her. An eerie feeling shrunk the room. I understood why she doubted the narrative that her brother had died in an accident. If she was correct, there might have been a cold-blooded killer involved.

"But why do you think this connects to Olav?"

"Because Geir met Olav at a rehab center. Olav had agreed to go to avoid prosecution for cannabis, and Geir to deal with his alcohol problem. They hit it off and often went fishing together. Olav even helped fix my roof."

She studied my face, her eyes narrowing. "An odd couple, but Geir and Olav clicked. I have no idea what their common interests were, but I suspect it went far beyond fishing and rehab."

After leaving, I sat in my car for a while. I had a lot to digest. Geir and Glette might have been involved in something illegal. Smuggling? Thefts? Not the embezzlement—too white-collar for a guy like Rosseberg.

I rested my head on the steering wheel and closed my eyes. This thing either seemed too complicated or extremely simple. Either Glette's explanation of his suicide was the truth, or the truth was far more cunning.

Did I possess the energy to untangle this? Did I risk digging up more dirt on Olav? Would it make the world better?

When I opened my eyes, the start button was the first thing I saw.

I pushed it.

Chapter Thirty-Seven

Dark clouds loomed over the city that Monday morning. I found no vacant parking spots near the police station, parked my car by a Catholic church, and walked a few hundred yards on foot. The traffic to and from the police station suggested the region had an abundant supply of troublemakers.

I lingered outside for a few minutes, unsure how to approach this. I mustered up my courage and entered.

The police station in Haugesund differed from San Francisco's. It was open, bright, and friendly, like a hotel reception. The noise level was subdued, and there were no signs of stress. The "priority club customers" had a separate entrance into the cellar.

I approached the desk and asked to speak with Jonas Vik. Then, I went sightseeing in the lobby.

A voice called out behind me: "So glad you dropped by!"

It was Jonas.

My phone pinged. A message from Anita: *"Hey Floki, I just wanted to remind you about the grant we discussed at the funeral. Can we talk soon?"*

I replied: "Of course, but busy right now."

I put my phone in my pocket and shook Jonas' hand.

I sat in Jonas' minimalist but bright office, with a fantastic seaside view. He had a modest stack of documents, a key, a keyboard, and two monitors on his desk. No personal photos or children's drawings.

He came in with a coffee mug in each hand and handed one to me.

"So, what's on your mind?" Jonas asked as he followed my gaze around the room.

I laid out my errand but omitted to mention Margit. I told him about Olav's friendship with Geir Rosseberg, his accident, the conspiracy theories, and a possible connection between Glette and a murder he hadn't confessed to in his suicide note.

I could hear how conspiratorial I sounded.

When I finished, Jonas sat rocking in his chair while tapping a rhythm with his pen against the armrest. He had only jotted down "Olav" and "Rosseberg" on the notepad before him. That's all.

He leaned forward with a caring look and cleared his throat with a short cough.

"We have no one to interrogate, no evidence to the contrary, just the autopsy report confirming Rosseberg drowned and the letter from Glette explaining what happened to your brother. Even if they were alive today, we'd have no reason to suspect anything other than what we currently know." He slumped, put his elbows on the desk, and rubbed his eyes. "I understand how hard it is to accept that someone close to you has done something so incredibly foolish, with such irrevocable consequences."

He met my gaze. "I know Olav was a fine kid. But he did some dumb things sometimes. Like when he experimented with drugs. I smoothed things over for him then because I saw he was a kid who'd gotten mixed up with the wrong crowd." He paused. "Those of us left behind sometimes have to accept the difficult, let it go, and move on with our lives. You've been in this situation before, Flokí. Sometimes the truth is what is in front of us, not the one we're craving."

I sat in the car, digesting Jonas' words. How would I have reacted if someone had told me such an absurd story?

I wanted to believe in Olav's innocence, both for his sake and the family's, but mostly because I wanted to see Dad straighten his back and lift his head.

But Jonas was right: Sometimes, letting go and moving on is the better option.

I drove home.

Dad was strolling along the walkway as I pulled up to his house.

"Did you get to talk to Jonas?" he asked.

I nodded.

"Let's make some coffee, and I'll tell you all about it."

"Tell me," he said when we had settled into the living room with our cups. He had already realized my conversation with Jonas hadn't gone as he'd hoped. I recounted my conversation in as much detail as I could.

"So, you're just letting this matter rest?" he asked.

I took a deep breath. "I don't see how we can move forward with this. Jonas is right. We so badly want Olav to have a better legacy; we're grasping at straws. It's taken me almost six years to take some small steps moving on after Jo-Ann passed. We must stay focused on the present and the future, not burden ourselves with the past."

"But Margit said Geir had evidence."

"I know, but nobody knows where this evidence is. If it ever existed at all. Margit has turned the entire house, the boathouse, the car, and the boat upside down without finding anything."

"Maybe it's hidden somewhere else. We have to find it."

"I hear you, but we need to let this go, Dad. We know Olav was a wonderful man, as did those in the church yesterday. But neither Jo-Ann nor Olav will ever come back. We must care for each other, for the living, and focus on building a future for Charlene."

He placed his hand over mine and fixed his gaze on me.

"You're wrong, Flokí. You're wrong again."

Chapter Thirty-Eight

I t was Monday afternoon. Charlene was doing her homework at the kitchen table. Dad was reading his newspaper, focused, his index finger sliding over the text.

Despite the events of the past few days, a new calmness had settled over my family. We found strength in each other and created moments of respite amid our grief.

Charlene glanced up from her homework and smiled at me. Dad turned a page in his newspaper and glanced at her. Pride flared up for a moment, bringing life back to his eyes.

The past weeks had given us a new perspective on life. Olav's passing reminded us of life's fragility. We have limited time together. It is so easy to forget in our daily hustles.

My watch vibrated. It was Anita. I sighed, grabbed my phone, and went to the terrace.

"Hey, Floki! How are you all doing?"

"We're managing," I said tersely.

She sighed with concern. "And your father? He seemed so lost at the funeral..."

"We're all lost... but Dad's crushed. It's not supposed to happen this way: kids dying before their parents. We didn't see it coming."

"Exactly why we're pushing for the foundation. We want to create a positive association with Olav's legacy. I won't bother you tonight, but would you like to come over for dinner on Thursday evening? We want to get to know you better... and Olav, of course. Who he was. We want to present a proposal and get your thoughts."

A PR disaster like this required a swift response. The market gods demanded a sacrifice. Helman-Larssen wanted to establish this foundation as fast as possible. I got it. But I wasn't sure how it would impact Olav.

Through the window, I saw Dad still hunched over his newspaper. Discussing a foundation with strangers would be too much at this point. It's not likely he'd be ready for it soon. But a foundation could give Olav redemption and associate him with something better. In time, it might turn into something positive. Maybe something that would make Dad straighten his back.

"I'll bring it up with Dad when he's ready."

She increased her pressure. "We can't keep this high on our agenda for long. I don't like pushing you, but I'm afraid Dad might shift his focus, and then it might not happen."

"Okay," I said. "I can come, and I'll ask Dad if he's up for it. But I'm afraid it might just be me."

"You just made me very happy," she said softly. "Come with an open mind. And... don't drive. We've brought a lovely vintage Sangiovese from our vineyard in Chianti."

She let out a low, conspiratorial laugh. "We'll talk tomorrow night."

For a moment, I pictured her soft, red lips.

When I returned, Charlene had finished her homework and left with Vidar. It was all good as long as she stuck to the rules we'd agreed: homework first and home by eight on school nights.

I put a hand on Dad's shoulder.

"Let's have a cup of coffee," I suggested.

We sat in the living room a little later, each with our cup.

"Who's on the phone?" Dad asked.

"Helman-Larssen," I said.

Dad eyed me from his coffee cup. "Anita?" He studied me. "Did she want to discuss the foundation?"

"Yeah, she invited us for dinner on Thursday night. To learn more about Olav, tell us about their plans."

He studied the rim of his cup. "So, what are you thinking?"

"I want to hear their proposal. Maybe there's something positive in this, I don't know."

Dad looked at me. He took his time weighing the options. "It's worth a try," he said. "It doesn't hurt to hear them out, but do you think a foundation will do any good?"

He slumped and shook his head. "I can't go anywhere. I can't handle being social. But you go if you think it might lead to something positive."

I nodded. "All right."

I texted Anita, and she confirmed a few minutes later,

"Looking forward to seeing you on Thursday night. Come to our house on Torvastad at 7 pm. Hope you like seafood. Dress smart. I'm planning to dress up for the occasion. Hugs, A."

I reread the message. The house on Torvastad was the Helman-Larssen family's stately reception home by the sea. What's with this dressing up? Was this a formal affair with a lot of people? I had understood it to be a private chat over some food.

I got this uneasy feeling that I might walk into a trap.

Chapter Thirty-Nine

Charlene savored each step on the narrow gravel path between the well-kept houses. The fall air was cool against her cheeks, and the scent of wet leaves and fireplace smoke filled her nose. She pulled her jacket tighter. Her stomach bubbled with excitement at the thought of her upcoming dinner with Vidar.

There was something special about cooking together, sharing laughter and small touches. She stopped to enjoy the sight of the cozy house where Vidar lived with his family. She smoothed her jacket sleeve as if to wipe away her sadness of the past few weeks.

The bubbling in her stomach became a knot as Vidar opened the door. His warm smile was gone. He looked sad, avoiding her gaze.

"Hey," she said.

Vidar nodded and stepped aside.

"You okay?" Charlene studied the half-packed moving boxes and cartons scattered around the room.

Her heart beat faster. This was no longer the cozy home she loved so much. "What's going on?" she asked worriedly.

Vidar shrugged, mumbled something indistinct, and went to the kitchen. She followed.

The kitchen was as chaotic as the rest of the house. Dishes piled on the counter. Charlene placed her groceries and turned to Vidar. He leaned against the counter, staring at the floor.

"Have you taken up a new hobby with all these dishes?" she asked crookedly.

Vidar shook his head. "No, it's just..."

Her frustration grew. She had been looking forward to this evening and was determined to find out his issue.

"What's going on? Talk to me, please."

He met her gaze. The pain in his eyes showed he was struggling, not knowing how to respond.

"I..." he began in a hoarse voice. "We're moving."

His words hit her like a punch. She stared at him in disbelief.

"Moving? Where? Why?" Her words stumbled over each other.

Vidar ran his hand through his hair. "My parents are getting divorced. Dad and I are moving back to Lillehammer."

Charlene tried to grasp the magnitude of Vidar's words. She reached out to comfort him, but he shied away. Her hand hung aimlessly in the air. She stepped closer to get his attention.

With a trembling voice, she said, "You don't have to move, do you? You're over eighteen."

Vidar shook his head and stared at the floor. "It feels hopeless. Everything's just a mess. I don't want to live with Mom and this new guy."

She sat next to him and tried to make eye contact. "You could get your own flat here."

"I can't leave Dad alone after this, and you here, me there; it won't work."

"Why do you say stuff like that? We love each other."

"Love is just a temporary thing. At some point, it's over, anyway."

Tears welled up. "But we're not them. We're us. We're different."

"How would you know? How do you know we won't end up like them in a few years? That we won't give up? Or end up hating each other?"

Charlene turned to the counter and began cutting vegetables with shaky hands. She glanced over her shoulder and saw Vidar standing with his hands in his pockets.

"Won't you help me?" she asked, trying to break the ice.

Vidar shrugged. "I'm not hungry."

Her irritation grew. She cut the vegetables with more force than necessary. The knife sliced through the carrots and made a sharp thump.

"Maybe we can watch a movie after dinner?" she suggested.

"Maybe," Vidar replied.

She put down her knife and turned to him. "Please, can't we try to have a good time together today?"

Vidar picked up an orange from the fruit bowl and started peeling it. "Want a slice?" he asked, offering her a piece.

Charlene accepted and smiled weakly. "Thanks." The sweet taste spread in her mouth.

Her cell vibrated in her pocket. The message from Dad could wait.

She straightened up. They sat at the table. She took a bite, but the food tasted like nothing. Vidar barely touched his food; he moved it around on his plate with his fork. This was far from the pleasant dinner she had envisioned.

Minutes ticked by, and despair grew. She tried to catch his eyes, but he avoided eye contact. It was as if an invisible wall was rising between them. She didn't know how to break it.

He got up and went to his room.

She put her fork down and followed. Half-packed boxes and suitcases littered the floor. She watched as he methodically placed clothes and belongings in the boxes as if he were closing off a chapter of his life.

She reached out to touch his arm, but he backed away. "We care about each other. Isn't that an awesome place to start?"

"I'm sorry," Vidar said, "but... I don't believe in it anymore."

She saw it in his eyes. Whatever she said, he'd already decided. Everything they had experienced over the last few months, all the beautiful memories, slipped like sand between her fingers. She tucked a lock of hair behind her ear.

"If we have a chance, we must want this together. But you've already decided?"

Vidar said nothing.

Charlene got up and moved toward the door. She heard tape being pulled over a box behind her.

When she reached the door, she paused for a moment. Part of her wanted to turn around, run back, and beg him to fight for them.

Chapter Forty

I pushed open the door to the bar called Stuelands Abothek and let my gaze sweep across the room. Cathrine followed with light steps, and I felt the warmth of her hand against my back. The lighting cast faint shadows over red chairs and dark benches. A mix of beer and perfume hung in the air.

We went through the half-full bar to an empty table in a secluded corner. I waved the waiter over and ordered a couple of beers.

Cathrine looked at the paintings on the wall before studying me. "I think we should investigate the issues Margit has raised."

I leaned back and ran my hand over my face. "We've dug up enough dirt on Olav. Let him rest in peace. We know the story by now."

"It's about knowing the whole truth."

I shook my head.

"Sometimes it's better not to know it all."

The waiter came with our beers. I took a long swig and let the bitter taste wash over my tongue. Cathrine waited while I gathered my thoughts.

"I understand what you're saying," I said. "But I'm scared of what we might find. Dad's been hurt enough. I don't think he'll survive if we uncover something more sinister."

Cathrine reached across the table and placed her hand over mine.

"It's the questions unanswered that beat us down."

I stared at my glass. She might have been right.

"Okay, let's investigate Margit's theory. But we need to be careful not to be destructive. Okay?"

Cathrine fiddled her beer glass before putting it back on the table.

"What's your deepest fear that we might uncover?"

I laughed briefly to brush off her question. Cathrine's eyes narrowed.

"I mean it. What do you fear the most?"

The voices and laughter disappeared. I saw only Cathrine's gaze.

"Can't we just enjoy our beer?" I said.

"No, be honest."

I hesitated. "I don't know, something dark. Something dire. Something that breaks my last hope of keeping Dad alive."

I made a helpless gesture with my hand.

Cathrine leaned forward, her gaze softening.

"I understand you're scared. But the truth can also set you free. Have you considered that?"

"But what if it makes everything worse?" I whispered. "Is it worth it?"

Cathrine was quiet for a while before changing the subject.

"Why can't we be open about our relationship?"

I gripped my glass tighter.

"We've discussed this before. It's not the right time."

"But when will it be the right time?"

She leaned forward. Her voice was low but intense. "We're not going to keep this a secret forever, are we? It's not illegal to love someone."

I closed my eyes and took a breath.

"Charlene has been through so much. I need to protect her from any additional stress."

"Charlene is smart. She's noticed something going on."

"I know, but..."

"She needs honesty, Flokí. Especially now. When you try keeping our relationship a secret, you tell her our feelings are somehow wrong. Is that what you want her to believe?"

Irritation rose in me.

"It's not that simple. You don't understand..."

"What is it I don't understand?"

She met my gaze, challenging. "That you're scared? That you think Charlene won't accept me?"

"That's not it. I don't want her to think you're trying to replace her mother."

Cathrine softened.

"Listen to me, no one can replace Jo-Ann. But Charlene deserves to know the truth about your life, about our lives."

I stared at the table, caught between two impossible choices.

"You may be right, but the timing is wrong."

"The timing will never be perfect. We can't wait for the perfect moment. Life is happening now."

"I promise to think about it, okay? Just... give me some time."

"Okay. But the longer you wait, the harder it gets."

She was right. But I was terrified of hurting Charlene. How could I balance my love for my daughter with this new and unexpected love?

Cathrine broke her silence after a while.

"By the way, I don't trust the Helman-Larssen family."

I frowned.

"How do you mean? They've been nothing but supportive."

"Exactly! It's too perfect, too smooth. Nobody's that helpful without a reason."

"They feel guilty about what Sture Glette did," I said. "The endowment in Olav's memory is their way of making amends."

Cathrine snorted.

"Or their way of buying a clear conscience. Haven't you noticed how eager they are to close this case?"

I shrugged.

"They just want to put it behind them. They're concerned about their public relations and try to turn negative news about a corrupt employee into something positive for the company. I get it."

"Or they want us to stop digging," Cathrine said. "What if they know more than they're telling us?"

"Now you're exaggerating. They've been open and honest all the way."

Cathrine's eyes narrowed.

"How can you be so sure? You barely know them."

"I trust my gut," I said.

"Well, my gut is telling me something else," she replied, frustrated. "And I thought you, of all people, would understand the value of asking the questions."

Again, I felt my irritation rising.

"What do you mean by that?"

"You are... you were a skilled detective. You should know better than to take things at face value."

I stared at my glass of beer.

"I know you have good intentions, but this interconnects and complicates things."

I ordered a bottle of red wine. She leaned back, arms crossed. "Is it as complicated, or are you making it complicated?"

"You don't understand the pressure I'm under. Charlene, my dad, this whole situation with Olav..."

"And where do I fit in? Just another complication?" she asked, meeting my gaze with wounded pride.

Suddenly, everything else became less important - the case, the problems, the past. The woman sitting before me had become an essential part of my life in a short time.

"You're important to me. More than I believed was ever possible."

She softened a bit but kept her skeptical expression.

"But not as important as you'd want to encompass me?"

I reached across the table and grabbed her hand. "Give me some time. I promise to talk to Charlene and be open about us. And maybe we should investigate Margit's ideas, too."

Cathrine smiled and squeezed my hand. "That's all I'm asking for. That we're a team again, you and I."

I raised my glass. "Here's to our team," I said.

Cathrine laughed and clinked her glass against mine. "To us."

The wine was full-bodied and smooth, and my shoulders relaxed. Cathrine took a sip and leaned back.

"Remember when we first met?" she asked.

I nodded. "At the airport in Málaga. You held up a sign with my name."

"I was anxious about whether you would show up. I could still feel our phone call in my bones. You were irritated about being dragged into it all," she said, smiling.

"I wasn't irritated," I protested. "Just... skeptical."

Cathrine laughed. "You were irritated. But you came."

We talked about our first days together in Spain. But beneath the amicable surface lurked those questions we had recently discussed.

I took another sip of wine and tried to push my unease aside.

"We've come a long way since then, haven't we?"

Cathrine nodded, but her gaze was serious.

"Yes, we have. But we still have a way to go."

"Let's enjoy this moment, okay? We'll worry about the other stuff another day."

Cathrine set her wineglass down hard on the table, her eyes frustrated.

"Are you even listening to me? If you cared about me, you'd understand how important it is for me to be part of your life!"

I leaned back, surprised by the intensity in her voice.

"I..."

"No, let me finish," she interrupted. "You can't just push my feelings and needs aside!"

I felt a lump in my throat.

"I understand this is important to you."

"Do you?" She leaned forward, her voice lower but just as intense. "Because it doesn't feel like it. It feels like you're keeping me at a distance from both you and your life."

I met her gaze and saw the vulnerability behind her frustration.

"You're right. I haven't been fair to you."

Cathrine nodded and waited for more.

"I promise to take a closer look at Margit's story. We'll do it together, okay?"

A small smile spread across her lips.

"And Charlene?"

I hesitated for a moment.

"I'll talk to her. Soon. About us."

Her disappointment was visible in her eyes. She shook her head.

"You don't mean it, Flokí. You're just saying what you believe you need to say to get some peace. Tomorrow, it'll all be back to normal."

"That's not true. I..."

"Admit it, you're scared," she interrupted. "Scared of what you might discover about Olav, scared to tell your family about us."

"You have no idea what you're talking about."

"Oh, don't I?"

She leaned forward. "You won't let go of Jo-Ann. That's why you can't be honest about us."

Anger flared up in me.

"How can you be this cruel?"

"You're using her as an excuse to keep me at a distance. It's the truth!"

I slammed my hand on the table. Several guests turned.

"This is madness, Cathrine. Your suspicions and digging into the past will destroy us."

She stood up abruptly with a hurt and proud expression.

"No, Flokí. It's your cowardice destroying us. You're letting me fight it on my own. I can't be with a man who won't fight for me and the truth."

She looked like she wanted to say some more but bit it back. She just shook her head, took her purse, and walked out.

Chapter Forty-One

I sprinted toward my car. The rain lashed against my face. I was face-to-face with the familiar Haugesund Public Library building and popped in. Wanted to check on a few things following Cathrine's outburst yesterday.

I brushed off the raindrops and put away my wet jacket. I acknowledged the librarian, and she smiled in recognition. "Let me know if you need any help," she said.

"Just checking some newspapers," I replied and strode toward the newspaper corner.

I discovered a vacant seat at a lengthy wooden table and scoured all the articles regarding Geir Rosseberg's accident. I assembled a sizeable stack of newspapers. An elderly lady sitting at a nearby table raised her gaze. "Are you writing a book?" she asked with a smile.

"Something like that," I lied.

Tracing the text, I could feel the newspaper crinkle beneath my finger. I smiled when I realized I was reading print newspapers like my dad.

The papers described the accident as a tragic case of drowning. While reading, I couldn't shake Margit's voice from my mind, but the articles revealed no link between Geir and Olav's deaths. They knew of one another and perished around the same period. Besides that, nothing specific.

I kept turning pages, searching for hints. A small notice captured my attention. They found Geir Rosseberg's boat at Torvastad, and they discovered his body near Hotel Maritime on the inner quay. I envisioned how the boat and the man, presumably together during the accident, could wind up so distant. I decided it was within the realm of possibility. The wind and the current might have impacted them differently.

I continued to dig through stacks of newspapers. According to an obituary in Haugesunds Avis, Geir achieved recognition as a skilled swimmer during his youth, winning several medals in national and international seamen championships. It was surprising how someone like Geir, a proficient swimmer, could drown after falling off his boat. Margit had a minor point worth considering.

I inspected the accident articles, searching for specific details to focus on. I discovered multiple articles about Geir Rosseberg in Haugesunds Nytt. According to a police source, one article reported Rosseberg's boat was found at a dock on Bakarøynå, contradicting another article that claimed it was at Torvastad.

Did the police provide conflicting information about the discovery site, or was it a mistake made by the journalist? It was a recurring problem. I made a mental note to consult Jonas about what was correct.

I needed to go home and get ready for dinner with Helman-Larssen. I got out of my chair and straightened up the newspapers. With a sudden snap, I closed my notebook. I'd had it for today.

While leaving, I called Jonas' number. He answered his phone immediately. I summarized the questions I had noted and shared them with him.

"I'm on a stakeout right now. We found his boat at Torvastad. I only received a verbal message initially, so I may have made a mistake."

I could tell he was surveilling from a car by the muted traffic and engine noise.

"I never investigated why the boat and Rosseberg ended up as they did. There was no reason to. Wind and currents are my theory."

He took a momentary pause. "The report from Gade is confidential but contains nothing exciting."

Chapter Forty-Two

I left my car parked outside the house. The rain had let up, although the air was wet and laden. I stepped indoors. Dad sat in the living room. With a wrinkle on his forehead, he tapped his fingers on his armrest.

"Charlene went to see Vidar," he said. "She wanted to talk to him but came home completely distraught. Ran to her room. She doesn't want me there."

I made my way to Charlene's room. Her door was shut. I tapped on the door. No response. I opened it and peeked inside.

The room was dark. Huddled in a corner, Charlene sat on the floor. I walked in, and she continued to gaze into the distance, not bothering to acknowledge my presence.

I sat next to her.

"What happened, honey?"

She wiped away her tears. "I went to see Vidar. They weren't home, so I put my letter in their mailbox."

She added, "I have had no word from him since. Nothing. It's like I don't mean a thing to him."

Her tears started flowing once more. I held her tight.

"Everything's falling apart. Everyone's disappearing."

Witnessing her in such pain was brutal. I had to take a deep breath to control my emotions.

"You'll always have me."

I placed my hand on her shoulder.

"I promise."

Charlene wiped away her tears and glanced at me with red-rimmed eyes. "Do you have to go to that dinner tonight?"

I tensed up. The dinner. I had almost forgotten about it.

"It's complicated. It's important for Grandpa and me."

"More important than me?"

Her words stung.

"No," I answered. "You're the most important."

"Then why can't you stay home?" she pleaded. "I need you here. I can't stand being alone."

I felt a pang in my heart. It was clear she needed me tonight. However, Olav's legacy and Dad's passion for life were in jeopardy.

Canceling with such little notice would cause issues. Dad had been so eager for me to go. Creating something positive from Olav's loss was his one shot at it. Could I take that away from him?

No matter what I chose, I'd be letting someone down.

"I know this is difficult, sweetie. But this dinner is important."

I kept caressing her hair while I carried on talking.

"It's more than just a dinner. It's about creating something lasting in Uncle Olav's memory. A way to help others, in Olav's name."

Charlene's eyes were wet with tears. I locked eyes with her and didn't look away.

"I know it feels like nothing makes sense anymore. But by attending this dinner, I can help turn all this pain into something positive. Something that can help others and make Olav's memory a force for good."

I embraced her.

"You have me. I'll come home if you can hang in there for a few hours. We can talk all night."

I gave her a tender kiss on her forehead.

"Can you do that?"

Charlene looked at me. "I think I understand. It's just hard."

She twirled her fingers. "Do you miss Uncle Olav as much as I do?"

I nodded. "I'm so glad you sent me to Spain, honey. Otherwise, we'd still be in the dark."

"Go to the dinner. But come straight home afterward."

I adjusted myself on the floor and brought Charlene closer to me. Her head leaned against my shoulder as she relaxed.

"You know what?" I said, stroking her hair. "I remember once when Olav was little. On a hot summer day, we decided to build a raft."

Charlene gave me a curious gaze.

"What happened?"

I smiled. "We spent almost the whole day finding planks and rope. Olav thought we needed a sail, so we stole one of Mom's sheets."

Charlene smiled softly.

"Did you get in trouble?"

"Absolutely," I replied, shaking my head. "But it was worth it. We got our raft in the water and sailed maybe thirty feet before it broke in two. We winded up in the sea but managed to scramble ashore."

"I miss him so much," she whispered. "And Mom."

It was my turn to wipe my eyes. I gave her a tight, warm hug.

"I do, too. But you know what? They're not entirely gone as long as we remember them and tell their stories."

I checked my watch. I was running late.

"Charlie, I need to go," I said. "But I promise to come home as soon as dinner ends. And tomorrow, how about we do something fun together? Just you and me?"

Charlene glanced at me with eyes that still had a hint of redness. A faint yet genuine smile emerged on her face.

"Sounds like fun," she answered.

With one last stroke of her cheek, I hurried down the stairs to the bathroom. Time was ticking away, and I was getting behind schedule. I opted for the express program while in the bathroom. Trembling, I struggled to button my shirt and grabbed the tacky tie Olav had given me as a Christmas present. It would have to do.

While struggling with my tie knot, Charlene's voice echoed in my mind: Go to the dinner. But what if Vidar responded to her, and she had another emotional collapse? I stared at my reflection in the mirror, but it didn't offer me any newfound wisdom.

As I was leaving, I heard fast footsteps coming from the stairs. Charlene sprinted toward me with energy and wrapped her arms around my neck. Her hug was so tight it made breathing hard for me.

"You'll come straight home after? Cross your heart?"

"I'm just going to this dinner, and then I'll be right back."

I kissed her forehead and wiped away a tear from her cheek.

"It'll be okay. Everything will work out. I promise."

I held her face and looked at her.

"Charlie, listen to me," I said. "I love you unconditionally, and that will never change. A lot can change, but you can always count on me. Always."

Chapter Forty-Three

Parking her car on the curb, Cathrine walked down a short walkway to the house. The worst part of the rain had passed, and the air was crisp and clean. Waves rolled against the stone pier below.

She pressed the doorbell. The lock clicked, and the door opened. Margit had a wide grin on her face. They held each other in a long-lasting hug.

Margit ushered her into the living room. She had arranged the table with tea and freshly baked buns. Cathrine slumped in a chair and felt at home.

"Thank you for coming. So good to see you," Margit said.

She poured tea for both of them.

"How are you and Flokí doing? Didn't he want to come?" she asked, placing her teapot back down with a gentle clink.

Cathrine smiled and tucked her hair behind her ear. She focused on a bun.

Margit cleared her throat. "It's an unusual name, but he seemed nice, and his daughter is adorable."

She hesitated. "But entering a ready-made family can't be easy, right? Not with such a backstory?"

Margit studied her over her glasses.

Cathrine tasted her bun and raised her gaze. "It's complicated. Can we talk about something else?"

Margit understood. "Of course," she said with a sigh.

"How about Geir?" Cathrine asked.

"I'm sure he was killed," Margit said. "People around here think I've fallen into the conspiracy pot, but I don't care what they think anymore."

Cathrine placed her hand on Margit's. "I believe you."

Margit took a sip of her tea. "I've searched everywhere for those documents. In his room, in his car, and on his boat."

Her hand trembled, and she set her cup down. "He gathered dangerous evidence, which could have major consequences for people of power. He was going to give it to the police, but then the so-called accident happened. Convenient for some."

Her voice grew more intense. "I don't believe the official explanation. Whoever killed him probably destroyed his documents."

She clenched her fists and stared out the window.

"Could he have made copies? Or left something else behind that could explain whatever he'd witnessed?"

Margit rose to her feet and smoothed out her dress. "Come," she said.

After making their way up a tight staircase, they arrived at a small room on the second floor. Margit heaved at the top of the stairs and scanned the sparsely furnished room. The air carried the fragrance of aged timber. The edges of the wallpaper were curled and faded. "Geir stayed in this room after his wife passed away. He sold the house and moved in with me."

A few memories from Geir's life rested on a dresser. Cathrine moved about the room, touching the furniture with her hands. She lifted a picture showing Geir and his wife. They were so young and radiant.

"He loved her, but his drinking ruined so much. He drowned his guilty conscience," Margit said. "After her death, he changed. He wanted to make amends for past sins, as he said, but he still drank."

She shook her head.

Cathrine picked up an open notebook from the dusty desk and sat on the hard edge of the bed. The pages contained hand-written notes, some almost illegible. She flipped through the pages. It was shopping lists, small accounts, and fishing lists with weight, location, and time. It wasn't worth killing him for, but it showed his fondness for keeping meticulous records.

Margit took an old photo album from a drawer and settled beside Cathrine. She turned the pages and found a picture of Geir showcasing a big trout. The picture's caption showed it was taken at Mosvatnet in Gullingen.

"He loved fishing. It was their shared passion that brought him and Olav together. This picture was taken last summer," Margit said.

Cathrine studied the picture. Geir appeared content, yet his gaze also held a sense of vigilance.

"It might have been Olav who snapped this picture. You ever visit the old farm your mother inherited by Sandsfjorden?" Margit asked.

Cathrine frowned. "No. I used to go there often as a kid, but not anymore, not after the divorce. Mom doesn't care anymore. Why do you ask?"

Margit turned to a picture of Geir in front of an old farmhouse. "Your mother owns this farm, but we split the costs, and we can use it as a cabin. Geir would stay at the farm while fishing in the mountains or fjord. He always said it was a special place to him," Margit continued.

"Could he have stashed something there, something too dangerous to have in the house?" Cathrine asked.

Margit held her gaze. "Only the family would connect this place to him, so it's quite possible."

They strolled through the beautiful garden to her boathouse. The scents of damp, freshly cut grass, lavender, and roses mingled with the sea air.

Margit pointed to the empty boat slip inside the house and said, "This is where Geir used to store his boat. I haven't retrieved it. Maybe you can help me sometime?"

"Of course I can," Cathrine replied. She allowed her gaze to take in the interior. Fishing equipment and tools filled the boathouse.

"He could sit here for hours. On his own," Margit said. "Polishing engine parts or fixing his fishing equipment. Switching from one fishing lake to another was quite a process."

Cathrine imagined Geir working here.

Margit beckoned her to a corner of the boathouse where an old wooden beam stood. "Let me show you something."

Three solid hooks were screwed into the wooden beam. Two had life vests hanging on them. Above each, a name had been carved: Geir, Margit, and Olav.

"Olav getting his hook was a major event," Margit chuckled. "It meant he could borrow the boat alone if Geir weren't home."

"Was Geir wearing a vest when he drowned?" Cathrine asked, pointing to the hook under Geir's name.

Nothing but a fishing rod hanging there.

"No. 'Only landlubbers need vests,' he once said. Maybe not very politically correct these days," she laughed.

She turned serious. "But then again, he drowned. If he'd been wearing a vest, it would not have been so easy to make it look like an accident."

In the dark sea, Cathrine spotted a slender fishing line slipping away. She tugged it upward. Seaweed and sea water made her hands slippery. The other end felt weighted. Her pulse was racing.

A small key ring with two keys emerged from the sea. Trembling, she pulled them up and studied them. One stood out from the rest. Although it seemed worn and rusty, she could still recognize it. The other was for a small padlock.

"Check this key," she said, pointing to the larger one. "It fits the door at the old farm by Sandsfjorden, doesn't it?"

Margit nodded. "That's my key—the one Geir borrowed. I haven't seen it in years. Geir must have hidden it here for a reason."

Cathrine's neck hair bristled. "I have to go check out that farm," she said.

Margit put her hand on her arm. "Be careful. It could be dangerous."

Cathrine put the keys in her pocket.

Later, they sat on Margit's terrace. "Geir was always careful about where he kept important things," Margit said. "As a child, he was skilled at hide-and-seek. He would never hide such items in a prominent place."

Cathrine took a bite of a pretzel. "How about the attic?" she asked. "Or the basement?"

Margit reclined in her seat and enjoyed a sip of her tea. "He could have hidden it anywhere."

Cathrine rose from her seat and began pacing on the porch, speaking aloud. "Maybe there's a secret room? Or a hidden trapdoor in the floor?"

Margit nodded. "It's possible. Geir always had creative solutions."

Cathrine was excited. "I want to go right now. I'm off until Monday. Even if I don't find anything, I can enjoy it as a pleasant trip and stay until Sunday evening."

With a look of concern in her eyes, Margit gazed at her. "Wait until the morning. It will be dark when you arrive, and searching won't be possible."

Clutching the key, Cathrine stood and gazed at the sea from her chair. "I'm leaving tonight," she said. "Then I can start searching as soon as it gets light tomorrow morning."

Margit handed her a small flashlight. "Take this. It's a bit of a walk, and there are no lights along the path from the parking lot to the house."

Chapter Forty-Four

I arrived at the Helman-Larssen's representative residence in Torvastad and parked in the driveway. Gothic windows and illuminated carvings adorned the façade, giving the property an almost eerie feeling on this windy fall night. It wasn't just a home but a fortress.

I took a deep breath, collected myself, and rang the door-bell. I did this for my brother despite my mixed feelings about Helman-Larssen—a last act to honor Olav's memory with the dignity he deserved.

The door opened.

"Glad you could make it," Anita said, smiling.

Her dark blue dress sparkled in the light. She ushered me in with a self-assured elegance.

"You drove?"

"I was running a bit late."

"Leave your car, and I'll have someone return it to you to-morrow," she said, leading me to the inner quarters.

Pictures of royalty and prominent businessmen on the walls signaled the family's power and influence. She guided me to a living room with low, wide, minimalist pieces from Scandinavian designers, complemented by light carpets over dark tiles.

Artwork from well-known contemporary artists hung on the walls. The enormous windows provided a panoramic view of the lights from Haugesund across the strait. Two champagne flutes sat empty on a silver tray on a small table in the corner.

"Father couldn't make it today, but I have full authority to negotiate if you have any specific thoughts," Anita said.

We sat on the sofa. Sank into the soft cushions. Anita retrieved a bottle of Dom Pérignon. The cork came off with a slight puff before she poured the sparkling champagne.

Anita sat beside me, her hip pressed against mine. An unexpected spark ignited between us. She smiled warmly at me while her gaze locked onto mine. It was as if she could read all my thoughts. It was not much of a feat, to be honest.

"To Olav's memory," she said, raising her glass.

I followed suit, raised my glass, and took a sip. While Anita talked, I tried to stay focused on honoring Olav's memory in the best possible way, but I stiffened with surprise as Anita placed her hand on my thigh.

"We'll do everything to keep Olav's memory alive in a good way, I promise," she said.

A senior lady entered the room and invited us to sit at the dining table. She showed no signs of having noticed our intimacy. She served our food and vanished just as invisibly as she had arrived.

The table had a beautiful setting for two, with a white tablecloth and decorations of candles and cut flowers.

"Your invitation surprised me," I said, taking a bite of the carpaccio.

"I get it, but our family wants to do something significant for Olav. He had such a unique passion for music," Anita said.

We continued with the main course, a perfectly prepared entrecôte with the family's Sangiovese.

Anita told me about Olav's memorial fund, a foundation dedicated to nurturing musical talents. She placed her hand over mine and looked me in the eye. She emphasized how deeply Olav's fate had affected the family and why Dad and I should be on the trust board.

With a perfect blend of coffee and mascarpone, the dessert melted on my tongue, but my sense of unease grew.

Anita had detailed knowledge of Olav's dreams and ambitions, which almost seemed too good to be true. I felt both flattered and suspicious. How did Anita come across so many details about Olav? This entire session seemed very well planned.

"I need to discuss all of this with my dad," I said, noticing Anita was topping up my wineglass again. I had lost count of how much I had drunk.

"Can I offer you something with your coffee?"

"I'd love a whiskey. Single malt if you have it. I'm not into cognac," I said.

"And how would you like your whiskey?" she asked.

"In a glass. Preferably."

She laughed, her sparkling eyes seeking mine. Next, she took a bottle of Balvenie and a whiskey glass from the display cabinet.

"Ice cubes?"

"One. A single cube for a single malt," I said to sound worldly.

We moved to the sofa again. Anita positioned herself closer, her hand on my thigh once more, casting me a warm and passionate glance. She breathed heavily through her nose. "I hope you see the value of what we try to do. It's more than just a memorial fund. It's a way to keep Olav's spirit alive."

She was quiet momentarily before she leaned in closer and kissed me. Her lips met mine with an unexpected softness that made me dizzy. I closed my eyes and surrendered to the moment. Met her passion with my growing desire.

Anita stood with an almost hypnotic movement, as if in a trance. I couldn't tear my eyes away.

"You can't drive home today anyway," she said, grabbing my tie.

I was already getting pretty buzzed but downed the rest of my whiskey. She led me by the tie to her bedroom. I heard Cathrine's warning from the night before, but just as quickly ignored it.

"Let me make you more comfortable," Anita said, removing my horrible tie and unbuttoning my shirt.

I didn't resist. My head was spinning in a fog of alcohol and emotional chaos. I felt a nagging doubt about what I had gotten myself into, but Anita continued to seduce me with an almost supernatural confidence. I questioned the intelligence of my actions, but I couldn't resist her. Swept up in a whirlwind of emotions, Anita's passion made it challenging to reason.

Just as she removed my boxers and sent another jolt of pleasure through my body, I came to my senses. I knew in my heart I loved Cathrine and had no business being in bed with Anita. What I was doing was just sexual desire and plain stupid.

I wriggled free and grabbed my clothes. "I have to go," I said.

All my uncertainty was gone.

I got dressed, hurried down the stairs, stumbled in my pants on the last few steps, and hit my chin hard. I was bleeding, but I didn't care.

"You have no idea what you'll miss if you leave," she shouted after me.

A few hundred yards from the property, I took out my phone to call a cab. I noticed a message from Cathrine. She was on her way to her family's farm by Sandsfjorden. Thought she might find something of interest there.

"Can we rewind to before we met yesterday? Sorry."

She ended with a heart emoji.

Chapter Forty-Five

During her drive through Haugalandet, she thought about the previous evening. She recalled the disappointed expression on Flokí's face and her own frustration and anger.

How could she be so harsh with him despite all she knew about his past? She sighed frustratedly and tapped the steering wheel. Despite the difficulties, her heart ached to feel his arms around her.

Then there was Anita Helman-Larssen. She had him wrapped around her little finger and had a plan. Couldn't he see what she was up to? He was even having dinner with the Helman-Larssen family tonight.

She glanced at her watch. They were probably on their dessert by now. And Flokí was footloose and fancy-free. She rolled her eyes, groaned, bitterly regretted herself and felt more lonely than ever.

Cathrine opened the car window to get some air, but it didn't help. She wished Flokí had been in the car with her and hoped they still could try to figure this out together.

At Knapphus, she had stopped, bought some food and drinks, and sent him a text message. She hoped he would reply quickly and come to the farm. But her phone remained silent.

She arrived, parked her car, and started walking up the path to the house. It had turned dark and raw. Soon, it would start raining.

The flashlight Margit had given her died after a few minutes. She cursed and continued in the dark. She thought she had heard footsteps and twigs snapping nearby. Cathrine stopped. Her pulse quickened. She stood still, listening, but heard nothing but the wind.

She took out her phone and used it as a flashlight. She ran the last few meters to the house and fumbled for her keys. Her heart pounded. Behind her, she heard a sound like twigs moving. In haste, she dropped her keys on the ground and had to turn and shine her light backward. She found them right away. She got the door open and locked it as quickly as she could, leaned against the door and exhaled before turning on the light.

After calming down and eating, she began searching through the rooms. She found no documents, just old letters and pictures. Her gaze swept from corner to corner, looking for hidden rooms and loose floorboards. She found nothing.

Cathrine found a better flashlight in one of the dusty cabinets by the front door. She took a round on the property, illuminating every corner and thicket.

Cathrine searched, increasingly frustrated and uneasy. She felt watched. She aimed the flashlight at the grove several times but saw nothing. An icy shiver crept up her spine. She zipped up her jacket.

As she was heading back to the house, she saw it. A hook similar to the one in Margit's boathouse was stuck in the well's frame. A fishing line stretched from the hook down into the old well.

She struggled to remove the heavy well cover. She had to fetch a shovel from the barn to pry it up before pulling the line back up. The end of the line had a solid rope attached to it. She hauled on the rope. It was heavier to pull up than the keys from the boathouse.

A waterproof A4 box emerged from the well, locked with a padlock. She pulled out the smallest key and tried it. It fitted perfectly. Her heart was pounding audibly as she opened the box.

Inside the box were pictures and papers. Many of the documents had endless records and neat columns. Cathrine scanned through the top ones. The light was poor, so she took the box inside the house.

The records comprised many sheets with data on loading and unloading in various cities, names, and weights. The sheets contained labels such as "Moroccan," "Colombian," and "Afghan," while the letter "H" identified some entries. Other papers listed presumably foreign account numbers, dates, and amounts.

The pictures showed plastic packages hidden in various cavities on a boat. These images also showed captains talking with customs officers and goods unloaded from large ships.

Cathrine understood that these documents were solid proof of drug smuggling, corruption, and money laundering. By following the money trail, one might even expose the puppet masters behind the scheme.

She took out her phone and started photographing. Excited, she called Flokí but had no coverage.

When she finished photographing, she went outside and sat in a chair on the porch.

Once again, a twig snapped behind her. She jumped and turned, her heart in her throat.

Chapter Forty-Six

I returned to my car, jumped in, and fired up the engine. I was far from sober and shouldn't have been driving, but this was an emergency.

My car peeled out of the driveway. The tires screeched against the gravel. The dark, winding road demanded all my concentration. I had no idea how much of a head start Cathrine had.

My heart was pounding, but this time for a different reason. If Margit's hunch was correct, and influential figures were connected to Geir's death by drowning, the act of collecting evidence could be dangerous for her. I couldn't risk leaving her alone on an isolated, abandoned farm.

I sped toward my destination, Sandsfjorden. The road ahead of me was a chaotic blend of darkness and light. My eyes danced frantically between the road and my phone, hoping for a sign of life from Cathrine. My heart pounded so hard it hurt. Sweat ran down my back.

I called Margit for more precise directions. Called Cathrine repeatedly with no answer. With every missed call, the fear grew more and more intense. Why didn't she answer me? Was she still mad at me?

I stormed out of the car and shouted Cathrine's name as I ran through the woods. The house was pitch black when I arrived. The place was silent. Nobody answered. The only movement I detected were the lights of a speed carrier darting across the fjord.

I bounded up the stairs, opened the door, and switched on the light. The house was empty. A bag of groceries sat on the kitchen counter.

I called her again. My phone had no signal. Could this be the reason for Cathrine's unanswered calls? I felt a slight relief.

I stepped outside and stood on the stairs. In the light from the doorway, I saw it—the bloodstains on the edge of the terrace. My ice-cold fear returned. Something was terribly wrong. I followed the trail out into the darkness.

The blood trail led me to an old well. In the dead of night, I found Cathrine lying lifeless on the ground. Panic hit me with tremendous force. I threw myself beside her, shook her with trembling hands, and called out her name. My heart was racing wildly.

I detected a slight pulse and realized every second would count. I searched for my phone to call for help.

Rapid, heavy footsteps approached from behind. I turned around. A dark character wearing a balaclava stood clenching a raised shovel. I spun around, and his shovel hit my shoulder as I tried to grab it.

I glimpsed his heavy boot coming at my head, but it was too late.

Chapter Forty-Seven

I woke up to my car shaking violently and whipped my head around as a figure moved into my peripheral vision. Cathrine was sitting next to me. Her head had fallen forward. A dark red streak of blood was forming a droplet under her nose.

The car sped up down a hill. I caught a brief glimpse of the pitch-black Lovrafjord far below on our right side.

I desperately reached for the steering wheel, but it was too late. The car hurtled toward a curve, veered off the road, and hit a curb stone. My body slammed against the steering wheel. My head felt shattered, as if by a sledgehammer. A warm liquid filled my mouth, leaving a taste of rusty iron.

Then our car came to rest. My heart was pounding as if it wanted to escape my body.

"Cathrine!" I cried as I stroked her cheek and searched for a pulse.

The car tipped forward, swung back for a moment, then tipped over the edge. We fell and spun for an eternity.

The rear of the car hit the water surface with a violent crash. The crash threw us back into our seats. I lost my consciousness.

When I came to, the car was underwater. An air pocket dragged it back toward the surface. The seat back had given way, and my head was in the ice-cold floor water. My lungs were burning. I coughed a mix of blood and seawater.

Cathrine was still in her seat. Her head bumped against the side window in sync with the car's movements. Her pulse was weak.

The car didn't reach the surface but descended into the dark fjord again. Anxiety gripped me, but my determination overcame my fear. I had to find a way out. No way in hell this would be our grave.

I pushed against the door with all my might, but the water outside pushed back with overwhelming force. I tried the window, but the engine was dead.

The water was still rising. I reached for my gun, but my holster was empty. I scrabbled on the floor, dunked my head in the water, and checked under our seats. Nothing. Damn it!

I kicked at the window with all my strength, but the glass didn't budge. I panicked and frantically searched for a solution. I needed to break a window and equalize the pressure to open the door.

I hit the window with my elbow but didn't get enough force behind the blow. I desperately looked for something to serve as a hammer.

Water was pouring in. I struck it again. The glass moved but didn't break.

I ignored the intense pain in my arm. I yanked a headrest loose from the back seat and hit the window with its metal rods.

Cracks! I hit it repeatedly until the cracks spread like a spider web across the glass, heard the glass giving way.

Air bubbled through the cracks, and the water rose faster. The car started sliding even quicker toward the depths.

I struck one last time. The glass shattered, and water flooded in. The car shot down toward the bottom.

I grabbed Cathrine's hand, clung to the door handle, and pushed myself out. Glass shards cut into my hand, and the sea struck me with icy claws. But I ignored the pain once more.

I dragged Cathrine out and kicked us away from the car. It sailed on down to the depths.

I kicked off my shoes, and we rose to the surface. I equalized the pressure by letting the air out of my lungs. I no longer felt the intense cold, but I felt indifferent and powerless. I almost gave up, but realized that would be our demise.

Desperate, I punched the water with my free hand and saw the faint light from the surface approaching. I broke the water's surface with one desperate burst of strength and inhaled the air with a violent thirst that filled my aching lungs.

A cramp seized one of my calves. I lay on my back to float while paddling us toward land with my arms. We weren't far from a small rocky outcrop where I hoisted Cathrine onto the shore.

She wasn't breathing, and I couldn't feel her pulse, so I started mouth-to-mouth and chest compressions. I kept the pace to the rhythm of "Stayin' Alive" while I wrung my soul in prayer to God for help. Nothing happened. No breath. No pulse.

A shooting star crossed the sky and faded. Did I witness Cathrine's soul leaving me? I cried like a lone wolf toward the moon above.

The lights from an emergency vehicle swept across the darkness behind me. I heard a car braking on the road and the shouts of voices approaching.

Chapter Forty-Eight

Charlene lay curled up in a fetal position on her bed, her curtains drawn shut.

She'd checked her dad's room and the living room, but he wasn't home yet. She ran her thumb over the picture she'd taken of him at Ryvarden. Remembered how he'd hurried to make the dinner in time last night. Remembered his promise to come straight home afterward.

But he didn't come home. It was almost five in the morning. His phone went straight to voicemail. And she hadn't slept all night.

Grandpa came into her room carrying a steaming cup of hot chocolate, like when she was little. He slumped in a chair.

"He'll be here soon," he said, stroking her hair. His voice quivered.

She glanced at her grandpa, doubt in her eyes. Her throat tightened; she swallowed hard.

"First Mom, then Uncle Olav…" she trailed off.

Grandpa leaned forward in the chair.

"I know you're having a tough time, buttercup, but don't give up."

She looked anxiously at him.

"Everything just keeps getting worse and worse?"

Grandpa took her hand, his rough skin against hers.

"I don't know what he's up to, but he'll be back."

Her grandpa stood and left the room. His heavy footsteps faded down the hall.

A phone rang somewhere in the house. She listened and heard her grandfather's muffled voice. His words were indistinct, but the tone seemed calm. *Was it about Dad?*

Footsteps approached again. Charlene opened her eyes as her grandfather reentered the room.

"That was Vidar," he whispered. "I messaged him, and he called me back. It's early, but he's on his way."

Charlene walked toward the window, unsure about seeing Vidar. She turned to face her grandpa.

"What if he hurts me again?"

"I understand it's scary. But you're not going to go through life without getting hurt. Take it from an old man: the journey's worth it, regardless."

She bit her lip hard.

"But Vidar let me down."

She looked desperate. "How can I trust him? Trust anyone?"

"Sometimes the bravest thing we do is take a chance. We must risk getting hurt to find the one worth it all."

She closed her eyes and let his words sink in.

"Think about how much fun you guys used to have," he continued. "I saw the two of you together. Maybe he's scared, too, but deep down, he knows he needs you?"

Charlene opened her eyes and met her grandpa's gaze.

"But what if I'm not good enough?"

"You're more than good, sweetheart. Shall we go downstairs?"

Charlene smoothed her clothes. She followed him down the stairs. The doorbell rang, and she stopped halfway. She closed her eyes, hyperventilated, and reminded herself of her grandpa's words.

With trembling hands, she tucked her hair behind her ears and straightened up. Vidar's voice reached her through the door.

They stood silent for a moment before Vidar stepped forward and embraced her. "I'm so sorry," he whispered into her hair. "About everything. Can we talk?"

Vidar pulled back and met her gaze.

"Maybe we could go for a walk? Talk things over?"

Charlene hesitated. But to her surprise, she said, "Yeah, tha t's... okay."

Vidar smiled. Charlene put on her jacket and turned to her grandpa.

"Go on," he said. "I'll call when there's news."

The cool breeze caressed her face as they walked side by side along the Coastal Path at Killingøy. She glanced at Vidar, but she didn't know what to say.

After a while, he broke his silence.

"I was so scared," he began. "When I found out my parents were getting divorced, it felt like my world was falling apart."

They approached a bench overlooking the sea. Vidar sat, and Charlene did the same. Without thinking, she leaned against his shoulder and let her gaze wander the endless ocean.

"Thanks for coming," she said.

He pulled her closer in response.

They continued along the gravel path and approached a viewpoint where the trail curved up a small hill from which they could see even farther to sea.

They stopped. Vidar took her hands in his. "I was an idiot. Stupid and scared," he said. "I'm sorry."

A moment of warmth filled her, but it didn't last long. An icy fear crept back into her heart, and her body tensed. Thoughts of her father and everything that could have happened to him came rushing back in full force.

She pulled her hands out of Vidar's grip and stepped back. Vidar reached out, but Charlene backed away.

"It's too much. I can't bear to lose anyone else."

"Please," he began.

Charlene turned away. Mom was gone, Uncle Olav was dead, and now... Dad? It was unbearable.

Vidar placed his hands on her shoulders.

Charlene closed her eyes. Part of her wanted to push Vidar away, build a wall around herself, and shut out all her feelings. But another part longed for his closeness and comfort.

She breathed through her nose. His familiar scent calmed her. She leaned back against him and opened her eyes. Looked into his warm, brown eyes.

"I'm scared, Vidar. So incredibly scared."

Chapter Forty-Nine

I twisted away from the harsh light above me. The smell of disinfectants revealed that I was in a hospital. Once again. It had become an unfortunate habit of mine.

My head was pounding. I couldn't move my left arm. It had colorful tubes and wires tethering it.

The faint light of day was breaking. I could see the silhouette of the mountains surrounding Sauda through my window. They stood motionless and eternal, contrasting the chaos I had experienced.

A man in a police tactical uniform entered with a notepad and sat by my bed. "Sheriff Selvik," he said with a nod.

I nodded weakly, still groggy from the painkillers. "Cathrine? She alive?" I asked with a strained grimace.

"Yes, she's alive and in the ICU in Haugesund," the sheriff said. "I'm afraid I don't know more right now. I'll notify you as soon as we know anything else."

He blew his nose in a handkerchief. "Are you two living together?"

"No, we met when I was in Spain searching for my brother. We got close."

"Did you find your brother?"

"We found him. Murdered."

He glanced over from his notepad. "Olav Wilhelmsen? The guy that got killed in Spain, and where his killer offed himself? I've read about it."

I confirmed.

"My condolences. However, I need to investigate the events at Lovra last night. Can you give me an account of what happened? Are you up to it?"

I nodded and closed my eyes to gather my thoughts. "Cathrine messaged late last night. She was heading to the farm by Sandsfjorden to look for some papers. I wanted to join, so I drove to the farm and found her unconscious by the well on her family farm. Then someone attacked me, and I didn't regain consciousness until my car was heading for the fjord."

Selvik took notes. "Who do you believe attacked you?"

I shook my head. "I don't know. But no doubt someone tried to kill us. It was a deliberate murder attempt disguised as an accident. It's got to be connected to my brother's murder and the potential murder of Cathrine's great-uncle."

Selvik raised his eyebrows. "How do you reckon?"

I told him about Margit's suspicions and why Cathrine went to the farm. Selvik leaned forward with an intense gaze. "Take me back to when you traveled to Spain. From the beginning. I need to understand the full story."

I took a breath. "It all started when my brother, Olav, went missing in Spain," I began.

Selvik nodded.

"I traveled to Spain to investigate his disappearance."

"And Cathrine?" Selvik asked. "How did she fit into all of this?"

"Cathrine knew Olav. She called me, told me he was missing, and wanted to help with her contacts when I arrived. That's why she helped me trace him," I explained.

I gave him a condensed version of the story from Cathrine's Sunday morning phone call to the dinner at Helman-Larssen's.

"Cathrine went to the farm looking for documents that might confirm Margit's suspicions. I know it all sounds incredible," I concluded. "I almost cannot believe it myself."

Selvik leaned back with narrowed eyes. "You're right. It's an incredible story."

He scrutinized me, weighing every word I said. "Are you sure this is everything?" he asked.

"That's all."

Selvik stood and strolled around my bed. "I've been around for so long, I can tell when someone's bullshitting me."

My heart beat faster. Had I forgotten anything significant?

Selvik put his notepad on the table. "I have this one thing I need to ask you," he said and sat by my bed.

"A witness claims to have seen you and Cathrine arguing at a bar in Haugesund a few days before the accident. Care to share what happened?"

I swallowed hard. My memories from the evening at Stuelands Abothek came flooding back. Cathrine and I had been discussing heatedly, but it wasn't an argument for me.

I hesitated. "We disagreed. But an argument? No."

Selvik raised an eyebrow. "My witness describes it as quite heated. According to my witness, Cathrine left the place in anger."

I felt flushed. No matter how I explained it, it could sound suspicious. "It wasn't anything like that," I said. "We discussed different theories, and emotions ran a bit high."

"Okay," Selvik mumbled and made notes on his pad.

I was sweating lightly.

"So this was just an 'intense but friendly conversation,' not a heated argument?"

I closed my eyes and tried to remember every detail from that evening. "It might be a bit more complicated than I first portrayed."

Selvik stopped at the foot of my bed. "How so?"

"It wasn't just about Olav. Cathrine and I... We have a complicated history."

"According to our sources," Selvik continued, "Cathrine broke up with you that evening."

He paused. "Some people at my office may believe that you, driven by jealousy and under the influence, forced Cathrine off the farm against her will. On the way back, you drove off the road and ended up in the fjord."

I stared at him in disbelief. "That's absurd! I can understand the logic, but it isn't what happened. It is not true!"

"We found quite a bit of alcohol in your blood. Enough to revoke your driver's license, by the way. Consider yourself a pedestrian from now on."

He glanced at me. "You should expect charges to be filed."

I shook my head, frustrated at how wrong this was getting. "Yeah, I had a few drinks that night but did not force Cathrine to go anywhere!"

"Then why did you decide to drive to the farm when you knew you shouldn't be driving?" Selvik asked.

"I was worried about her. It was an emergency!" I exclaimed. "She messaged me, letting me know she was going to the farmhouse. With a heart emoji. I went to help her, protect her, and maybe resolve the issues between us."

I waved my arms. The tubes and wires attached rattled.

He sighed. "Some might think she rejected you. Or she never invited you to come. So far, we only have your side of this story. And your claim that messages were exchanged between your phones, which currently reside at the bottom of a 1500-foot-deep fjord."

I felt a surge of anger welling up inside me. "Do you think I would do anything that might hurt Cathrine? That I would risk both her life and mine?"

Selvik met my gaze without blinking. "Mixing considerable amounts of alcohol with powerful emotions can make people do crazy stuff. However, I know this is just one possibility of many we are investigating. Cathrine may wake up soon and corroborate your story. That would resolve this issue."

I stared back at him, shocked by the accusations. "This is madness. I love Cathrine. I would never..."

Selvik leaned closer. "Consider this from my perspective," he said sharply. "Your story reads like an awful crime novel. A conspiracy? Mysterious attacker? A staged accident? In Suldal?"

Panic tightened my chest.

He shrugged. "Or you might just be this crazy, jealous idiot, drunk as a skunk, driving too fast, and losing control of your vehicle on this narrow, winding road along the fjord."

Chapter Fifty

I must have passed out as the sheriff left. A crack of thunder reminded me of the crash as we hit the curb, Cathrine, and the car sinking. I woke up, clenched my fists around the edge of my bed, and jerked upright.

A sharp pain radiated from my ribs. With my left hand, I fumbled for my cell phone on the nightstand but couldn't find it.

I let my gaze sweep across my room. I found neither phone, wallet, nor car keys. Everything was at the bottom of Lovrafjorden. Reality hit me. I was stranded.

"Dammit!"

I hammered the call button. A nurse came running.

"Can I talk to the doctor?" I asked.

"He's almost done with his rounds..."

"Can you let him know a miracle's happened and I've risen from the dead? I'm leaving."

She nodded and disappeared. A middle-aged man in a white coat entered a few minutes later. He introduced himself as Dr. Bakke.

"I need to get out of here," I said firmly.

The doctor frowned. "Your body needs rest."

"I need to go home... to Cathrine," I said, trying to sit.

Dr. Bakke sighed. "At your own risk, but it could be danger-ous."

Doctors worldwide were apparently reading from the same script.

"I understand the risk, but I have no choice."

The doctor shook his head but realized I wouldn't be per-suaded. He went to get the discharge papers.

I forced myself up. Cathrine had risked everything to help me find Olav. It was my turn to be there for her.

Dr. Bakke returned with his papers. "I hope you know what you're doing," he said as I signed.

"I do," I replied, but I knew better.

"One small thing: We called that number you provided for your father..."

He flipped through his notes. "Olav Wilhelmsen in Hauge-sund. But he's not picking up."

"Dad's name is Godtfred. Let me see that number."

He handed me his chart. I had given him Olav's number. He wouldn't be picking up anymore.

"I need to borrow a phone and let my dad know I'm okay."

"Serina can get one for you," he said, nodding toward the nurse before he left.

I ran my hand over my face. My arms and legs ached. My head felt like cotton. How was I going to get to Haugesund?

"Can you check the bus schedules for Haugesund for me?" I asked the nurse.

She nodded and checked her iPad. "The next bus leaves in two hours, and the trip will take about two and a half hours."

She left and returned with a cell phone. I called Dad.

"Oh, thank God! We've been beside ourselves. Charlene's been inconsolable. She's sure you're dead. She hasn't slept all night. I called Vidar this morning. He came over and picked her up, bless him. Where the hell are you? I don't recognize this number as being yours. Did you get a new phone?"

I couldn't remember him swearing before, but he finally shut up and gave me a chance to update him.

"I want to visit Cathrine at the hospital as soon as possible. We can meet there. I'll call you when I'm on my way."

We hung up.

I had no cell phone of my own, no money, no way to get out of this place. I found myself trapped while Cathrine battled for her life.

I had to call Torstein. Asking for help wasn't my strong suit, but this was the second time I had to ask him in just a few weeks. Still, I had no choice but to dial his number.

I waited for Torstein to answer with a mix of relief and anxiety. Relief at having the energy to move forward. At the same time, I felt anxiety gnawing in my stomach following my conversation with the sheriff. It was like before a thunderstorm. You know it's coming, but you have no idea how bad it's gonna be.

Torstein had been there for me through all the crises in my life—Jo-Ann's death, moving back to Norway, and everything that had happened over the past few days. Along with my dad, Charlene, and Catch, he had been one of the life rafts I could cling to.

I was ashamed I had never told him how much he meant to me and promised to tell him at my first opportunity.

Torstein's voice came through on the other end.

"I need help."

"Floki? What's up?"

I explained my situation.

"Damn. It's a freaking miracle you're alive. We'll get the details in the car. I'm on my way home from my cabin at Vågslid. Just passed Røldal. There's a back road to Sauda from here. Give me about an hour, and I'll be on your doorstep."

Relief washed over me. "Thanks. Once more."

"Relax. I'll be sure to bill you through your nose. Ha-ha."

He hung up. I turned to the nurse entering.

"I'm getting picked up in an hour and would like to wait in the reception area."

She frowned. "You should be resting in bed."

"I can't stand it. Promise I'll behave."

Reluctantly, she agreed.

I waited impatiently in the reception area. There was a time-piece on the wall. The second hand moved ever so slowly around the dial from one notch to the other. Its other hands seemed to stand still.

A nurse returned half an hour later with a serious expression. "Flokí Wilhelmsen? Sheriff Selvik called. He wants to talk to you."

I froze. "Tell him I'm on my way to see Cathrine. I'll call him later."

The nurse frowned. "The sheriff seemed quite insistent about speaking with you."

"I'm not charged with anything, am I?" I snapped.

She shook her head. "Not that I'm aware."

"Then I have the right to leave, don't I? My severely injured girlfriend is fighting for her life in the ICU in Haugesund, and I've told him all I know. I'm leaving."

She hesitated. "You can. But..."

"No buts," I interrupted. "I'm leaving as soon as my buddy picks me up."

As the nurse left, doubt crept in. Would it look suspicious if I left? I decided I had to go. I had to be with Cathrine. I couldn't let Selvik and his groundless, twisted suspicions stop me. He already had me pegged as a suspect. Nothing would change that, and staying would only slow me down.

A while later, Torstein's Audi pulled into the parking lot. Relief washed over me.

Finally!

I got up. Pain shot through my ribs. With a shaky hand, I grabbed my jacket. As I turned toward the exit, I froze.

Sheriff Selvik came marching in with his gaze locked on me. "Flokí Wilhelmsen!" he shouted. "We need to talk."

I broke into a sweat and had to steady myself. "I need to get to Haugesund," I said.

"This is serious!"

Then I heard a familiar voice from behind him. "Excuse me, Sheriff Selvik. I'm Torstein Trømme Jr., Floki's attorney."

Torstein positioned himself between us. "Unless you have formal charges against my client, he has every right to leave this hospital," Torstein said, calm but firm.

Selvik hesitated, his eyes darting between the two of us. "He's a witness, and we have some questions..."

"Which can wait," Torstein interrupted. "My client has been through a trauma and needs to be with his girlfriend at the hospital ICU in Haugesund. If you have charges, present them. If not, we're leaving."

I held my breath and waited.

The sheriff pressed his lips together, then shook his head. "No charges... yet. But make sure he doesn't get to see her until she has confirmed she wants him to. There's some uncertainty surrounding Mr. Wilhelmsen's explanation. He may have forced her into his car against her will and may even have an interest in her demise. You should not leave him alone with her until she corroborates his story."

Torstein glanced from the sheriff to me.

"Duly noted. Now we're leaving," he said.

Part Four

Forfatterfabrikken Forlag AS

Chapter Fifty-One

Charlene rested her head against Vidar's shoulder. The salty air opened her lungs, allowing her to breathe.

Vidar wrapped his arms around her as if trying to hold her together. Her thoughts raced through everything that had happened over the last few days. She needed some positive news.

Charlene stood, brushed her clothes, and took Vidar's hand. They hurried back toward the car.

"Do you think Dad's been staying over at Cathrine's place?" she asked. "But then, why hasn't he told me?"

Vidar squeezed her hand. "Could be. Do they have something going? Could he do something like that without telling you?"

Charlene frowned. "Why are they trying to hide it? Do they think I'm stupid?"

She kicked the gravel in frustration. "Cathrine is good for my dad, but why would he visit her yesterday? He knew how important it was for me that he came straight home. He promised."

Vidar nodded. "He'd better have a fucking good reason."

"But why didn't he answer me when I texted him and called him? What if something terrible has happened to him? He and Grandpa are all I have left, and Grandpa is not well. I can't survive losing either of them."

Her cell rang. It was Grandpa. Her heart beat faster. She hesitated before putting it on speaker.

Grandpa sounded tense. "Dad and Cathrine have been in a car accident."

She froze.

"Are they... are they...?"

"They're alive," Grandpa said. "But they've admitted Cathrine to the hospital in Haugesund. She's in the ICU. Dad's on his way over. Can you and Vidar pick me up?"

Charlene nodded. "We're on our way."

She hung up and glanced at Vidar, her eyes wide. "We need to go. Now!"

They sprinted the last hundred yards toward the car. Charlene grabbed her door handle and turned to Vidar. She fought back her tears.

Vidar got behind the wheel. "Your dad is alive and on his way to the hospital. That's most important," he said. "We'll pray Cathrine will be okay, too."

Charlene held on tight as Vidar drove. "Can you drive a little faster?" she asked, glancing at the speedometer. She knew Grandpa was sitting alone at home, as worried as she was.

"We're almost there," Vidar said.

"Dad might be hurt... Grandpa sounded worried."

"Your dad's a rock. He can take a hit."

They turned into Grandpa's driveway. Charlene threw herself out of the car as it stopped. Grandpa met them. He seemed unwell.

"Are you feeling sick?" she asked, examining him.

"Don't worry about me. We need to go," he said. "But your dad messaged me to bring Cathrine's tablet. I couldn't find it."

"I know what to look for. Let me check it for you."

She rushed inside and searched the living room, bedroom, and kitchen.

"It must be around here somewhere," she muttered, yanking open drawers.

She spotted its black metal edge under a newspaper on the kitchen table. Yes!

She ran to the car. Grandpa slumped back in his seat, sweating. Vidar drove off.

She glanced at her grandpa in the back seat. "You don't look too good, Grandpa. Dad and Cathrine will be okay. She's a fighter. She'll make it."

Charlene clutched her tablet as Vidar swung the car into the hospital parking lot. Grandpa struggled to escape his back seat, and Charlene helped him. Vidar placed a supportive hand on his back, and they hurried toward the entrance.

The automatic doors opened slowly. Charlene raced into the lobby in search of her dad. He was nowhere to be found.

They headed for the reception. Charlene leaned on the counter.

"We're looking for Cathrine Runevik," she said, breathless.

The receptionist typed on her computer. "She's in the intensive care unit at the end of that corridor," she said.

The nurse in the ICU seemed puzzled. "I'm sorry, she's not here. I believe she transferred to another unit."

She checked a list. "Hold on, I'll check in my system," she said, disappearing into a smaller office.

Charlene drummed her fingers against her thigh. She alternated her gaze between the empty corridor and her grandfather.

"What's keeping her?" she muttered, glancing at her watch for the third time in one minute.

The nurse returned, smiling. "She's in the neurology ward, fifth floor."

As the elevator moved slowly upward, Charlene could barely keep still. On the fifth floor, as the elevator doors opened, an orderly with a face mask and a hospital bed blocked her way.

Charlene stood motionless, her gaze fixed on the blanket drawn over the patient's face. A shiver ran through her as the bed passed. It was a grim reminder of the reality of a hospital.

They maneuvered past and hurried toward Cathrine's room. A nurse confirmed Cathrine was on the ward and pointed toward her room.

They arrived and came to an abrupt stop in the doorway. Cathrine's room was empty. Not even a bed.

Another nurse approached them. "I'm so sorry, but Cathrine was picked up for surgery. It was some kind of emergency procedure."

Charlene's legs gave way, and Vidar caught her.

Chapter Fifty-Two

I pushed through the automatic doors of the hospital. Torstein followed close behind. Adrenaline was still pumping through my body, but fatigue was setting in.

I scanned the reception area. Nurses rushed by in rustling uniforms. Patients and visitors sat surrounded by the smell of hot dogs and coffee in the kiosk area.

"Do you see them? They said they would be here," I said.

He shook his head.

I ran down a corridor, searching for my family. At the end of the hallway, Charlene stood by herself. She turned and spotted me. Her face lit up, and she ran toward me with outstretched arms.

"Daddy!" she cried, throwing herself around my neck.

I held her tight against me and felt her body shaking with relief. My arms ached, but the embrace was fantastic.

"It's okay, Charlene. I'm with you now."

"I've been so scared," she whispered to my chest.

I thanked higher powers for being close to Charlene again. A brief peace settled over us despite the surrounding chaos.

I stroked her hair. "There was an accident, but I'm okay. Cathrine is—"

Before I could finish, the door to the staff bathroom opened. Dad came out, supported by Vidar. Dad was pale, but his face brightened when he saw me.

"Flokí! Thank God you're…"

He scrutinized me. "More or less all right," he said and walked toward me with unsteady steps.

He glanced back at the sign on the door and shrugged. "It was an emergency. Sometimes you gotta break the rules."

He turned his attention back to me with a worried expression.

"You heard anything about Cathrine?"

I shook my head. "Not yet. We still need to locate her."

Just as I headed toward the reception, a nurse hurried toward us. "Are you the ones looking for Cathrine Runevik?" she asked.

We nodded.

"I'm sorry, but they have transferred her to another department."

"Which department?" I asked.

The nurse glanced at me. "She's listed in a department that no longer exists and, frankly, shouldn't be in the system anymore. We've had some issues after transitioning to our new IT platform."

"How can a hospital lose track of a patient like this?"

"Cool down, Daddy."

The nurse was sorry. "I understand this is frustrating. Wish I could provide more information, but our system hasn't been updated yet. I can only apologize."

"Any way to figure this out? They said she was going to surgery," I said.

"I'll do my best to find out more, but right now, I'm afraid I can't give you a better answer."

I clenched my fists in frustration. "I can't just stand around and wait. I'll track her down on my own."

"Dad, wait a second. We have to trust that the hospital can locate her."

I shook my head and started walking. "I don't have time for this."

"Dad, please. Don't do anything stupid."

"Charlene, I—"

A familiar voice cut in. "What's going on?"

It was Jonas. "I need to talk to Cathrine about what happened at the farm before you arrived, but I can wait if you want to visit her first. It's just a few minor things," he said.

"Cathrine is missing. No one seems to know where she is."

"Missing? In the hospital?"

"Yeah, and no one seems to care!"

I needed to do something. I couldn't passively wait for the "system" to find Cathrine.

"We need to find her," I said, turning to Torstein. "You ready?"

"Sure. Where do we start?"

"The surgical department. That's where Cathrine was supposed to go when they picked her up. Maybe we'll find something."

I paused for a moment and closed my eyes. Amid all this chaos, I had to force myself to stay calm. I met Torstein's gaze and knew he would always have my back.

"Wait," Jonas said, grabbing my arm. "I understand the gravity of your situation. I can assist and use my police authority if necessary."

"Thanks."

"Be careful," Charlene said.

"I will. I'm leaving Dad with you and Vidar. Liaison with the staff and call me if you get any updates," I said.

"Of course. You go find Cathrine."

I pictured Cathrine. When we found her, I'd tell her I loved her—to her and everyone else. That was a promise.

My gaze fell on Vidar, standing next to Charlene. He was taking care of her in a reassuring way. Her face showed she felt safe. Maybe I had judged him too harshly.

Before us stretched the corridor to the surgical department, lit by flickering fluorescent lights. We hurried past doors with incomprehensible medical terms, searching for a doctor to help us with Cathrine's records.

A nurse came out of a room, and Jonas grabbed her arm.

"Excuse me, we're looking for a patient, Cathrine Runevik. Can you help us?"

She frowned and checked some papers several times. "Cathrine Runevik? She was supposed to be in the operating room over an hour ago. But she never showed up."

"What do you mean she never showed up?" I asked.

"They prepped her for surgery on the ward, but when they went to get her, she had disappeared. We've searched everywhere," she said and hurried on.

Panic smoldered in my body, and my voice turned hoarse. "We need to find her. Right this minute!"

We slipped through a nearby door as it was closing. A nurse blocked our way.

"Stop! This area is off-limits to unauthorized personnel."

Jonas showed his police badge. "We're looking for a missing patient. It's a critical situation."

The nurse straightened. "I don't care who you are. You're disrupting our work and compromising our sanitation procedures. I'll call security if you don't leave this area immediately."

"Listen," I said. "My girlfriend is missing somewhere in this goddamn hospital, and—"

Torstein grabbed my arm and pulled me back. "Easy now."

Jonas positioned himself between us and turned to the nurse. "We understand your situation, but this is an acute emergency. Please cooperate."

The nurse hesitated but didn't give in. "You have no right to be behind this door. This is a restricted area. Leave now, or else—"

Jonas turned back to me and Torstein. "We need a fresh approach."

He pulled me along. "Come on, I have an idea."

We ran through a maze of hospital corridors until he found a door marked "Security." He knocked. A burly man opened.

"Bjørn, we're looking for a missing patient," Jonas explained. "Can we see some of your footage from the last few hours?"

Bjørn hesitated.

"This is an emergency," Jonas said.

"Concerning a breach of security protocols," Torstein added.

Bjørn sat at a computer and started scrolling through the footage.

"Stop! There! Look!" I cried.

On his screen, we saw Cathrine being wheeled out of the hospital, sitting in a wheelchair with her head hanging limply forward.

"Who's that?" I exclaimed, pointing at the veiled woman pushing her.

"Dad!"

Charlene was standing in the doorway.

"I've seen her before," she said. "She was wheeling a bed out of Cathrine's ward earlier. The patient was dead."

Chapter Fifty-Three

We stared at the tablet as I logged in to track Cathrine's smartwatch. Torstein, Jonas, Charlene, and I waited for the app to load. Dad sat in a chair. Vidar kept him company.

"Come on," I muttered to myself.

A blue circle appeared on the map.

"Gotcha!" I exclaimed, pointing. "She's on the move."

I zoomed in on the map. "Cathrine's heading toward a property on the northern side of Ålfjorden," I said. "Any of you familiar with this place?"

"I've hiked a lot in that area. It's an extensive property, kind of secluded. I know a parking spot and a trail that leads unseen onto the property," Torstein said.

Jonas turned to Torstein. "I'll get my car. Since you know the area, you and Floki take your car and lead the way."

He pulled out his phone. "And I'm mobilizing the cavalry," he said, running off.

"Two seconds. Gotta drain my lizard," Torstein said.

I held onto my seat back as Torstein's Audi flew along the narrow Ålfjorden Road with Jonas on our tail. I glanced over at Torstein; he was calm and focused.

"How much farther?" I asked.

"We're close. I'm unsure where the trail begins, but it should be somewhere close."

Jonas turned off his flashing lights, and the patrol car behind him did the same. I clenched my fists. *We're on our way, Cathrine. We're coming.*

I leaned forward in my seat. "We're on a tight schedule when we arrive. Every second counts. They've tried to kill her, kill us both, once. I don't want to give them another chance."

"There might be civilians around. We can't just storm in. We have to let the police do their job."

"You planning on staying in the car?"

"No... and I get your concern, but the police need time to do some reconnaissance, right? You're a bit of a cowboy sometimes. Don't fuck this up."

I said nothing.

"Did we agree to aim for the place I suggested?" Torstein asked as we approached. "It's not too far off, within walking distance."

"We did."

Torstein swiveled off the road onto a narrow path. I clenched the seat back. Through the windshield, I glimpsed an old barn.

"We are out of sight behind this barn," he said.

I nodded. We opened the doors, slid onto the gravel, and ran through the tall grass behind the police officers.

My mind filled with a horrible image: Cathrine, lifeless and cold in a dark basement. *No, don't believe it. She's alive. She has to be.* I picked up the pace. Jonas was right in front of me. I focused only on the goal ahead of us.

My heart pounded as we crept toward the house. Jonas nodded. The police ran to the entrance and broke down the door with a loud bang.

"Police!"

We stormed into the room. An elderly couple and two frightened teenagers stared at us with wide eyes.

The man raised his hands and slowly stood. "What's this? Some stupid Halloween prank?" he stammered.

Jonas gathered everyone in the living room. I ran up the stairs and checked each room. Bedrooms, bathroom, closet - nothing. No trace of Cathrine.

Jonas shook his head when I returned to the living room. "Have you had any visitors?" he asked the old couple.

"A woman?" I added.

They looked at each other before the wife answered. "No, we've been alone all day."

I panicked. Where was Cathrine?

"Check the basement, boathouse, and outbuilding," Jonas shouted to the other officers.

I followed, desperate to find a clue. We searched everywhere but still couldn't find Cathrine.

Exhausted and frustrated, we met outside. Jonas gave me a worried glance.

"She's not here. We must have made a mistake."

I sank to my knees. Where on earth could she be?

I stared out at the fjord as my frustration bubbled inside of me. Jonas stood beside me on the porch, just as disappointed as me.

"Damn it! We must have missed something!"

I slammed my hand on the railing.

Jonas sighed. "We've searched the entire property. The dogs have found no trace of her. She's not here."

I shook my head. "But it must be something we missed. A secret cellar, a hidden room, anything!"

Jonas squeezed my shoulder. "Maybe someone placed her watch on this property to mislead us?"

My frustration grew as I stared at the tablet. The police were doing the last searches on the property, but I knew it was futile.

"Check this," I said.

He came over, and I showed him the map on the screen. "The signal's gone. It's like someone turned off the watch or..."

"Or destroyed it," Jonas finished.

An icy dread gripped me. What if we were too late? What if Cathrine was ...? I refused to finish my thinking.

"We must have missed something," I said. "A clue, a hint, anything."

Jonas looked worried. "We've checked everything. We should consider other possibilities."

I shook my head. I refused to give up, but my doubts were killing me. Had we been chasing a red herring all along? Was this just a diversion?

"We're heading back to the station," Jonas said. "Cathrine is not here. These poor retired teachers and their grandkids deserve to be left in peace."

I felt helpless. We'd been played, and time was running out. Cathrine was out somewhere, in mortal danger, but we had no clue.

I stared out over the fjord as frustration boiled. Something didn't add up. I turned to Torstein. "Wait a minute," I said, grabbing the tablet.

I zoomed out on the map and let my gaze wander over the terrain. The fjord line, the roads, the small islands... My eyes stopped at a detail. A peninsula jutting out into the fjord. Why hadn't I noticed it earlier?

I zoomed in and out several times, studying the area around the peninsula. My heart beat faster. Was it possible? Could we have been this close but still raided the wrong place?

With trembling fingers, I traced the route we had driven. Then, I compared it with the signal we had observed from Cathrine's smartwatch. My breathing quickened as I realized the mistake.

"Torstein!" I shouted. "We're on the wrong side! Look!"

I pointed at the map and explained. "I think the signal came from the other side of this peninsula."

Chapter Fifty-Four

We lay on our stomachs, staring at the neighboring property. The fjord was still and dark. A faint breeze moved the pennant, carrying the earthy scent of fallen leaves. A few outdoor lights were on. The place was idyllic, but something growled inside me.

"You got a lead on something?" Torstein asked.

I shook my head. Time was running out. My pulse quickened. I could feel Cathrine's presence and flexed my fists.

I turned to Torstein. "Closer?"

Torstein nodded. "By the looks of it, this place is vacated."

I pulled him toward me and whispered, "We need to find out where they are holding her. Then we'll improvise."

Torstein pointed. "That's the main building. To the left is some kind of event space, and behind that one is a guest annex and boathouse."

I followed his gaze and noticed the yellow signs on the walls. "Alarm Systems. Sensors on most windows and doors and motion detectors on the ground floor. We need to avoid triggering them too early. Guards are at least half an hour away, maybe an hour if we are lucky. I don't see any outdoor surveillance cameras."

"Do we have a plan?" Torstein whispered.

"Observe from outside first. If we need to go in, we'll have to find a blind spot in their alarm system."

Torstein turned serious. "Got it."

We tiptoed out of our hiding spot. I scanned the surrounding area, looking for signs of movement. It was as quiet and still as a grave.

"No cars," I whispered to Torstein, pointing toward a parking lot. "You might be correct."

He confirmed with a brief nod. "Place seems deserted."

I signaled Torstein, and we sprinted across the lawn. The grass muffled our steps as we approached the main house.

We pressed ourselves against the wall and peeked inside. A living room. The lights were off. The room was empty. Next window. Kitchen. Just as abandoned and dark as the living room.

Where did they keep Cathrine? Did they move her elsewhere?

We checked out the annex and boathouse. Just as empty. Just as dark.

I leaned closer to Torstein and whispered, "I need to get inside."

I pointed toward the upper floor.

Torstein grabbed my arm. "How do you avoid the alarm systems?"

I pointed to the second-floor windows on the short wall. "No easy access. Maybe no sensors on those."

He glanced around. "Okay, but how will you get up there?"

I pointed to a tree standing near the house wall. "I'll climb that tree and jump over to the balcony. The door and window facing the balcony will have sensors, but I can climb along the cornice and access those windows."

"Are you sure you can manage this in your condition?" Torstein mumbled.

I squeezed his shoulder. "I promise to be careful. We need to get moving before anyone shows up."

He cupped his hands in front of him. I took a deep breath. I used his hands as the first step, then his shoulder, before grabbing the first branch. Pain shot through my ribs, but I gritted my teeth and continued climbing. I calculated every grip and movement to avoid unnecessary noise and pain.

"This is crazy," Torstein said.

I ignored him and focused on the next branch. Slowly but surely, I approached the second-floor balcony. With a careful jump, I landed on the white-painted wooden floor.

This was the riskier part. I crept along the narrow cornice and pressed myself against the wall. One misstep would mean a fall of ten feet. In my condition, that wouldn't be advisable. Finally, I reached the short-side windows.

I broke the pane with my elbow. No audible alarm. I removed the glass shards, found the latch, and opened the window.

I glanced at Torstein standing guard before I sneaked inside the house. My adrenaline numbed my pain.

I stood still in the small bedroom. The door was open to the hallway. I closed my eyes and listened for the slightest whimper or movement.

Nothing. I sniffed the air but couldn't catch Cathrine's scent. I knew the search would be fruitless, but I had to be sure.

I tiptoed through the hallway.

The first room I came to was an elegant bathroom. Empty. The next room was an oversized bedroom. I opened the closet doors. I pushed the clothes aside. Empty. Under the beds were only dust and forgotten socks.

The last room was a guest room. Just as empty.

I sank onto the bed. Cathrine was nowhere. Was this just another mistake?

I exited the bed, went to the window, pressed my head against the cool glass, and examined the garden.

Something caught my eye. An unpainted, weathered wooden door was visible at the edge of the woods, well hidden by trees and bushes from ground level. It stood like a mysterious entrance to something resembling a huge rock. At the top of the rock, a long pipe protruded. A smokehouse? I squinted and focused. Yes, it was definitely a chimney up there.

I climbed out of the window. I found footing on the cornice, gripped the edge, and lowered myself. Ignoring the pain in my ribs, I dropped onto the grass.

"Found anything?" he whispered.

I shook my head and pointed toward the edge of the woods. "But I saw something interesting over on the other side."

We sprinted across the lawn and reached the door. We found the door locked with a padlock.

"Damn it," I muttered.

Torstein examined the surroundings. "Should we quit while we're ahead?"

I shook my head. "No, Cathrine might be inside."

My gaze fell on a small rebar lying behind the annex. I grabbed the iron and wedged it in behind the fitting. With all my strength, I twisted the iron. The screws holding the hasp in place gave way to a crunching sound. The door was open!

An engine roared in the distance. A car was approaching.

"Shit, I must have triggered an alarm," I hissed.

Torstein seemed stressed. "Fuck! Let's abort."

I hesitated momentarily, weighing the risks, but we had no choice.

Chapter Fifty-Five

I ran through the door with Torstein right on my heels. My adrenaline pushed away my pain. The iron bar felt heavy in my hand. I clung to it.

The darkness was suffocating. The smell of smoked fish and old wood filled the room. My eyes struggled to adjust to the dim light.

"Cathrine?" I called out into the darkness.

The silence was absolute. Not a sound came from the inside. No sound from the outside. These walls were solid.

We felt our way along the rough stone walls. The contours of the surrounding room emerged. Rusty hooks hung menacingly from the ceiling. Old barrels lined the walls. The smell of old smoke and salt reminded me of the harbor in San Francisco, but it was staler.

I found a switch and turned on the light.

A faint sound came from a side room. Cathrine? Without hesitation, I moved toward the sound. Torstein followed close behind.

We reached the door to a side room. I grabbed and turned the handle, but the door didn't budge. It was locked. I roared in pure frustration.

"Cathrine? You there?" I shouted. No one answered.

I glanced at Torstein, unable to think. His gaze met mine. "We need to get this door open," I said, trying to find a spot for my iron bar.

Torstein pointed to a key hanging on a nail on the wall. "Try that one."

The key fit the lock, and I opened the door. The room was dark, but my heart raced wildly as I glimpsed Cathrine on a mattress on the floor.

"Cathrine!"

I threw myself beside her. She lay motionless, gagged, and with her hands zip-tied behind her back. I brushed her hair away from her face. Her eyes darted around in confusion before focusing on me. She tried to speak.

Relief washed over me. Cathrine was alive. Then her eyes widened in sheer terror. I turned and followed her gaze. Torstein was standing in the doorway.

She mumbled in panic and tried to crawl away from him. I studied her. Her terrified eyes flicked between me and Torstein. Did she see Torstein, or was she hallucinating?

I removed her gag. "Don't listen to him! He isn't like you think he is!" she cried.

Torstein shook his head. "What the heck have they given her? She's out of it!"

My stomach churned. I broke out in a cold sweat. Cathrine's eyes were still wide open, and her body was shaking.

Torstein stood like a statue, not moving a muscle.

I looked at her. "He... he's a murderer! He killed Olav!" she stuttered.

Torstein sighed. "She's really off her rocker. You know me. Would I hurt Olav?"

My gaze flickered between them.

"Please, listen to me!" Cathrine pleaded.

Torstein put a hand on my shoulder. "Let's get her to the hospital. She needs medical attention."

I glanced around for something to cut her zip tie with. A knife lay on the floor under a massive workbench. I was about to pick it up when I heard the unmistakable sound of a slide racked behind me. I froze.

Slowly, I turned around. Torstein was pointing a gun at me. I stared down the barrel of my Glock.

His face had become expressionless and cold. His eyes that met mine were no longer those of a friend.

"What the hell, Torstein?" I stammered.

"This wasn't the plan," he said, his voice as cold as his gaze. Cathrine had been right. My world spun as the truth sank in.

"Why, Torstein?"

Torstein shrugged. "It's complicated."

My best friend for over thirty years had utterly conned me.

Torstein kept his weapon aimed at me. I held my gaze fixed on Torstein.

"Small favors for shady clients… that's how this started?" I asked, as if putting together a puzzle.

Torstein nodded. "I guess."

"Did you kill Olav?" I asked, my voice trembling.

Torstein frowned. "No, it wasn't me. Olav's death was… something else."

I stared at Torstein, and yet another piece fell into place. It was as if a fog had lifted from my eyes.

"You sent us over the cliff?" I asked in disbelief.

Torstein met my gaze without blinking. "Might have been me."

Nausea rose in my throat. "Why?" I pressed out.

"Cathrine found and read Rosseberg's papers. She got too close to the flame. I had no choice. Then you showed up right after. Very inconvenient, for sure."

He shrugged. "But also… an opportunity, I guess."

His betrayal hit me like a sucker punch. "For how long?" I asked.

Torstein didn't answer. He pointed my gun at a thick pipe protruding from the floor to the ceiling and extended a bit from the wall.

"Sit down over there," he said, fishing another zip tie from his pocket. "Put your hands behind the pipe and fasten this," he commanded.

With trembling hands, I did as he told me. Torstein checked and tightened the zip tie further.

"You, of all people? My best buddy? The one person I was absolutely sure I could trust?"

"Says the guy who went to America, married 'Barbie's sister' and became a real 'American Hero'? The rest of us soon forgotten."

I said nothing.

"You could have asked Olav," he said. "That boy sure didn't take it well when his brother left. He had to fight both his internal demons and others to survive."

I said nothing.

"Have you stopped talking crap and feeling sorry for yourself? Gone quiet as a clam?"

I still said nothing.

He gave up with a shrug and disappeared from the room. I listened to his footsteps moving away. Cathrine was still lying on the floor. The zip tie cut into my wrist as I tried to loosen it. The adrenaline dulled my pain, but it was futile.

Then, I heard voices outside. Torstein was talking to someone. I pricked my ears, desperate to listen to what he said. I recognized the other voice immediately. I'd heard that voice before. It sent an icy shiver through my body.

The man spoke quietly but with authority. His tone was calm, almost pleasant, but with an underlying threat that made the hairs on my neck stand.

Heavy footsteps approached the door, and my heart sank.

Chapter Fifty-Six

The windowless room was cramped, and the air was stuffy and warm. Sweat dampened my back and face. I twisted my wrists, and my zip ties cut even deeper.

The pipe I was bound to was old and not fastened to the wall. I hooked the zip tie into a clamp and pushed myself upward with my knees. To my surprise, the pipe gave a little. I pushed harder, ignoring my pain, and felt the pipe loosen more.

The voices on the outside sounded closer. I held my breath and strained my ears. The doorknob turned, and I slid back into the position I'd been in when Torstein left the room.

The door swung open, and light from the hallway cast long shadows into the room. John Helman-Larssen's silhouette stood in the doorway. He exuded an icy presence.

He took in his surroundings. His calculating gaze swept over us. "Well," he said. "So, what do we have here?"

Torstein entered and positioned himself behind him. He held my gun at his side.

Helman-Larssen came closer. He bent his head and stared at me. "Flokí," he said with a crooked smile. "Always so curious, always so stubborn. Why did you have to stir things up?"

I said nothing.

Helman-Larssen shrugged. "I tried to make it simple for you. I offered you money to restore Olav's honor and gave you a simple explanation everyone could buy into. But, of course, you had to complicate things, didn't you? See what you've forced us to do now?"

I said nothing.

He walked over to Cathrine but kept his gaze fixed on me. "I thought you knew what might happen to the people you care about when you mess with things that don't concern you. Torstein thought you'd learned, but he was wrong. You just have to stick your nose into everything. And those around you pay the ultimate price."

I said nothing.

He leaned over Cathrine. "This time, you've made life difficult for little Miss Detective over here. Poor girl. So sweet. So unfair."

I clenched my fists and tensed my body. Helman-Larssen didn't turn. "Don't try anything stupid, Wilhelmsen," he said threateningly. "Lead supplements to your heart won't help your circulation."

He addressed Cathrine again. "Sorry we had to meet like this, honey."

Her body stiffened.

He stood and looked at both of us, then turned to Torstein. "You'll have to come up with something creative—an accident or two. You're the best. And don't let old friendships mess things up."

"A bit tricky with those strip marks. We'll rather add an episode to *Without a Trace*," Torstein said.

"As you please," Helman-Larssen said.

He turned and walked toward the doorway. With each step toward the door, he signed our death warrant.

Stop him! Distract him!

Cathrine half-raised herself on the mattress and asked him, with a defiant expression: "So, what will you tell the journalists from *The Daily Business* when they call?"

Helman-Larssen stopped short of the door. He didn't turn. "Why would they call me?"

"To ask you to comment on the revelations the paper is about to publish." She sat straight. "Based on the documents Geir had collected."

He snorted. "Do you smell that scent of smoke in here? That's all that's left of those documents."

He gripped the door handle.

"But that's *not* the smell of the pictures I took with my phone."

He paused and turned around. He shot Torstein a questioning look. Torstein signaled he knew nothing.

"If I'm not mistaken, the bottom-feeders in Lovrafjorden borrowed that phone," Helman-Larssen said.

"But all the pictures are also in the cloud. I sent a link to a friend of mine at TDB with some explanations. He can download everything and publish his article when he gets to work tomorrow. It will be the scoop of the year. Your picture will be on the front page for a long, long time. And then your genuine problems begin."

"What friend of yours at TDB?" he snarled and slammed his hand on the pipe I attached. Dust fell from the ceiling.

Cathrine pressed her lips together and refused to answer. Helman-Larssen grabbed her chin.

"I asked you something."

"Leave her alone!"

Helman-Larssen still held onto Cathrine and stared at me. "This is between Cathrine and me."

I said nothing. Just stared at him.

Cathrine pressed her lips together, still refusing to answer. He gripped her harder. "I'm starting to lose my patience."

"This is madness. You won't get away with this," I said.

He turned to me, his eyes narrow. "Don't delude yourself. This is nothing. I've gotten away with much worse."

Cathrine's gaze darted between Helman-Larssen, me, and the room, searching for a solution. Time was running out.

"Last chance," Helman-Larssen said, turning back to Cathrine. "Tell me about the pictures, or your sweetheart will get to test how long he can hold his breath underwater. Did you time how long Geir lasted before he caved in, Torstein? Maybe we'll set a record tonight?"

Cathrine stared at him, terrified. "Wait," she said in a trembling voice.

Helman-Larssen stopped and raised an eyebrow. "Well?"

Cathrine nodded.

"And?"

Helman-Larssen leaned closer to her.

"We will have no evidence if I delete my pictures from the cloud service. We can claim stuff, but we won't be able to prove anything. Neither can TDB," she said.

Helman-Larssen oscillated between rage and fear. He didn't know whether to believe her. "Tell me who this journalist is," he said.

Cathrine held her breath for a moment before answering. "You will not figure that out until you see his article in the paper. Your clock is ticking. What's your choice?"

Helman-Larssen signaled, and he and Torstein left the room. The door slammed shut behind them.

"Good thinking," I whispered to Cathrine.

She nodded. "But it's only a delay."

"Yes, you've bought us some time. Are those pictures you mentioned really in a cloud?"

"Yes," she confirmed. "But I haven't sent them to any journalist. What do you think they will do next?"

"They'll try to force you to delete the pictures," I said. "But you just need to delay long enough for us to find a way to get out of this place. Delay them as much as possible so I can have some me time."

Cathrine nodded, this time with more determination in her eyes.

The door opened. Helman-Larssen and Torstein entered the room. I met Cathrine's gaze for a moment before turning my attention to our captors.

"So," Helman-Larssen said with a strained smile. "Let's talk about these pictures."

I took the initiative. "Before we get into that, let's discuss what these documents prove. For instance, how you've financed the buildup of your shipping company with drug trafficking."

A glint of irritation showed in his eyes.

Cathrine stared at Torstein. "And how you helped launder his money."

Torstein crossed his arms over his chest.

"That's what these documents prove," I said, holding his gaze. "They link the two of you to these illegal activities."

Helman-Larssen said nothing.

"And how about the murder of Geir Rosseberg?" I said, turning to Torstein. "Was that you?"

Torstein clenched his jaw. "He was a sly and stubborn bastard. He wanted to go to the police. Not good for his health. Downright unhealthy."

"And Olav? Was that you?" I asked Helman-Larssen.

He laughed, but it was a laugh without humor. "You surprise me. I thought you were smarter than this."

"I'm smart enough to know you don't want to let us go, but you can't kill us either without the truth getting exposed," I said.

Helman-Larssen stared hard at us, his gaze wandering between Cathrine and me. The pressure built in him as he considered his options. He sighed and let his shoulders drop. "Damn both of you," he said.

Helman-Larssen took a threatening step closer to Cathrine, his eyes icy. "I've heard enough. How do we delete those damn pictures? Talk!"

She said nothing.

He turned to me and grabbed my index and middle fingers, locking his gaze on Cathrine.

"You have five seconds to tell us where the pictures are, and the password, or I will cut off his fingers one by one."

Cathrine gasped and closed her eyes. Then she straightened up. "You'll need more than my password," she said. "You'll need my prints, too."

He let go of me. I hit the floor hard. He turned to Cathrine. Torstein took out a knife. My stomach knotted as they looked at each other.

Something terrible was about to happen.

Chapter Fifty-Seven

The antique chandelier cast a soft light over the library. Countless books lined the shelves, looking untouched. Among the titles were *Great Expectations* and *Wuthering Heights*. Cathrine couldn't imagine Helman-Larssen leafing through any of them.

A dark wooden desk dominated the center of the room, a closed laptop sitting on top. Cathrine lost her footing but regained her balance as Helman-Larssen shoved her toward the desk. Her wrists throbbed under the zip ties.

Cathrine pictured Floki's desperate face as they dragged her away. She hoped he had found a solution by the time she returned.

"Give me your god damned knife," Helman-Larssen said.

Torstein handed him his knife, and Helman-Larssen cut her zip ties without a word.

Helman-Larssen stood so close she could hear and smell his breath. She struggled to concentrate.

"I want those pictures deleted," Helman-Larssen said. "Immediately," he added, leaving no room for objection.

But those pictures were the only thing protecting them from death. She considered making a quick dash for the door.

"Don't even think about it. You'll never make it to that door," Helman-Larssen growled.

"The network isn't working," she said, pointing to the screen where the login page was still loading.

Helman-Larssen signaled to Torstein, who disappeared.

"He's restarting the router," Helman-Larssen said.

Time was on her side. Once she had deleted those pictures, it would be game over for both of them. If she refused, they would use Flokí as leverage. She had to keep them busy for as long as possible and hoped Flokí would find a solution.

"What are you waiting for?" Helman-Larssen roared, pointing at her screen, which displayed a cloud service login page.

"I'm doing my best," she said. "Can I use the bathroom? I need a quick break," she added, pleading.

"No breaks. Delete the pictures."

Cathrine turned and met his gaze with an intense, desperate expression. "Please. I haven't been to the bathroom since I woke up. I can't concentrate."

"It only takes a few seconds to type in a password. You can go to the bathroom after."

"On my PC, I don't type in the password. The browser remembers it for me. Now I have to try to remember the password. That's going to take some time. I can't work miracles."

Helman-Larssen hesitated before nodding.

"Fine. But no tricks. Your door stays unlocked and open. It's a long fall if you try to jump through the window. I will haul you back in if you try."

He signaled for Torstein to escort her upstairs.

Cathrine slumped on the toilet, thinking about Flokí. She thought about everything they had survived. It cannot end this way!

She finished her business, straightened, and stared at her pale reflection in the mirror. She returned with a strained smile.

In the library, she met Helman-Larssen's impatient gaze and sat in front of the laptop. Her fingers rested on the keyboard. She deliberately mistyped the password several times. The login locked and required a ninety-second wait before her next attempt.

Helman-Larssen drummed on the desk, his eyes narrowed.

"Don't fuck with me. I'm giving you one minute after those ninety seconds. Then, no mercy."

Twenty seconds left.

She squeezed her eyes shut, breathing rapidly, her body shaking.

"I can't breathe..."

"What the hell is happening?" Helman-Larssen shouted.

Torstein glanced at Helman-Larssen.

"Seems like a panic attack," Torstein said.

"I... I need some air," she gasped.

Helman-Larssen yanked open a window. He was irritated but unsure how to handle her. He dragged her over to the window.

"Breathe, damn it!" he commanded.

Cathrine nodded weakly and let her breathing calm down. She was walking a fine line. Too much would give her away; too little would force her back to the laptop.

"I... I think it's getting better," she whispered. "Just give me a moment."

Cathrine flinched as Helman-Larssen slammed his fist on the table.

"This is it!" he roared, his voice hard and threatening.

Helman-Larssen's grip on her arm was like a vise; his fingers dug into her skin.

"This is your last warning," he said and tightened his grip until Cathrine cried out in pain. "You have five seconds to access these files, or we're going back, and you'll get front-row seats when we test how long Flokí can hold his breath underwater."

With trembling hands, she turned back to the laptop. She slowly typed in her password, sweat running down her neck. She couldn't make any mistakes this time. Helman-Larssen gave Torstein a sign, and he began the countdown.

"Five... four..."

Helman-Larssen leaned over her, his breath hot on her ear.

"Three... two..."

The screen reflected Helman-Larssen's impatient gaze.

"One..."

As Torstein reached zero, Cathrine hit Enter. The screen flickered, and a message appeared: Loading...

Helman-Larssen's growl filled the room.

"Are you trying to make a fool of me?"

"No, I'm not," Cathrine assured him with a shaky voice. "The system is just slow."

The login screen disappeared. Her file structure appeared, and any hope of further delays vanished. Helman-Larssen brutally shoved her aside.

"Finally!" he shouted. His fingers flew over the keyboard.

Helman-Larssen deleted her folders while she watched in despair.

Chapter Fifty-Eight

My eyes had adjusted to the darkness. I got my bearings in the room, paying close attention to every detail that could be useful.

I could make out the contours of the massive workbench. Remembered the knife I'd seen on the floor behind it.

A dark shadow outlined the door on the other side of the room. The door was a solid construction. Made to keep unwanted visitors out—and prisoners in.

I spotted the distinct outline of an oversized plastic fan high on a wall. There had to be some kind of duct behind it.

I took a deep breath and started working on the pipe. I rocked my body hard against the wall, grunted, and fought to keep my eyes open despite my stinging sweat.

It creaked. The pipe moved. I doubled my efforts, pressing my shoulders against the wall to increase the power of my movements. The metal scraped against the brick wall, coming loose bit by bit.

With one last jerk, the pipe came free. I fell forward and hit my head on the floor, but it didn't matter. I was finally loose.

A showdown with Torstein in this room would be too dangerous. He had my Glock. The outcome of a shootout in a cramped room with stone walls would be catastrophic.

They might even decide to kill off Cathrine first, then return for me. I couldn't let that happen. I had to find my way out of there.

I fumbled along the wall for something I could use. There was an old broom propped up against the wall in the corner. Perfect. Gripping the broom, I made my way to the workbench.

I hunched over and used the handle to search for the knife I had seen earlier. After a few attempts, I pushed the knife out from under the bench. It scraped against the concrete floor as it slid forward.

With the knife held between my knees, I diligently worked on sawing through the zip ties around my wrists. The plastic gave way, and the zip ties fell off.

I rubbed my wrists and enjoyed this moment of freedom. Then I grabbed my broomstick and turned toward the air duct.

The fan in the duct looked old and rotten. I threaded the broom handle between the fan blades and pried the fan outward. It resisted, but the plastic creaked and bent. I increased the pressure. The fan came loose with a thud and landed on the floor.

I grabbed the edge of the duct and tried to hoist myself up, but my wrists gave out. With all my strength, I pushed that workbench against the wall, climbed on top, and reached for the opening.

It was a tight opening, but I forced myself in. The stone walls pressed against my skin as I twisted my body inside.

My breathing became faster and shallower in the confined space. I hated it intensely. I wriggled forward. Dust and cobwebs covered my face. The air was heavy. I hyperventilated to keep my panic at bay and pushed on.

A spider crawled over my hand. I jerked and hit the ceiling of the duct with my head. I had to stifle my scream that was trying to break free.

Hang in. Think of Cathrine. You're almost through.

I inched forward. As the air improved, I heard a scurrying sound in front of me. A mouse darted past my face. I closed my eyes, trying to control my panic by breathing slower.

The duct curved to the right. The passage became even tighter. I could barely breathe. My chest pressed against the sides. My hands were shaking. I had to stop for a moment to regain control.

Giving up was not an option. I pushed on. Every inch felt like a mile.

At the end of the duct, I saw a faint glimmer of light. It gave me the added energy I needed. I fought my way forward, getting my claustrophobia under control.

I reached the end of the duct. But my joy was short-lived. A solid and brand-new grate blocked my exit. My heart sank.

I pressed my fingers against the metal, desperately trying to find a weakness.

Chapter Fifty-Nine

I lay stretched out in the narrow air duct, staring at the grate—the last barrier between me and freedom. I closed my eyes.

There had to be a solution. The screws holding the grate in place were on the outside and out of reach. But the fasteners were screwed into the stone walls of the air duct. That was my way out.

I fished out the knife from my pocket. With trembling fingers, I twisted the first screw. It came loose after what felt like an eternity and fell to the duct floor.

Three to go...

The remaining screws gave way one by one. I removed the grate and maneuvered my head out. I dropped the grate into the bushes. The sound of metal hitting the ground cut through the night.

I listened intently. Had anyone heard it? Time crawled by, but I heard nothing—just the sound of my heartbeat.

I fought my urge to throw myself into freedom. Take it easy. Think. I squeezed myself out of the air duct, landed on the ground, and rolled under a lilac bush.

Where would Cathrine be? Was she in the main building?

My knife. Where's my knife?

I must have lost it when I fell. I searched around in the dark, but it was gone.

Damn. Damn. Damn.

A door in the main building opened, and light flooded out. I held my breath and listened from under the bush. My heart was pounding so hard I feared it would give me away. I saw the light from the hallway through the gaps in the foliage. An outdoor lamp came on.

Two figures came out. Torstein pushed Cathrine in front of him.

She's alive.

Cathrine stumbled but didn't fall. John Helman-Larssen followed close behind them, his face contorted with irritation.

I focused on the three standing under the lamp outside the house. I held my breath and listened. Torstein and Helman-Larssen were talking. Helman-Larssen's cold, calculating voice cut through the night.

"Get rid of her first. Then take care of Floki."

"I'll handle it," said Torstein.

I struggled to breathe.

Torstein, you cold-blooded bastard!

I had to do something. But what? I was unarmed, alone against two men with a hostage and a Glock.

I hid behind a corner of the house. I stuck my sweaty back to the cold wooden wall. I sank to my knees to hide behind the vegetation when I poked my head out. It gave me a safer viewpoint.

Torstein studied my gun. He studied both sides of the weapon for the safety lock. He didn't know about the Glock's particular trigger safety. It gave me an edge. A small one, but still an edge.

I assessed the distance between us, calculating my timing. Torstein and Cathrine were walking on the gravel path and approaching my corner. Time stood still. The only sound was the footsteps on the gravel.

It's now or never.

I tensed my muscles, ready to lunge forward. The Glock still distracted Torstein. His eyes were on the weapon, not his surroundings. Cathrine walked in front of him with her head bowed.

The distance shrank.

Five meters. Four. Three.

Cathrine was in line with the house wall. Had she turned her head, she would have seen me. Her body language revealed she'd given up.

Two meters. One.

I stood still to avoid being detected in Torstein's peripheral vision. I let him pass me by a few meters.

Now!

I ran three steps and threw myself forward.

Torstein didn't have time to react before we hit the ground. A deafening shot pierced the night. The bullet grazed my arm, but I forced myself to ignore my pain and focus on his weapon.

We rolled around on the ground, a chaotic mass of arms and legs. Torstein fought like a madman to hold on to the gun, but I was driven by sheer desperation. My fingers clung to his hand, holding the weapon. My nails dug into his skin.

"Let go, you bastard!" I said through gritted teeth.

Torstein responded with a gurgling roar and tried to turn the gun toward my face. I strained my muscles to the breaking point to hold it back.

Gravel and dirt scraped against my skin as we continued to roll. The world was spinning, and I lost all sense of direction. The only thing that mattered was holding onto the gun hand and preventing Torstein from gaining the upper hand.

Rapid footsteps approached. Helman-Larssen. He had heard the shot. Time was short.

"Get away, Cathrine!" I shouted. "Run!"

I gathered all my strength and gave Torstein a stiff knee to his stomach. He gasped for air, and his grip on the gun loosened for a moment. It was all I needed. With a violent twist, I turned the gun away from me.

I reached for the gun as Helman-Larssen grabbed my shoulders and tried to pull me away. I desperately held onto the hands clinging to the weapon.

"Damn you! Let go!" Torstein roared.

Cathrine got to her feet and grabbed a flower urn. She lifted it above her head.

"Stay away!" I shouted.

But she didn't listen. She threw the urn at Helman-Larssen with all her might. It hit him on the side of his head with a crash and shattered into a thousand pieces. He roared in pain.

In the chaos that followed, another shot went off. The sound was deafening. Helman-Larssen let go of me and staggered backward. He collapsed on the ground with a muffled groan.

Adrenaline pumped through my body. I fought my way up to my knees, still with a death grip on the hands clinging to the weapon.

With my last ounce of strength, I forced the weapon toward Torstein's head. My index finger lay over his on the trigger. My heart was racing. Torstein met my gaze. In his eyes, I saw fear, but also something else. Regret? Despair?

I stared at Torstein, the man I had once trusted with my entire life. Rage boiled inside me, but something held me back. My finger rested on the trigger.

I pictured Torstein as a little boy, as a teenager, and as my best man. How could he have gone so wrong?

Seconds felt like hours as I made up my mind. Sweat dripped from my forehead, mixing with the blood from my injuries. Torstein stared up at me.

"Flokí..." he said, shaking his head.

My hand trembled. I pressed my gun harder against his forehead; my knuckles whitened around the grip. But something inside me rebelled and refused to pull.

What have you become, Floki? A killer?

"Floki! No!"

Jonas' voice cut through the night. I jolted, aware of what I was about to do. My fingers eased the pressure on the trigger. I locked my eyes on Torstein's. For a moment, I saw a glimpse of my old friend—the boy I had grown up with.

What was I doing? The sound of Jonas reminded me that the law still prevailed, even in this chaos.

Time remained at a standstill. Torstein's eyes met my gaze. For a moment, I saw resignation and regret in them.

"Sorry, buddy!" he said.

Before I could react, he jerked the gun into his mouth. I couldn't hold back.

"Don't do it, Torstein!"

The deafening bang drowned my cry as Torstein pulled the trigger. Blood sprayed, and his body fell limply to the ground.

Chapter Sixty

The blue lights of police cars and ambulances cast flickering shadows across the house walls and the surrounding forest. An ambulance door slammed shut, and the driver set the vehicle in motion. Sirens cut through the night as the ambulance carrying Helman-Larssen disappeared down the road.

We sat on a garden bench, watching the foamy waves from the fjord. A nearby aspen tree shook and trembled, and tiny raindrops hung in the air. A blanket over our shoulders muffled the chilly wind. I held Cathrine, who'd curled up close to me. We were both quiet.

Police officers and paramedics moved in controlled chaos with murmuring voices, crackling radios, and crunching footsteps on the gravel, but it all felt so distant.

"What now?" Cathrine asked.

I held her hand. "It's over," I replied, hoping I was right.

Cathrine's hand found mine and held it tight. She rested her head on my shoulder. Her tears moistened my skin.

I stroked her cheek and let my gaze wander. This place, which was a veritable death trap a few hours ago, now had uniformed personnel collecting evidence and securing the crime scene.

It was so surreal to be alive. I glanced at Torstein, still covered by a white sheet just ten feet away. The traitor. My best friend. Gone forever.

I closed my eyes, trying to shut out Torstein's face as he pulled the trigger, but his last gaze would forever remain frozen in my mind.

"Flokí..." Cathrine mumbled.

Her voice broke. I understood. We had survived. I pulled her closer and let my silence do the talking.

Jonas came walking toward us and sat on the bench. He said nothing for a while, studied the waves rolling in.

He pulled himself together. "Helman-Larssen is on his way to the hospital. The injuries are severe," he said. "We don't know if he'll survive. Even if he does..."

He let his sentence hang in the air, but I understood. The bullet had penetrated his neck and grazed his brain. It was a miracle that he survived.

"What's next?" I asked.

"I know you're exhausted, but if you're up to it, I would appreciate a debrief while it is all fresh. I'd like to note the sequence of events from when we left the neighboring property until the first shot. Ole and I got the rest. We'll take care of it."

Cathrine caught my eye. She was dead tired, but agreed.

"Why did you return?" I asked.

"Your dad called me. He and Charlene were worried since you didn't come home. I remembered Torstein's car was left in the parking lot when we drove off, so I called him. He didn't answer, so we returned. We heard the first shot as we exited the car."

"I need to call my dad. Can I use your phone?" I asked. "To let them know we're okay," I added.

Jonas nodded. "Of course. Take the time you need. I'll start with Cathrine, and we'll talk afterward."

When I returned to the bench, Cathrine and Jonas were waiting. Cathrine's eyes sought mine. I nodded. "They were relieved to hear we were safe," I said. "I didn't give them all the details. We'll do it face-to-face later."

Jonas cleared his throat and opened his notebook. "Cathrine doesn't recall much since the accident. She's been heavily sedated. But she remembered Torstein. He must have had a tracking device on her car. He followed her to the farm, attacked her, and sedated her. She tried to escape, but he knocked her down. Then you arrived on the scene. The rest is history."

"No description of the woman who abducted her from the hospital?"

"No. The only thing Cathrine remembers is dreaming about an angel. The woman we saw was no angel."

"Tell me what happened after I left you guys," he said, looking at me.

I went through the events, told Jonas how Torstein and I found Cathrine in the smokehouse.

"I woke up when you shouted my name. I heard your voice before you entered," she said.

"We heard you, too. Torstein knew about you and the key on the wall, of course, but I didn't realize it. He played me so well."

"I was terrified when I saw Torstein," Cathrine continued with a trembling voice, "but I couldn't warn you."

I felt a lump in my throat. "He tried to convince me you were hallucinating. I didn't know what to believe. The implications were so crazy I couldn't wrap my mind around it."

Jonas took notes as we talked. "And then?"

"Torstein pulled his gun. Then John Helman-Larssen arrived. They admitted everything. The drug trafficking that founded Helman-Larssen's shipping empire, that Torstein sent our car off the cliff, that he had killed Geir, and the illegal services he provided for his criminal clients, such as money laundering."

I didn't bother him with minor details, like who owned the gun.

Cathrine gripped my hand. "He said I'd come too close to the truth."

I nodded. "You had to be 'neutralized,' I guess."

I told him about my escape and the confrontation in the yard. Jonas leaned forward with his elbows on his knees as he studied his notes. Then he looked at us with a serious gaze.

"Based on your account and the evidence you've gathered, it appears Torstein committed all the murders, including Olav," he said.

I had been waiting for Jonas to conclude like that. It was a logical deduction. Still, I felt an unexpected reluctance to accept it.

"Are you sure?" I heard myself ask. "I can't make it add up."

Jonas nodded. "I know it's difficult to accept. But everything points toward him."

"I understand your thinking, but something doesn't sit right."

"Torstein's confessions, his involvement with Helman-Larssen, and his desperate actions tonight—it all suggests he was involved in everything that's happened, including your brother's murder."

I shook my head. "Yes, but Olav... Torstein and his wife had no children, and Olav was like a son to him. How could he...?"

I grew restless, stood up, and paced as I spoke.

Jonas followed me with his eyes. "I don't know, but Torstein must have been exceptionally cold. And he had access to information and resources."

The thought of Torstein as Olav's killer crushed me. Yet I couldn't ignore the logic of Jonas's reasoning. I hoped for a different truth but knew Jonas might be right. The realization hurt more than I thought possible.

Cathrine put her hand on my arm. "What's on your mind?" she asked. "You don't seem convinced."

I glanced at the window before meeting her gaze. "I... I don't know. Something doesn't add up. I can't put my finger on it, but there's something sinister to this. I know it."

She nodded. "Try me," she said. "Don't overthink, just talk it through."

I sat. "Jonas, I get where you're going with this, but neither Helman-Larssen nor Torstein admitted to being involved in Olav's murder. They felt so secure they admitted to all other crimes. All of it. Except for that one all-important issue. The murder of Olav. They both denied it."

Jonas frowned. "Well, we know they were involved in covering it up."

"When I asked Helman-Larssen if he'd killed Olav, he laughed it off and said he thought I was smarter. I thought he meant he was too smart to believe he would admit it to me. But he meant I was smart enough to figure out the truth."

"Or you got it right the first time, and Torstein killed him on Helman-Larssen's orders," said Jonas. "He had no qualms about killing you and Cathrine. He wasn't the friend you thought he was."

"When I asked Torstein if he killed Olav, he denied it, almost as if it was an insult. He said it was 'something else.'"

Cathrine nodded. "You're right."

"I bet Torstein wasn't even in Spain the day Olav was killed," I continued. "Maybe not at all. I don't believe he drove, and the authorities may confirm he didn't fly."

"But if Torstein wasn't in Spain, then who killed Olav? The murder took place in the villa outside Marbella. That's a fact. Glette was staying in that villa and involved in the cover-up.

Do you believe Olav pressured him for money, after all?" Jonas asked.

"I don't know. Maybe Glette was killed because he might expose the drug trade to receive a lighter punishment for his murder," I said.

I sat silent for a while. "Or maybe it was something completely different," I said.

Jonas leaned forward and narrowed his eyes. "I understand you want to find a better explanation, but sometimes the obvious is correct."

"And sometimes it ain't. Something doesn't add up."

"Like what?"

"I don't know. Glette might have had the opportunity if he had been in Spain at the time of the murder. You might want to check on that, by the way. There's always the possibility someone fabricated his motive in a fake suicide note to cover up something else, like this drug business."

"Listen, I understand it's hard to accept Olav did something so stupid. But sometimes…"

"There's more to this," I said sharply. "I owe it to Olav to figure this out."

Cathrine leaned in toward me. "But if the scoundrel they carried out of here winds up as a vegetable, we might never know the truth."

Chapter Sixty-One

I t was four-thirty on Saturday morning. The house glowed with light as if the evening had never ended. My jaw was tense. I rubbed my face. My skin felt tight, and my eyes burned after a long, sleepless night.

Streetlights cast long shadows across the well-manicured lawn. An icy wind tore at my hair. I pulled my jacket tighter around me, more to steel myself than to keep warm. I was uneasy at the idea of what could wait for me.

I walked with determined steps toward the front door. I rang the bell and waited. After a couple of minutes, Anita opened the door wearing a silk nightgown. She pressed herself against me, pushing her hips against my groin and placing her hand on the small of my back.

It could have been sexy, but the smell of sweat and cigarettes, combined with her empty, sad gaze that stared past me, ruined it all.

I had a flashback to when I was staking out Johns in the bars of North Beach. That desperate last dance.

I nuzzled her away. She looked both surprised and suspicious.

"Why are you here... this early?" she asked, trying to focus on her Hermès watch, but she gave up.

"If you're back for what you didn't get the other day, forget it. That ship has sailed," she said coldly.

I pretended not to notice. "May I come in?"

She pulled her nightgown tighter, as if the thin silk could protect her from what was coming.

"I need to talk to you. It's important," I said.

She hesitated for a moment before opening the door. "Come in," she said, leading me into her living room.

She went over to the bar in the corner. "Can I get you a drink?" she asked. Her voice was clearer and more tense.

I shook my head. "No, thanks. I'm here on serious business."

She shrugged and poured herself a stiff G&T. Her hands shook as she lifted the glass to her mouth.

"So, why are you on my doorstep at the crack of dawn? Cathrine didn't want you after all?" she asked, sinking into her expensive leather chair.

I met her gaze. Locked it in. "Your father is dead, Anita. Torstein shot him about an hour ago. Outside your family's country house in Ålfjorden."

It was mean; I knew it. Her father wasn't dead. Not yet.

She turned pale and dropped her glass, which shattered on the floor. "You're lying," she hissed.

I shook my head. "I wish I did," I lied.

She stood. The nightgown fluttered around her. "It was you!" she screamed, pointing at me. "You were behind this! You got your old buddy to kill him!"

I raised my hands in a calming gesture. "No. I..."

"Out!" she roared. "Get out of my house!"

"Please, listen to me. I had nothing to do with your father's death. It was Torstein who killed him. A negligent discharge," I said.

She sank back into the chair, her eyes wet with tears and anger. "Why should I believe you?"

I took a deep breath. "Because I was there, and I saw it happen."

Anita froze. Her hands clutched the glass so tightly that her knuckles turned white. "And you're lying," she said.

"No. I'm not lying. Your father and Torstein were holding Cathrine and me captive. They wanted to kill us."

Anger replaced the fear in her face. "Bullshit!"

I weighed each word, trying to avoid escalating the situation. "I know more than you think. You are well aware that Cathrine was held captive on your father's property in Ålfjorden because you were the one who kidnapped her from the hospital. You drove her there."

"Have you been drinking?"

"I also know about your father's drug trade and the money laundering. I know that Torstein killed Rosseberg to keep him quiet."

She was trembling. Her eyes were wide with shock and fear.

"And I know he was involved in covering up Olav's death. Torstein then arranged Glette's tragic 'suicide.' They were neighbors, after all."

Anita stood. "I have no idea what you're rambling about! I'm calling the police."

I met her gaze. "I also know that you were in Marbella when Olav was killed."

"I was in Copenhagen. Even I can't be in two places at once," she snorted.

"You killed him, didn't you?"

Anita froze. Her eyes narrowed in anger. "You must have lost your marbles in that other whore's bed!" she snapped back.

The panic was building behind her facade. Her hand shook as she reached for another glass. "I have no idea what you're talking about," she said, strained. "You should leave. Right now."

I stood motionless, my gaze locked on her. "I'm not going anywhere until you tell me the truth."

She snorted and turned away. "The truth? You and this endless pursuit of truth. Hasn't the cost of truth been high enough for you? Glette killed Olav. Then, the coward committed suicide. End of story."

"That's a lie," I said. "You were there. You killed Olav. Glette came to Marbella to clean up your mess. He got nervous when we came knocking. Then they killed him, too. No loose ends."

She closed her eyes. "I want you to leave. Now," she said.

I sat on the sofa and looked out at the lights of Haugesund. "Not until you tell me what happened."

For a moment, Olav's face appeared before me. "Let's talk about when we met at the airport. Interesting timing, wasn't it?"

She snorted. "I've already told you. I'd been to Copenhagen. What else do you want?"

"Maybe an explanation for why you came back so tanned and lovely after all that bad weather you'd had?"

Anita stiffened. "I went to a tanning salon. In Copenhagen."

I raised an eyebrow. "And those passenger lists from Malaga to Copenhagen in the days after the murder? Will they confirm your story?"

She swallowed hard. "Of course they will."

I studied the skyline of Haugesund. "You were his new girlfriend, weren't you?"

Anita's eyes widened. "You're crazy!"

Anita backed up against the wall, her breathing fast and shallow. Cornered like an animal.

She walked over to the liquor cabinet. I monitored her in the reflection of the large panoramic windows. She poured herself another G&T, opened a compartment in the cabinet, and pulled out a small revolver with a pearl grip.

The air in the room became too heavy to breathe. I sat motionless.

Anita came quietly from behind, her weapon pointed at my head.

"You don't understand anything," she hissed. "Olav... cheated on me. With Victoria."

I said nothing.

"I asked him, and he just laughed it off. He said I was overreacting."

Anita laughed bitterly, a sharp, cutting sound.

I said nothing.

"She drove him in that fancy whore mobile of hers. Dropped him off a long way down the road. Then he came to me, the bastard. Said he loved me oh so much. And that he needed money. A lot of money. He was an evil, irresponsible con artist. A bastard. Only going after my bodily pleasures and money."

She sniffled and wiped her nose off on her arm.

I still said nothing.

"He denied it, of course. He said she'd just given him a ride. There was nothing between them. But I knew better. He was only after our money. He even knew about our side business."

I swallowed hard. "The drug trade?"

"Call it whatever you want! Geir had ratted us out to him. Olav wanted me to break with my dad blah-blah-blah," she spat. "He was a faithless bastard who knew too much. He deserved exactly what he got!"

I turned around on the sofa and met her gaze. I tried to keep my voice calm. "So you killed him?"

"He gave me no choice!"

Anita's hand shook, and the revolver quivered in her grip. At this short distance, her weapon was lethal.

I need to be careful. One wrong word or movement, and everything will go sideways.

I stared into the muzzle of her revolver. My adrenaline sharpened my thoughts. I could see reality had left her eyes by now. She was trapped in her fear, desperation, and paranoia.

Perhaps I'd pushed her too hard.

"And now you're planning to kill me, too?"

"It will be self-defense," she said. "You came in the middle of the night and tried to rape me. I had to protect myself."

She held the gun against my head.

"So, I was sitting on the sofa trying to rape you while you were standing over me with a gun? Self-defense with a shot point-blank to my head? Come up with something better."

I pulled out my phone. "Maybe you'd rather talk to Jonas? He and his friends in uniform are on their way over. While we wait, you can talk to him."

I put it on speakerphone.

"Put the weapon down. We're turning into your driveway right now, and we're armed. Put it down immediately," Jonas's authoritative voice sounded.

The sirens blared outside. Anita came and stood before me with her feet spread and the weapon raised. She prepared to pull the trigger.

"Turn around and enjoy the view. I'm not falling for this shit. Nice try, smarty pants!" she said through gritted teeth.

I didn't turn around. Most people on a battlefield get shot from behind.

Someone kicked open the front door with a crash, and we heard running footsteps and radio communication coming from the hall.

She pointed the weapon at her head. Held it with her eyes closed.

Chapter Sixty-Two

"She put down her gun and threw up. Not a pretty sight," I concluded.

Margit shook her head. "Unbelievable," she said. "The entire case is unbelievable. But I'm so grateful you figured it out, for Olav and Geir's sake."

On the cutting board in front of us lay piles of sliced bell peppers, cucumbers, and tomatoes, ready for tonight's tacos. Next to me, Dad was kneading the dough. The smell of yeast and butter filled the kitchen.

Cathrine was setting the table on the terrace. Charlene and Vidar were playing cards in our living room. Catch lay at their feet, following the game with half an eye.

My shoulders relaxed as I watched my family. After everything we'd been through, being together and having a regular family Friday felt good.

Dad kneaded the dough in silence, then cleared his throat. "By the way, I met Erik Lea today. The defense attorney. He has an empty office space you could use as a base if you'd like to work as an investigator. How does that sound to you?"

I stopped slicing tomatoes and studied him. "Private investigator? Don't think that's my cup of tea."

"Why not? You've got both the experience and the skills."

I frowned and continued chopping vegetables. "I don't know, Dad. Sounds like a lot of paperwork and boring assignments with cheating spouses and insurance fraud."

Dad chuckled. "You never know what might happen. Sometimes, you just have to take the plunge."

I was about to answer when laughter from the living room interrupted me. Charlene and Vidar were sitting close together on the couch. He whispered something in her ear, and she smiled.

I bit my lip. My little girl wasn't little anymore. Cathrine was right. I had to deal with it. Maybe Dad was right, too — it was time to focus on something else.

Cathrine came into the kitchen with a smile and a curious sparkle in her eyes. "Why do three of you look so sly?" she asked, leaning against the kitchen counter.

I explained Dad's suggestion. Cathrine raised her eyebrows and studied me. "Why not? Are you interested?"

I shrugged and continued chopping vegetables.

She moved closer, put her hand on my arm, and our eyes met. "You've shown us what you're capable of. You're plenty good."

I opened my mouth to protest, but closed it. She had a point.

Cathrine interrupted my thoughts. "You don't have to decide today. Just consider it, okay? You don't need to sit in your office every day, but it'll be good to get out now and then."

I nodded. Thunder rolled in the distance. I turned to the window; the sky over the ocean darkened, and tiny raindrops gathered on the windows.

"Flokí! Charlene! I need help!" Cathrine called from the terrace.

I dropped my knife and headed for the door with Dad behind me. Cathrine struggled with the tablecloth in the increasing wind while plates and glasses slid close to the edge.

"Take the glasses!" I shouted to Dad as I grabbed the other end of the tablecloth.

Cathrine and I struggled to hold the tablecloth while Dad, Vidar, and Charlene ran to collect the dishes. Vidar grabbed a wine bottle just before it slid off the table.

We struggled to save our dinner as the rain increased around us. Even though the rain was pelting down, I couldn't help but smile. We were like a family—everyone pitching in.

Dad came carrying a bowl of salad, water droplets glistening in his gray hair. "Anyone seen the taco shells?" he asked.

"They're still in the kitchen," I replied. "I'll get them."

Vidar came carrying the taco meat with Catch wagging around his legs. "No, Catch, this isn't for you," he said, lifting the plate higher.

Finally, everything was in place, and we could relax and gather around the table.

"Let's eat," Dad said, reaching for the taco shells.

As we ate, I considered becoming a private investigator. The thought of endless paperwork, boring surveillance assignments, and frustrated clients didn't appeal to me, but I wanted to help people in genuine need.

"Is everything okay?" Charlene asked.

"Yeah, just a bit distracted."

Cathrine met my gaze across the table and raised an eyebrow. I knew she could read me like an open book.

Margit glanced over at me, and Dad leaned across the table.

"Sometimes you have to take chances, son. You're ready for the next step," he said.

Cathrine placed her hand over mine.

"I've made up my mind," I said, putting down my fork.

Everyone around the table stopped eating and glanced at me.

I looked at Dad. "I'll accept Erik's offer but choose my assignments carefully. Family always comes first."

Cathrine squeezed my hand and smiled slyly. "How about a partner? I've got some experience, you know. Might even have some pretty good references, too."

I smiled and shook my head.

"One thing at a time, Cathrine. One thing at a time."

He sat alone at a table, savoring an espresso. His eyes scanned the people walking across Union Square.

On the table in front of him lay today's edition of The Chronicle, folded around a small article with the headline:

"Former Homicide Detective Exposes Major Corruption Scandal and Multiple Murders in Home Country."

The article featured an old photograph of Flokí Wilhelmsen in full SFPD uniform, taken during his days as a celebrated homicide detective in San Francisco.

The man ran his hand over the article.

You just couldn't stay out of the spotlight, could you? Didn't learn a damn thing the last time. There's no running from this one.

He stood, downed his espresso, crossed the square, and vanished into the crowd.

Afterword

First, before I forget, if you have enjoyed this story, or if you are very disappointed, please give the world your honest review here:

https://amazon.com/review/create-review?&asin=B0DPN DHVB3

And, let's make sure we keep in touch! Please sign up for news about my future releases and events here:

https://forfatterfabrikken-forlag.kit.com/sign-up

Thank you so much!

I grew up in the small town of Haugesund, Norway. One day during my childhood, a classmate took me to an old wooden building in the center of town. It was the old library.

That became a pivotal moment in my life. At the library, I could borrow books to take home. Completely free of charge.

That's how the magic world of books opened up to me.

I devoured mystery series like The Bobbsey Twins, The Famous Five, and The Hardy Boys, but eventually moved on to classics, contemporary authors, hobby books, biographies, and political analyses.

I became a genuine bookworm, a nerd long before it was cool, and I still am.

Good books, even lighthearted tall tales like this one, tell stories that give us insight. Stories that teach us about the society around us and people in different life situations. Stories that teach us how fragile life is, what's important, and what's less so.

Good stories give us insight into psychology, worldviews, and how our values affect our lives and the lives of others. Good stories let us step inside other people's shoes for a while. We see the world through fresh eyes, from a different perspective. It changes us.

You must literally open your eyes to read. And when what you're reading engages your emotions, it also opens your heart.

If you've read *Anne Frank's Diary* as a young person, you're more resistant to arguments that devalue and dehumanize other groups of people.

If you've read *Uncle Tom's Cabin*, you won't readily accept that one human being can exploit another as a slave.

If you've read *All Quiet on the Western Front*, you understand more about the horrors of war, its impact on people, and the importance of avoiding it.

Well-written stories act as a vaccine against the indoctrination of evil. It's no coincidence that authoritarian movements and cults, both religious and political, often burn books.

That's why I still love books, I love what books do to us, and that we still have libraries where they can be read for free.

When you love reading books, it can quickly develop into a dream of writing one yourself. I've dreamed of writing a book since my teens but didn't start writing until well into adulthood.

My writing journey began with a course in narrative structure in Los Angeles. Later, I became a student in the first class of Cappelen Damm's Mystery Writing Academy.

Being close to the industry and getting a glimpse into a major publishing house was exciting. We met accomplished crime writers and received guidance from two fantastic teachers: Torkild Damhaug, triple Riverton winner, and Bernt Roald Nilsen, author, journalist, blogger, and writing instructor. The latter has also been a consultant on this book.

The legal stuff: This story is entirely fictional. Any resemblance to actual persons, living or dead, is purely coincidental, with one exception: Erik Lea. He's an accomplished defense attorney and a living legend in my hometown, who has generously allowed me to use his name in the final chapter.

Unfortunately, there's no longer a hospital in Sauda, but I've allocated enough fictional money to keep it running in this book. Hope the people of Sauda appreciate that.

Antonio's restaurant in Puerto Banús closed down a decade ago, but not in this book. One of the joys of writing fiction is that you can spin yarns to your heart's content and even revive old restaurants like that.

Many people deserve thanks for making this book possible. First and foremost, I thank my wife, Ingunn, who has supported me through the ups and downs of the writing process. As a former Norwegian teacher, she has also read the manuscript with her magnifying glass many times and has been very generous with her red marker.

Thanks also to Cappelen Damm's Mystery Writing Academy for new inspiration when I was about to lose my heart.

Thanks to Bernt for the harsh, honest, and constructive feedback, which was delivered with good humor and a genuine desire to improve the manuscript.

I also want to thank Chris Chinchilla for his thorough feedback on the storyline and my English translation.

Finally, a massive shout out to Marlene McPherson, accomplished screenwriter, TV producer, and Emmy Award winner, for essential advice and inspiration in the project's initial phase.

Lastly, a huge thank you to you, the reader, who took a chance on reading a book by an author you've never heard of. I've spent over twelve years completing this book you're holding. After such a long pregnancy, I'm glad the book is finally born and making its way into the world on its own.

That's why it's so inspiring that you've taken the time to read it. Now it's up to you to judge whether the child turned out well-formed and whether you've grown as fond of Flokí and his family as I have.

I'm crossing my fingers and hoping we'll meet again in my next book.

Paul B Bergquist, Author